The Cleveland Indian

The Cleveland Indian
The Legend of King Saturday

Luke Salisbury

The Smith ⚒ Brooklyn

Published by The Smith
69 Joralemon Street, Brooklyn, N.Y. 11201
Typography by Pineland Press
1074 Feylers Corner Road, Waldoboro, ME 04572-5710
Printed at Capital City Press
P.O. Box 546, Montpelier, VT 05602

Cover design by Jakob Trollbeck
Cover photograph digitally composited by R/GA Print
Photographs courtesy of National Baseball Library, Cooperstown,NY

Library of Congress Cataloging in Publication Data:

Salisbury, Luke, 1947 —
Fiction
ISBN: 0-912292-95-4

92-080447   CIP

First Edition, May 1992

Also by Luke Salisbury:

The Answer is Baseball,
Times Books, 1989, and Vintage, 1990

Contributed to:

Ted Williams: A Portrait in Words and Pictures
Walker, 1991

Baseball and the Game of Life
Birch Brook Press, 1990, and Vintage, 1991

Sections of *The Cleveland Indian*
appeared [in a slightly different form] in *Pulpsmith Magazine*

This book is dedicated to:

David L. Brandt
William Brevda
Leslie Epstein
Michael Fahey
George Fifield
Robert Gurland
Dick Johnson
John Robert Lee
Sam Leiken
Christopher Lydon
Jake Shearer
Glenn Stout

who stand with me like brothers

And

Mason Salisbury

Barbara

Ace

Part One

1

They're all dead now — the Indian, Ned Phillips, Frank Ember, and probably Annie too, though she may be in San Francisco. I have what I said I wanted — a ballclub. It's not a big league club, but we're on our way to winning the Eastern League and I own the club. I have what I want, but my friends are dead. Like most men, I'm guilty and not guilty.

It's been ten years since King Saturday, a Penobscot Indian, appeared in uniform for the Cleveland Spiders and tore up the National League for half a season. Saturday had the most talent any baseball man had ever seen. John McGraw of Baltimore said so. So did Frank Ember, the Spider third base coach, and neither was easy to impress. King Saturday disappeared a week after the Fourth of July in 1898. I was a lawyer for the Spiders. The club gave me a check for $10,000 and sent me to find him. It would have been better for both of us if I hadn't.

I was twenty-seven that summer — full of ambition, wild to get my hands on a ballclub, a bit of a dandy, and hellbent on being as great a friend to King Saturday as a self-absorbed, hero-worshipping Harvard lawyer could be.

2

He was my friend.

He was my friend from the night I met him in August '97, until that wretchedly cold day in '99 when he disappeared for the last time. By the calendar that's only a year and a half, but time swirled or stood still around the Indian in a way it doesn't around other men. I knew Saturday for a summer, tracked him through the fall, and now it seems, must try to understand him forever.

I met King Saturday in a hotel room in Hooper, Pa. a little after midnight on August 11, 1897. He was touring with Ned Phillips' Eastern Collegiate All-Stars and had signed with the Cleveland Spiders. I was supposed to accompany him to Toledo, where Saturday was going to finish the Association season and then join the Spiders in September.

The Indian was out cold. Ned Phillips, my Harvard roommate and sponsor of the Stars, watched over him with two men from Harvard's nine. Saturday was so still he could have been laid out for burial. The Harvard men were so apprehensive they might have been trying to keep the devil from stealing the Indian's soul. I stood at one corner of the bed and suppressed a smile. I didn't like Ned's ballplaying friends. The big catcher Schmidt was a bully. Shortstop Krueger was a snob. I felt I was on Saturday's side. He and I belonged to the big league.

"He's been drinking," said Schmidt. "Any more and he's no good tomorrow." The Harvard men exchanged glances. This was the night before the last game of their tour, and Ned had bet heavily. The Stars were going to play a team of the best players from teams they'd beaten. I didn't like Schmidt's insinuation about Indians and liquor. Having been a scholarship student at boarding school and college, I was sensitive to innuendo and used to not saying anything about it. King Saturday, I soon learned, didn't need anyone to speak for him.

The room was lit by a candle on the sill of the one window. The night in those Pennsylvania hills was chilly but five men in a small room made it warm. We were under the eaves and the roof slanted over our heads. The floorboards were rough and warped. King lay on a bare mattress. He was naked to the waist. Saturday was six feet but in the unstable candle light he looked gigantic. His chest was immense and his hands were as big as any man's I've ever seen. Saturday had scars on his arms and his black hair was as luxuriant as a woman's.

I tried not to stare and watched the other men. Ned's horsy, patrician face looked worried over his high collar. Ned was the scion of an old and wealthy Pittsburgh family. He was the most prim and starched man I ever met. Ned was a great krank, as fans were called then, but he could be aggressively formal and overlay every move with a patina of snobbery. A lot of Harvard hated him. If Ned liked you, your background was inconsequential. If he didn't, he had eyebrows like knives and a manner of dismissal which, even for someone raised with servants, could only be termed cruel. Like many rich young men, Ned Phillips seemed to be waiting for something. He assumed destiny couldn't avoid him and baseball occupied him while he waited.

Schmidt's thick neck, heavy German face, and unpleasant stare offered little to distract me from the Indian, nor did Tuck Krueger's neatly parted hair and habit of folding his arms across his chest and rocking back on his heels. Perhaps I sensed that one friendship and part of my life was ending, but I may be reading too much into the past. I know I stared at the man on the bed.

His face was remarkably ugly and remarkably handsome. I'd never seen one like it. Even in the shadows I saw the deep eye-sockets, the big nose — a huge nose — big ears, and a big, aggressively angular chin. The mouth was big too. Everything about that face seemed to jump out, yet it also held a deep oriental calm. Saturday's face, even in shadow, was a mixture of violence and indifference, cunning and oblivion. Whatever character was to be read there, whether savage or angel, was in signs I couldn't decode.

3

I've often wondered how much of the future could have been foretold by the events of that night. The great Emerson says ten minutes of any man's life holds its whole history, past and future, but I think the Concord philosopher was better observing mankind from afar than in hotel rooms. Perhaps I could have read my history with the Indian in the events of that night and the following day, but I didn't want to be warned. I wanted to be his friend.

Saturday opened his eyes a little before one. Schmidt and Krueger tensed. They were athletes and tensed with a supple yet threatening movement of forearms and fists. Ned raised his famous eyebrows.

"What do you fellows want?" said Saturday.

"Go back to sleep," said Schmidt.

"King," said Ned, as a breeze reduced the candle to a point of light and made the trees rustle. "Tomorrow's big. I bet our money home on it." Ned, of course, could get more money, but he liked the challenge of a wager.

The Indian sat up as the wind subsided and candle rose. His skin looked black. His hair almost reached his shoulders. Saturday rubbed his eyes and said, "I've had enough sleep." His voice wasn't as deep as I expected. Its pitch was remarkably like my own. His accent wasn't the "Down East" Maine inflection commonly thought to be the standard peasant speech of New England but more like Quebec. Saturday wasn't as Indian as I expected. Everyone called him "the Indian," but this is a vague and ominous title which makes me think of a Plains Indian with a bow on his back stalking a white man on a lonely trail. King Saturday was an eastern Indian. He was from Old Town, Maine and, as I learned, the last full-blooded Penobscot died the year he was born. Saturday was raised a Catholic, or at least attended a school run by Jesuits. He also went to Holy Cross College for two years on a baseball scholarship after being spotted in a Bangor summer league by Doc Powers, the big league catcher and Notre Dame man. Saturday looked Indian, he was Indian, but his voice and manner were more like a Canadian lumberjack.

"Who are you?" Saturday's black eyes got bigger and he gave me a smile which seemed to imply that he and I were in on a great joke.

"Henry," I said, and put out my hand. He reached up slowly and muscles in his arm and torso rippled. I saw a scar on his right hand which ran down to his wrist and another which curved toward his left nipple. In spite of these marks, the man's skin looked very fine. Like that contradictory face, Saturday's skin could look rough one moment and silky another. He had a knot of muscle in his forearm bigger than my biceps. The Indian squeezed my hand so hard I almost cried out.

"I'm with the Spiders."

"We'll be together," he said. Saturday's stomach was all one smooth, flat muscle. He was one of the few men I ever saw who looked better without a uniform.

"If I can keep you out of jail," I said.

King laughed but the other men didn't even smile. I knew Saturday's reputation as a wild man. Anyone who followed college baseball knew it. The Spiders knew it and had sent me to get him to Toledo after the All-Stars' last game.

"Let's get some sleep," said Ned, but Saturday reached under the bed and pulled out a pair of black boots.

"You've got to be ready for tomorrow," said Schmidt, his arms still folded across his jersey. Horse, as he was called, but not to his face, was said to be the "toughest man at Harvard College." Schmidt played football, as well as baseball, and beat

16

up two Yale men under the stands after the game in '94. He put both of them in Springfield City Hospital. Tuck Krueger rocked on his heels. He looked impatient and irritated at having to depend on someone as irresponsible as Saturday. I didn't know Schmidt, I knew Tuck Krueger. He was a member of the exclusive Porcellian Club and used to call me the "nobody from Cleveland."

"I'm going downstairs," said Saturday.

"We all need to sleep," said Ned.

"Then sleep," said Saturday. He stood up and took a white shirt off a peg. The room, with its sloping ceiling, bowed floorboards and unstable light, seemed smaller, and Saturday towered over the other men. He rolled up his sleeves but didn't button the shirt. He wore coarse beige trousers which, with the open shirt, made him look Mexican.

"We can play without him," said Krueger.

"He'll wake the rest," said Schmidt.

"The rest?" said Krueger, making his voice huskier. "He'll wake the dead if he gets started."

Saturday put on his boots. He reached under the bed and brought out a bottle.

"No, King," said Schmidt.

"Why not after the game, sport?" said Ned.

Saturday held up the bottle for our inspection and drank. He threw back his head and his hair touched the white collar of his shirt. "Who wants one?" said King Saturday.

"I do," I said.

My fellow Harvard men turned to me as if I were Judas. I swallowed a mouthful of cheap whiskey and crossed one of those metaphorical lines that break friendships and reveal the heart. I crossed a number of lines that night and each one was a stand against Ned Phillips. These stands were only gestures, but like most gestures they had inward implications. A minute later, King Saturday made a considerably less subtle gesture, but subtlety is to my life what danger was to his. I began to go over to the Indian's side with that drink. You might ask what I was giving up since I had my degree, a job, and the world likes the sound of the words "Harvard man," but Ned Phillips had been the center of my life for five years. I hadn't been his equal but I'd been his friend. He wanted to lend me money to go to law school. He liked to say he would buy a ballclub and we would run it. I knew this was a dream shared in box seats and whorehouses. As overbearing and difficult as Ned could be, we had some fine and reckless times at Harvard, but the rest of the world is another place. Ned offered me a job when I graduated law school and didn't understand when I said, "I thought we were friends."

Horse Schmidt reached across the bed and took the bottle. "Get out of here, Harrison," he said.

"Give it back," said Saturday.

"He don't need it anymore than you do."

The Indian was very still. There was no expression on his face.

"I'm tired of looking after you," said Schmidt. The catcher's jersey was open like Saturday's shirt. He was powerfully built — bull neck, compact shoulders, heavy, slightly bowed legs. Schmidt was several inches shorter than Saturday, and didn't rely on eyebrows to make a point.

King stepped toward Schmidt and the small room seemed even smaller. Horse had the bottle by the neck.

"Gentlemen, please," said Ned.

The catcher crouched in front of the door like an end about to make a tackle. "I ain't afraid of you," he said, and tossed the bottle into a corner. It broke. Schmidt closed his fists and lowered his head.

The Indian's left hand moved. A knife came out of the beige pants and the point went to Schmidt's throat. The catcher stepped back and bumped the door, knocking the knob to the floor. The point touched Schmidt's Adam's apple, the blade glistened, and for one awful moment, the "toughest man at Harvard College" thought he was going to have his throat cut.

"One day," said Saturday, in a low voice, "you lose your tongue."

Tuck Krueger, an agile shortstop, didn't move. Ned's mouth was open and, he told me later, mine was too. I remember the stillness. The whole world lost the ability to make a sound, except for Horse Schmidt, who breathed.

There were tears in the catcher's eyes when the knife came down. Saturday picked up the knob and opened the door. Schmidt backed out. Krueger and Ned looked numbly at each other. Perhaps, like me, they had never seen a knife drawn in anger.

4

I crossed another line when I followed Saturday down an oak staircase to the hotel bar. Ned said later, "He was your job," but I didn't follow a man who'd just pulled a knife into a dark room because it was my job.

Saturday struck a match and lit a lamp by the door. He smiled again, perhaps he appreciated being followed. He always liked an audience and that may have been the great joke we shared — he needed an audience and I needed a star, but I'm getting ahead of myself. Saturday opened the windows by the bar and we heard the trees. The night was cool, especially after the room under the eaves. Patches of mist drifted through that coal-mining town like irregular bands of spirits. The lamp sputtered and filled the mirror behind the bar with those unreal, silvery shadows which inhabit a dark glass and have always seemed to me the very picture of the realm of sleep and dreams. The horns of a buffalo head over the fireplace reached up and disappeared into the darkness. A Tiffany lamp hanging in the middle of the room was supported by a chain that might have hung from somnambulist regions. By the single lamp I saw that a billiard table by the windows had legs which ended in ornately carved claws. Saturday and I sat at the bar. His reflection floated over a ghostly row of bottles.

I asked him about playing Harvard when he was at Holy Cross, making my voice deeper so it wouldn't sound like a whisper in that empty place. Saturday vaulted over the bar and began checking the bottles. He lit another lamp, one of a half-dozen which bordered the mirror, and the second light began to dispel the occult play of mirror and shadow. The walls were red, the mirror draped with Fourth of July bunting, and the room decorated in that most provincial of styles: the patriotic. The owner was a German immigrant who, it seemed, had combined the Teutonic weakness for the martial with a reverence for trophies from his adopted homeland's Civil War. The red walls sported crossed swords, regimental flags, plates illustrating the careers of Sherman and Sheridan, and maps of the United States at different moments in our sweep across the continent. The second light didn't entirely remove the tavern from the realm of shadow to the red region of vulgarity. Etchings of Lincoln and Grant brooded in dark corners as if those northern gods had been Commanders-in-Chief of the Land of Nod.

"I saw the throw you made against Harvard the papers called 'lightning,'" I said. "Two professors measured it at 414 feet."

"I beat Harvard," said Saturday, turning around. His hair was lit from behind and looked blue-black, even purple.

"No big leaguer's ever thrown more than 430 feet," I said, referring to the mark Gil Hatfield set in a contest.

Saturday held up his left hand and spread the fingers. "I can throw five hundred feet."

I doubted that but wasn't about to contradict him. Saturday returned to the bottles. I watched his hands in the silvery depths of the mirror. "Who's your favorite player?" I asked, too nervous not to talk, and anxious to show off how much I knew. Saturday continued to pick up bottles, inspect the labels, and return them like an angler not satisfied with his catch. A green one finally met his approval and he put two shot glasses on the bar. The Indian poured, threw down a shot with a lustrous toss of the head, and said, "Me."

I disposed of my whiskey with a modest toss, and said, "I mean in the League."

"I don't watch," he said, and drank.

"What about this fellow Scott?" I said. "He's pitching tomorrow. He beat you in Potterstown. The Giants are interested in him."

Saturday came out from behind the bar. He walked this time, and went to the billiard table. I didn't know that he didn't like to talk baseball. If the game excited him, it did so only on the field. Saturday took down a cue from a rack by the fireplace and arranged the balls on the table. He leaned on the white-tipped instrument and studied the shot. The man had the ability to be absolutely still. I'd been around ballplayers enough to know that most of them couldn't be still unless they were asleep. Saturday was motionless. I later heard him say he could see in the dark and having watched him study those billiard balls in that country tavern, I almost believe it.

I tapped my foot and peeled the label off a whiskey bottle. Saturday's silence did that to me. He could create an aura that all hell was about to break loose by being quiet. His silences were like lightning on the horizon seen from a small boat: one felt precautions should be taken. The click of billiard balls rang through the room. Saturday watched the balls move over the green table, rearranged them, and studied the new combination as Ned Phillips came down the stairs. Ned looked elegant in his white, English suit as he crossed the lobby. He entered the bar like the hero of a play who's been off-stage for the fourth act and appears for the fifth, but Saturday didn't look up.

"Whiskey," said Ned, taking out a cigar as if it were a treaty, and putting his foot on the brass rail under the bar. "Tuck says he won't play tomorrow."

"And Schmidt?" I said.

"He's angry but he'll play. Playing's a matter of pride with Horse. Tuck's moaning about the goddamn principle of the thing." Ned puffed and watched Saturday. "If those prinkers can just stand the sight of each other for another day, we'll be all right." He sounded worried, but the way he held the cigar, the cut of his suit, and the tilt of his aquiline nose and hard jaw, suggested that nothing could rattle Ned Phillips. Nothing, at any rate, I could do.

"We may not," he said, keeping his eye on Saturday, who banked the cueball off two sides of the table so that it struck a ball, which struck another, "play at all."

"We'll play," said the Indian, without looking up.

Ned pointed his cigar at Saturday. "The night is young."

"Well," I said as Saturday studied the results of his shot, "we'll find out who can play with a hangover."

"He can," said Ned.

We were joined by the hotel-keeper. Fritz wore a black coat over a nightshirt, striped pants and red slippers. He had a red beard and shrewd, little eyes. "Gentlemen, gentlemen!" Fritz waved his hands and rushed around the bar. "It's late. Late. Very late."

"I'll cover it," said Ned.

"Someone must pay for the viskey. Mr. Saturday, you play tomorrow. Do not drink tonight." King laughed. Fritz fussed over the glasses and pretended to be irritated but he knew Ned had money and was impressed that "die Spielen" attended "the Harvard" and "the Yale."

The All-Stars began to come in. Schmidt and Krueger didn't appear but the rest of the lads, including pitcher Bill Duryee, said hello to Saturday in an easy way that indicated they hadn't heard about the knife. The lights around the mirror and all the wall-lamps were lit. Left fielder Cates stood on a chair and lit the Tiffany lamp. Fritz's tavern shone in all its red, jingo vainglory. I noticed headlines announcing the news from Antietam and Gettysburg, Appomattox, and even Vera Cruz. No Pennsylvania public house was complete without some embroidered wisdom of Franklin, and this was to be had if any of the lads cared to read it. King Saturday went behind the mahogany bar and, framed by lights which might have lit a stage, and red, white and blue bunting, served his teammates. Two salesmen, both wearing suspenders and shirts without collars, marched in and complained about the noise. They were palliated with whiskey.

The Indian grinned and told his teammates what to drink. His hands glided over bottles, poured shots, drew beer from a keg, and sent foaming steins down the length of the bar. When everyone had a drink, he arm-wrestled Lefty Adams and slammed the first baseman's fist into the bar. No one else wanted to arm-wrestle, so Saturday downed three quick shots, took a towel and rubbed the bar until it shined.

"The bets are in jeopardy," said Ned.

The shorter salesman, a commercial cherub with pudgy, pink cheeks, made his way past Lucius Cates and tapped Ned on the shoulder. Ned raised an eyebrow. A tap on the shoulder was not his idea of an introduction.

"This the way the boys train for a big game?" The cherub had bright, small blue eyes in his pink face. He snapped his suspenders.

"Always," said Ned, turning away.

The salesman tried my shoulder. "The folks in town are takin' this pretty serious." The suspenders snapped again. "They're closin' the mines and half the county'll be there." The pink face and bright eyes moved closer. "They don't want to be beat by a bunch of college boys," he lowered his high-pitched voice, "and an Indian."

I felt like snapping his suspenders myself and telling him how highly I valued his profession, but Saturday spied an accordion hanging from the wall by a leather strap, sprinted around the bar, and took it down. "Nein!" cried Fritz, "Nein!" The Indian pumped the instrument. It groaned and produced a God-awful noise. If any guest still slept, he might have thought the Final Trumpet had sounded. Fritz snatched the accordion. "I play vat you vant! Vat you vant! Anyting! Promise!" Saturday laughed and might have snatched the instrument back but two young women sleepily joined the company. "Mr. Saturday," said Fritz. "Meet Fraulein Fanny and Fraulein Rose." The "frauleins" were country girls with broad faces and yellow dresses. They yawned and smiled shyly. Fritz looked at Saturday and began to play "Turkey In The Straw."

The Indian grabbed Rose, the more buxom of the two, and pulled her into the middle of the floor. His teammates grinned and raised their glasses. They clapped as Saturday took the young woman in his arms. They stomped as he began to whirl her about that crowded room. Rose gave a little shriek and then proved to be as nimble as Saturday. Fritz pumped harder and the salesmen whistled. Even Ned tapped his foot. The Indian's open shirt and blue-black hair flew as he high-stepped with that agile barmaid, and they went round and round, as if they'd known each other for years. Rose's yellow frock brushed the bar, the billiard table, and the irons in the fireplace. Saturday slid by Lucius Cates and kicked over a chair. He spun Rose into Oscar Harris, who let out a hoot, guided her by Ned, and stopped her in front of me. Rose gathered up her dress with a sort of country curtsy, took Saturday's hand, and spun him around. They went arm-in-arm under the blue Tiffany lamp. Saturday's forearm was a moving knot of muscle. Rose's curly, corn-colored hair bounced on her shoulders and a mustache of perspiration formed over the little blond one on her upper lip. They must have circled the room twenty times, and when the song was over, Saturday hugged her and everyone cheered.

After a round of libations, Fritz dropped the pace with a melancholy "Blue Danube." Fanny told me the song reminded Fritz of his wife, who'd run away with a railway conductor. Saturday took Rose in his arms and waltzed her about as properly as ever I was taught at Miss Walker's on Euclid Avenue.

5

Ned walked proudly through the Stars in his white English suit. They slapped backs and sang college songs in a state of happy disarray. They wore shirts without collars, jerseys or those striped undergarments which make a man look like a lifeguard. Ned looked like a prince among his subjects, which was the way he always wanted to look. He was white and confident and greeted the possibility that the Eastern All-Stars might tomorrow be a troop of sots and cost him his bets with a smile of pure *noblesse oblige*. Ned was enjoying himself.

He ignored me. I stood against the bar and watched Saturday play billiards. Ned must have talked to everyone in the room before he acknowledged me. Had the night ended with the Indian waltzing and the lads drinking themselves into a stupor, our friendship might have attenuated into the sad formalities of men who've changed, grown, or just aren't young anymore, but as Ned had said, the night had just begun.

"Loaded already?" he said, as I leaned against the bar.

"No," I said. "Should I be?" which was one of those remarks friends who aren't going to be friends anymore make.

"Since when do you need an excuse, Henry?"

I didn't answer right away. Ned Phillips was a man I'd tried to be like. I copied his accent, dressed like him, and wanted people to know he liked me. My father died when I was ten and a world died with him. Mother managed to provide the trappings of that world: dancing lessons, boarding school, Harvard; which meant borrowed clothes, slights, and scholarships. When I met Ned Phillips I thought he was inviting me back.

"Better keep your pitcher sober," I said.

"Sometimes you say just the right thing, Henry," Ned said, and walked away.

Saturday was betting teammates that he could bank a ball off two sides of the table, around a glass of beer, and into another ball. Fanny and Rose held the money. The Indian's chest looked bronze against his coarse shirt. His eyes were glazed. The mystery I'd seen in that contradictory face had been replaced by a sort of wild shrewdness.

The shot misfired and the ball knocked over the glass making a large stain on the green table. "Who vill pay?" yelled Fritz, and the accordion stopped, but Saturday went by the little man with the leather instrument around his neck, and stood under the Tiffany lamp. The blue light made his thick hair black and purple. His teammates stopped their back-slapping, betting and arm-wrestling.

"Who's betting the game?" shouted Saturday. "How 'bout you, Pop? Win some money! Clean the table."

Fritz shook his head. His beard was red as fire and he looked ready to stomp through the floor like Rumpelstiltskin. "Never bet," he said. "Never bet."

"You'll never be rich," said Saturday, tossing his head so his profuse hair fell on his shoulders. "You!" he pointed at the commercial cherub who, fortified with free whiskey, had been telling all in earshot he sold soap. "I bet both sides," said the salesman, winking. "I can't lose."

"A jackass has two ears," said Saturday. "How 'bout you, Chief?"

The taller drummer hooked his thumbs through his suspenders. "I like the miners. You fellas are breakin' training."

That brought a hearty laugh. Fritz played "A Hot Time In The Old Town Tonight" and lustily swung the accordion. Like Orpheus, the German thought his influence came from song. Second baseman Harris and Lucius Cates grabbed Fanny and Rose and the Stars turned to Saturday to see if he would halt or encourage a dance floor free-for-all with the young ladies. The Indian did neither. He pulled Ned onto the floor.

Saturday put his arm around Ned's linen waist, took Ned's hand in his large hand, and made him waltz. Ned was surprised. He made an ironic face and laughed. Ned was frequently ironic. He waltzed a few steps but Saturday wouldn't let him go. Ned tapped the Indian's shoulder with his free hand. He wasn't angry. He was making a suggestion, asking a favor, but Saturday gave no quarter and Fritz played harder. Ned's disdain flared into anger. He pushed Saturday but couldn't get away.

I was fascinated — utterly caught in the absurdity of the moment. Fritz played, Ned pushed, and that horribly exotic couple moved across the floor. I didn't walk out. I didn't grab a partner and act the harlequin to outjoke the joker. I watched and Ned never forgave me. Perhaps he was right. It wouldn't have hurt him so much if I hadn't been there.

I couldn't take my eyes off them: Saturday's iridescent hair, his chest pressed against Ned's chest, his cruel hands. The Indian must have been very strong. Ned was solidly built — he played a year of "club" football, something I refused to risk my round, Welsh face at, and took his licks too — but he couldn't break Saturday's hold. He could only slap the Indian's chest.

The lads clapped with the music just as they had for Saturday and Rose. They clapped with a vengeance. They might not have if Schmidt and Krueger had been there but Ned's lieutenants were upstairs bemoaning the fact there were no trains after midnight. The Stars clapped and Ned was stripped of his egotism before their very eyes. Some of them grinned, others looked frightened. Later, everyone said it was a joke.

Saturday threw back his head and laughed. He wheeled Ned against the bar, shoved him and caught him, so Ned tipped backward in the classic pose of a lady swept off her feet. Ned hit Saturday's shoulder. The Indian laughed. They spun under the blue lamp, twisting through the cigar smoke, past the grins and stares. Saturday's shirt flew, his scar throbbed. Ned's face burned. They went round in a dizzy solitude. It was as though there were only the three of us, or maybe just two. Saturday could have been something supernatural — a Caliban or Mr. Hyde, who acted out my basest instincts and exposed Ned's worst fears. He made Ned pay for every pretense, and destroyed me too by showing my friend how mean I was.

27

Saturday bounced Ned off the bar and caught him. "Enough!" shouted Ned. His shout was a gasp and a cry. Saturday looked as though he thought Ned were having the time of his life. "Enough," said Ned in a hoarse whisper, and Saturday dropped his arm. "Damn you," said Ned. His face changed from red to white.

The Indian released him and Fritz stopped playing. "OK," said Saturday, and looked at his teammates as if waiting for someone to tell him what he'd done wrong. "OK." Then, almost as an afterthought, Saturday ripped Ned's vest and shirt in half.

Ned looked at the Indian, straightened his cuffs, and walked out.

6

I stood at the bar and drank. I could have followed Ned but I had nothing to say. Our friendship was over. Had I gone to him and said the Indian was a drunken son of a bitch and an invert to boot, it wouldn't have made a difference. My friend had been insulted in front of men in his pay, two frightened girls, a shopkeeper, and an old friend. Saturday had cut him in a way that allowed no apology. He had made a joke out of Ned Phillips. He had made a joke out of Ned's confident, Eastern, ironical style. Saturday had cut to the quick which was one of his talents — an uncanny willingness to go for the jugular. King never treated me like that. He always treated me like a friend, which could also be difficult. I was a man who, for whatever reason, didn't offend him.

Fritz was behind the bar with the two girls, apprehensively serving whiskey. Saturday looked at each man in the room and they smiled cautiously. Only the salesmen continued to drink as if nothing had happened.

Lucius Cates broke the silence by yelling, "Long live the King!" Lefty Adams doused him with beer and all the men shouted, "Long live the King!" They banged their glasses and steins, happy to break the tension. Saturday seemed pleased and raised his glass. He smiled and his gaze fell on a pair of swords. In two strides he was on the bar pulling them down.

"Nein!" cried Fritz, looking fearfully from one "spieler" to another.

"Who can stick it in the wall?" said Saturday, waving the sword.

"Herr Saturday, please," pleaded Fritz, who was literally at the Indian's feet.

"That!" said Saturday, pointing the sword at a portrait of Cap Anson, the famous Chicago White Stocking, which hung next to a calendar for the year 1895 and a picture of President Cleveland. The shorter drummer — the cherubic representative of that class which upset Henry James for having no soul, no language, and no earthly purpose but the pushing of shoddy merchandise — looked at Fanny and said, "Swordplay and a drunken Indian are too much for me."

I don't know if the man was trying to impress Fanny, or felt he was speaking for the group and perhaps the whole nineteenth century, but he made a mistake. The Stars jumped at the opportunity to be on Saturday's side. The drummer started for the door and Lefty Adams blocked his way. The salesman looked at his commercial brother, then at Fritz who was contemplating a charcoal rendering of Lincoln, and was pushed back to Saturday.

"You," said King, jumping off the bar and taking the drummer by his once clean shirtfront. "Try it." Saturday ripped the man's shirt open and gave him the sword. The drummer stared at the saber as if he'd never seen one before. The lads yelled, "Go on!", "Be brave!" and called him a fool. The other salesman slipped out. Saturday pushed the cherub against the bar. The drummer dropped the sword. "Need courage?" said the Indian, and taking the man by the nose, yanked his head back, and forced him to drink from a bottle until the salesman gagged and spat whiskey all over the bar. The lads roared with laughter and Lefty Adams slapped the man's face dry with a towel.

"Let me go!" cried the drummer, but no one had hold of him. Oscar Harris poured beer on his head.

"Pick it up," said Saturday.

The drummer wiped his eyes. His wet, thin, brown hair was pasted to his scalp like a wig. He tried to part his hair with his hands and Saturday grabbed him by the nose again. He pinched that short, pink nose, pulled the drummer's head back and stuck the bottle down his throat. Lefty Adams tried to pull the man's pants down but a thick, black belt held them up.

"Let him go," said Fritz, but no one even turned to look at him.

Saturday took the drummer by his wet hair and made him bend over and pick up the sword. The salesman's plump face was white. He held the weapon by the bell with the blade pointed down. Saturday raised his hand. The drummer took a step forward and threw the sword. It sailed through the air, bell first, and clattered into the mantel, smashing a porcelain mug illustrated with *Washington Crossing the Delaware*.

"I'm going to be sick." The drummer put his hand to his mouth and started for the door. Saturday raised his boot and gave him a kick which drove the man toward the fire. The cherub stumbled and might have fallen into the flames but Lefty Adams caught him and sent him back to Saturday, who gave the man another boot and sent the purveyor of soap at the door. Several lads imitated Saturday and the unfortunate drummer was literally kicked into the hall where he landed face down.

"Like this!" Saturday jumped on the bar and took down the other sword. He balanced it on his index finger the way I used to balance a knife before throwing it. Saturday took the weapon by the blade, pulled it back over his head, and let fly. It did two complete revolutions like a chariot wheel and landed point forward, shattering glass, skewering Cap Anson, and sticking in the wall.

"Who vill pay? Who vill pay?" howled Fritz, waving his arms. Lefty Adams grabbed Fritz and hoisted him onto the bar. Oscar Harris put a towel in Fritz's mouth and Lefty pinned his arms behind his back.

More swords came down. Lucius Cates and Harris tried balancing them on their fingers. Cates hurled his sword at a buffalo head over the mantel. It missed but broke a plate commemorating the surrender of Richmond. The other sword smashed a blue mug. Lefty Adams picked up a billiard ball, and the Stars headed for the door. Cates and Harris picked up balls. Saturday jumped over the bar and pulled Rose down. I fell to my hands and knees as a billiard ball crashed into the mirror. I crawled behind the bar as another hit the bottles in front of the mirror. Saturday and Rose were rolling in a puddle, Fritz and Fanny scampered behind the bar and through a door which led to the front hall. I stumbled over Saturday and Rose — she was kissing him — and we were showered with whiskey and splinters of glass. I got over them and made my way into the hall.

With a great yell, Oscar Harris hacked away at the buffalo head. After several lusty strokes, the head gave way and fell to the floor as a cloud of sawdust rose in the air.

I stood in the hall with alarmed guests and cheering ballplayers. Rose joined me and we stood over the fallen drummer. Saturday was under the blue lamp, waving a sword. The room was empty. Ned watched from the stairs. Schmidt and Krueger were with him. His shirt and vest hung down and his face was still red.

With the barroom to himself, Saturday leapt on the billiard table and cut down the curtains. Fritz moaned and pulled at Ned's coat but Ned paid no attention. Saturday jumped off the billiard table and leapt onto the bar. He cut down the bunting over the broken mirror. He slashed the necks of bottles. His white shirt swung as he ripped down maps and cut Grover Cleveland. His eyes were fierce but strangely calm. He had made the storm but its center was still. Saturday broke plates and hacked down a headline announcing the end of the Civil War. He leapt from bar to floor to billiard table and back to the bar. The saber flashed — its point danced brightly through the air.

Everything came down: the USA, 1895, a bellrope, embroidered wisdom, lace, bunting, and even the American flag. The spectators winced as the flag was ripped. They groaned as frame, glass, and George Washington were cut with three glistening strokes. Lincoln wasn't spared. Everything was hacked, struck, or sliced. There was nothing woman-like about the shining black hair as this bronze marauder strode across the bar to the tables and back to the bar. His knotty forearms flexed, his chest rippled, and his skin looked rough and dark. He laughed and cut and leapt until nothing remained but the Tiffany lamp. He stood on the bar and contemplated it while Fritz said, "Nein, nein," in a pathetic voice. King sliced the cord and the blue treasure crashed to the oak floor.

Saturday doused the burning remains with the contents of the beer keg and then threw down the keg. He surveyed the wreck of the barroom and spied the oil lamps which flanked what was left of the mirror. The Indian carefully lifted the glass shades off each lamp with the tip of the saber, and flung them against the wall.

The lawn, as well as the main hall, was full of spectators. They gaped through the open door and at the windows. Thirty people watched Saturday, who stood on the bar, lit by naked flames, surrounded by a broken mirror, a decapitated buffalo, a pile of Tiffany glass, shredded lace, torn bunting and so much broken glass that he might have been in an icehouse. The Indian looked dark as an African: a sort of glistening, ebony Ajax.

7

The evening wasn't over. Saturday sat on the billiard table in the brilliantly lit bar. I sat on the stairs, thinking my bridges to the past and future had been wrecked along with Fritz's tavern. I hadn't learned that the Indian could give any evening one more twist.

Saturday was alone in the bright, ruined room. Glass sparkled and glittered around him. He had stuck the sword in the bar where it stood like Excalibur awaiting Arthur. The red walls were scarred and stained. White shreds of curtain littered the floor. A pile of blue glass stood in the middle of the room like a burial mound. Ned and Krueger watched him from the hall, their backs turned conspicuously to me. They nodded and smiled with grim satisfaction, convinced, I'm sure, that their preconceptions about everything from nobodies-from-Cleveland to Indians had been vindicated. The rest of Ned's nine were scattered. Several lads watched Saturday but several had gone to bed. Oscar Harris sat next to Fritz on the first stair and tried to stop the German from crying. Lucius Cates was draped around the newel post and sang a song I didn't recognize.

King gave me a sly smile and slid off the table. He walked out of the bar, crunching glass under his boots. He nodded as he passed Ned but Ned looked through him and didn't even bother to raise an eyebrow. Saturday came to the stairs and put his hands on the balusters.

"Where're the ladies, counselor?" His hands were scratched and nicked but not bleeding. The coarse pants were stained.

"Something frightened them."

"Their loss, Harry."

Saturday leaned over and picked up Fritz by the armpits. Fritz babbled and covered his face with his hands. "You're going to be rich," said Saturday in his Canadian tenor voice. The Indian's eyes were bright and shrewd like a Hebrew pedlar. Cunning made his angular face handsome.

"I'm ruined," said Fritz. Saturday removed Fritz's hands from his wet face and stood him against the wall. "Rich, Fritz, rich. We'll all be rich." King brought the hotel-keeper to Ned.

"Let's talk," said Saturday.

Ned raised an eyebrow and looked at Krueger, but Saturday wasn't put off. He put a hand on Ned's shoulder and said, "Outside." Ned looked skeptically at his Porcellian chum but let himself be guided into the dining room.

"Come on, Harry," said Saturday. "You too, Fritz."

We stepped over the drummer into the dark room. Fritz looked anxiously at the plates in an oak cabinet and even put out a hand to steer Saturday away from it, but King didn't look at the cabinet, or the long table set for breakfast with straw mats and earthenware mugs. Saturday wasn't interested in breaking dishes. He had his arm around Ned's shoulder and talked in a low voice as he led him through a Dutch door into the chilly August night.

We might have been in another world outside. By the light of a moon barely above the trees, I saw an arbor, a well and several apple trees. We heard people walking on glass but they seemed far away. Their hoots and guffaws were muffled by the wind in the trees and got lost in the dark Pennsylvania countryside with its white moon and night-rustling leaves.

Saturday released Ned and said, "Did you bet?"

Ned's hands were in his pockets. His shirt and vest swung as he walked. Ned exaggerated this with his gait, which I think was meant to be an ironic commentary on his plight as Saturday's victim. "I did," he said, "in an ill-considered moment."

"Bet everything," said Saturday. "The odds will be fantastic."

"My club couldn't beat a lady's nine," said Ned.

"Leave that to me." Saturday turned to me. "Harry, bet all your money. We've got to pay for Fritz's barroom. I owe Ned a suit."

We were some distance from the hotel. The sound of sweeping and tinkle of glass could barely be heard over the crickets and cicadas. A voice carried on about a "drunken Indian," but in the wind it sounded like incantation or a ghost. King Saturday was interested only in Ned. They walked a few paces in front of us. I heard King apologize for ripping Ned's coat. Ned gave him a cigar, lit one himself, and they took a turn through the apple trees. Saturday's face was a dark blur in the intermittent glow of the cigar. His skin looked silky. He talked and pointed — at the hotel, the moon, his head, and Ned. He shrugged, took Ned's arm, pulled away, and then threw back his head and laughed. Ned puffed on his cigar. Saturday's gestures became wider. It was a virtuoso performance. King had a plan and Ned listened. Saturday told him the evening's antics were all "planned," and that he'd ripped Ned's coat and demolished Fritz's tavern to make the locals think he was crazy to change the odds for tomorrow's game. I don't know if Ned believed it. I know Ned wanted to save face and it was easier to be angry with me, who he understood, than Saturday, who he didn't. I don't know if I believed it. Saturday kept saying the evening was his "design" and, like Ned, I wanted to believe him. I still want to believe him. Later, the Indian's motives and my ability to discern them became, quite literally, matters of life and death.

They walked in front of us. Ned's white suit shone in the moonlight while Saturday seemed to blend into the darkness. Ned appeared to have forgiven this unpredictable giant who pointed, talked, and spread his arms like wings. Saturday put his hands in his pockets and strolled at Ned's side as if they were businessmen cutting a deal. He thanked Ned for inviting him on the tour. He apologized for the suit again but said it was his "plan." Saturday turned to Fritz and told him he would "pay for everything," even if he had to use the money the Spiders were going to give him. He asked me to be his lawyer.

Fritz sobbed.

Saturday raised his left hand. "Trust me."

Fritz kept sobbing and the Indian shrugged. Our host had his own tricks, and no doubt wanted a check from the Mellon Bank, not an option on a wager from a man with liquor on his breath. "I don't bet. Nein. Nein."

"You'll be taken care of," said Ned.

"How do you propose to beat the miners?" I said, unable to restrain my credulity.

"Get their pitcher into a throwing contest before the game," said Saturday.

"Tom Scott won't allow himself to be drawn into a contest," I said.

"Challenge him in front of the crowd, Harry," said Saturday. "He won't back down in front of his people."

8

The field was a half mile outside town. When we got there it was ringed by wagons, carriages, and spectators, which enclosed the field of play in an impromptu stadium. The line of carriages and crowd was broken only in dead center field by a barn, the roof of which was covered with kranks, one of whom waved an American flag. I had on white flannel trousers, a blue jacket, a new pair of white bucks with red rubber soles, and the snappiest straw hat that side of the Charles River. I was dressed like Ned Phillips ready for a stroll with a belle. This seemed appropriate for the last day we would act like friends.

I wasn't the only person dressed for the occasion. Some of those country kranks wore war-bonnets and whooped like Indians. Despite the bonnets, whoops, and cracks about drunken Indians, it was a beautiful afternoon. A few high, puffy clouds drifted toward distant mountains. Families sat on wagons parked along the foul lines. Enterprising lads climbed trees beyond the spectators in right and waved and shouted. I'd never seen a country ballfield with such a large crowd.

The Hooper nine, wearing new yellow jerseys, was loosening up in the outfield. The Stars were taking infield practice. As little as I cared for Tuck Krueger, it was good to see him scoop up grounders at short and make hard throws to Lefty Adams at first. Adams looked pale but moved gracefully, spurred on by shouts of "Rummy!" and "Drunken Indian!" which came from both base lines, and a particularly vocal group near the newly whitewashed backstop. Horse Schmidt hit grounders, Rogers of Harvard bounced agilely off third, and Bill Duryee, who seemed to have completely escaped the night's ravages, threw easily by first.

King Saturday stood with Ned by the visitors' bench. The Indian's arms were folded across his chest and he paid no attention to the crowd. He was so completely in control of himself I was willing to believe he had planned everything. He calmly discussed Bilk Duryee's motion while a grandstand of yahoos called him a "redskin," a drunk, and anything else they could think of.

"We're starting late, counselor," he said, and pointed at the wagons, pedestrians and stragglers that were packing the area behind the grandstand. I couldn't discern any effects of his drinking, but then I never could. It was impossible to tell if the crowd bothered him. With a nod, Saturday went out to short right field and began loosening up an unsteady Oscar Harris.

Ned and I sat on the bench with Lucius Cates who looked about to be sick. The fellows behind the backstop rode him unmercifully. Ned and I exchanged the coy grins of men who know each other well but aren't friends.

Tom Scott, the man I was to challenge, was throwing with his catcher. Scott was a lanky fellow with a mean jaw. The catcher was chewing a wad of tobacco with professional expertise and had the gnarled, clawlike hands of a man who plays ball for money. The local heroes were hitching up their pants, spitting in their gloves, and rubbing dirt on their hands as if they couldn't wait to get at us.

A tall fellow with a bugle blew the cavalry charge and the crowd responded with a chant of "Injun! Injun! Drunken Injun!" I studied those squinting, pallid men who had been let out of the mines and were so ready to yell at an Indian or a man with an education. There must have been a thousand of them standing, sitting, in trees, on shoulders, behind the backstop, and pressing five rows deep around the infield.

"Let's go," said Ned, who was wearing a spotless white suit. He must have been traveling with two of them and, I'll say this, I never saw him look better. We walked out to the pitcher's mound. Ned waved the Stars to the sidelines and pointed to Horse Schmidt.

"Get those stiffs out of here!" yelled a man with a tom-tom, who had stationed himself behind third base.

"Go back to college, sonny!"

"Sissy!"

Schmidt brought me a milking stool and a miner's bucket. We had something to offend everybody and heard obscenities which made Ned frown. With great ceremony I put the stool on home plate, examined the bucket as if it smelled, and put it on the stool. The crowd was really yelling. Ned walked off the field. The Indian joined me. I raised my hand and turned to Tom Scott. "My man can knock that bucket off with two pitches and you can't do it in three."

The locals answered for the big fellow the Giants liked.

"He can do anything that goddamned Indian can!"

"And he ain't been to college!"

"Neither's that Indian!"

"Tom can hit that with a cow patty!"

I bowed. This was one of the great moments of my life. I thought of precisely the right retort. "Sir, despite your proficiency with manure, I propose a baseball."

I tossed the ball to King Saturday who was standing on the mound. He caught it with his huge bare hand, wound up, threw easily, and knocked the bucket off with a resounding clang. Schmidt retrieved the ball and threw it to me. I walked over to Tom and handed it to him.

Tom stomped out to the mound squeezing the ball so hard his hand turned white. Next to the Indian, Tom looked ridiculous. The sleeves of his uniform were too short while Saturday filled his uniform like a big leaguer. Tom wound up with a grimace, all elbows and legs, like a sailboat with the sheet flapping, and cut loose a tremendous fast pitch.

There was no doubt this gangly fellow could throw. The ball came in twice as fast as Saturday's and missed by two feet.

"Gimme the damn thing!"

Horse whipped the ball back to him. Tom stood on the mound and stared at the bucket. The rube knew his craft. He got control of himself, rocked back, didn't throw as hard, and hit the bucket cleanly.

"How 'bout that, city slicker?"

"Good enough for you, college boy?"

"Want to trade your hat for my jackass?"

I doffed my skimmer to the crowd. Tom started back to his mates. He didn't see King Saturday at second base. Ned reassembled the bucket and stool, and I, with elaborate ease, threw the ball to King Saturday. He threw without a wind-up and knocked the bucket off.

"Are you up to it?" I said to Tom. The blood was pounding in my ears but I thought I cut a fancy figure.

"Here, sir!"

Tom went out to second base. He was furious. The fellow with the drum yelled, "Don't let an Indian beat you!" Men began to wager. The crowd was enjoying our trick. Tom had to gauge his throw. He was a pitcher and used to 60 feet 6 inches. Now he was at second and everything was different. He wound up and threw from a normal pitching motion. The ball was true but sank at the last moment and bounced off to the left. Schmidt retrieved it and threw it back.

This time Tom reared back like a man at a country fair trying to scatter a pyramid of wooden milk bottles. He missed by five feet.

I stepped into the breach. "Give him three! Give him three!"

Tom got the ball and didn't waste time. He threw without a wind-up and hit the bucket.

The crowd cheered but wanted more. King Saturday was fifty feet behind second base and someone yelled, "Tom's got his work cut out for him!" Schmidt put the bucket on the stool and I threw the ball to King Saturday. He eyed the bucket. His first throw had been tauntingly easy. His second had been harder but not much. This time Saturday put the ball on the ground, backed up, came in, picked it up as if a runner were breaking for the plate, and cut loose a bullet which made the crowd whoop.

The throw came over second base three feet off the ground but so hard it rose like a fast pitch and flew dead center into the bucket. That peg had more on it than most pitches.

Tom walked out to the Indian with his head down. I threw him the ball without fanfare. He took a step and threw.

Scott had a good arm. The pitcher is usually the best athlete on his team, and Tom, despite the gaggle of elbows and legs,

42

was an athlete. His throw came in like a bullet but missed. Tom made two more hard, impressive throws, and each missed.

"That round goes to Mr. Saturday!"

The Indian moved out another fifty feet. The crowd was really excited. Even if they knew what we were doing, they were caught in the rhythm of the contest. This was man against man, champion against champion: a ritual as old as Homer. Again Saturday put the ball on the ground. It was brown and nicked, which made it harder to throw straight. Saturday moved back, came in, swooped, and threw in one graceful, muscular motion. I love to watch outfielders throw. It's such fine, singular business. Throwing is like making love, anyone can do it, doing it well is another matter. Saturday had an amazing arm. The ball came in on a line. It missed and went all the way to the backstop which it hit with a sharp crack.

The crowd loved it. They were already entranced by that muscular body and those murderously hard, accurate throws. Saturday threw again and missed. Then he hit a leg of the stool and sent the bucket down.

I felt sorry for Tom. He was in front of his people and had to throw from every distance Saturday chose until the Indian backed him up to the barn. Tom had a strong arm but wasn't used to this. They went out another fifty feet. Tom threw three times and missed. Saturday hit the bucket. They went out another fifty feet and Saturday's throw came in even harder. He hit the bucket on the bounce. Tom tried and missed.

"Reach the plate on the fly!" I yelled, and waved the bucket away.

Tom tried. He was straining but wouldn't quit. They were three hundred and fifty feet out and Tom threw five times. Saturday had him mesmerized. Tom was one of those country boys who, like John Henry, can't believe they can be beaten. He finally made a tremendous throw which came in high but made the plate on two hops. Saturday threw a strike.

There was no place for them to go. Someone shouted, "Move that wagon!" and people started yelling, "Clear center field!" Everyone was standing and shouting. Two wagons were moved which opened a four hundred foot corridor. Saturday handed Tom the ball but Tom shook his head. The man who'd never been beaten stepped aside. The crowd went wild. Only one man was going to try from this distance and that man was their champion. Men who'd cursed Saturday were yelling for him. The Indian asked for the bucket and studied the distance. I was in the field and the bucket was the size of a toy. The drum beat frantically. The bugle blew. The whole crowd, even the Hooper players, were on his side.

King Saturday gave Tom a nod of camaraderie, took two steps, and threw. He put his whole tremendous body into it. The ball was never more than ten feet off the ground and had the trajectory of a cannon shot: level, straight, a white blur; it didn't sink, sail or veer. And it hit the bucket.

I don't think the crowd could believe it. Then they roared. The kranks on the barn waved their flag and danced. Lads in the trees climbed higher and shook the branches. I think every man thought he'd seen the limit of what can be done with a baseball.

Part Two

1

No one saw the Indian until spring training. He disappeared after the All-Stars thrashed those western Pennsylvania men, and I returned to Cleveland with a glowing report but no Saturday. The Robison brothers, who owned the Spiders, weren't sure whether my services would be needed for 1898. I spent a long, unhappy winter lawyering for a coal company whose owner was trying to marry my mother. She liked him better than I did, and the match would have been more than prudent, but the lady remained faithful to a blue-eyed ghost who, for her, was forever a twenty-three year old soldier left for dead by two armies in the Antietam cornfield.

I cursed King Saturday. It appeared he'd cost me my position with the Spiders as well as sealed a nasty ending to my friendship with Ned Phillips. I didn't blame him for Ned. My Porcellian friend and I were lost to each other before that difficult August night, but Frank Robison was very unhappy when Saturday didn't report to Toledo.

The Indian took and the Indian gave. He walked into training camp at Hot Springs, Arkansas, and demanded to know where I was. Manager Tebeau said, "Where the hell were you?" Patsy let Saturday play in an exhibition against the Giants, and the Indian doubled twice and threw two runners out at the plate from right field. I received a telegram stating that if I paid my way to Hot Springs, I had my job again.

Rookies weren't treated well in 1898. The veterans were an old guard who were as loyal to each other as Napoleon's had been to him. They resented anyone trying to take one of their jobs. Saturday was good-natured about their pranks, but someone had to fight him after each one. He didn't know Cupid Childs had sawed his heavy brown bat in half, so he knocked a tooth out of Lou Criger's head. When something that isn't mentioned in books found its way into his shoes, Saturday laughed loudest and then hit Jimmy McAleer, who laughed second loudest, so hard in the gut the center fielder didn't catch his breath before his head went in the round item in the water closet. McAleer almost drowned. The veterans stopped the hazing but didn't speak to Saturday, so he and I were frequently together. The Indian was as alert and cautious in Arkansas as he had been audacious in Hooper. It was the only time while I knew him when he was a "student of the game." Saturday watched everybody, especially manager Tebeau. He did what he was told and didn't drink. King ran every morning at dawn and went to bed early. He took extra batting, even offering to pay Frank Ember to pitch to him late in the afternoon, but the third base coach just smiled, threw the practice and said, "Don't let anybody fool with your swing." It was in Arkansas that he began referring to me as "Little Brother," in a half-patronizing, half-contemptuous voice. I never knew exactly what he meant by it. After a week the Robisons sent me back to Cleveland, but my reputation as Saturday's friend was established.

The Spiders opened in Louisville and King Saturday tripled home the winning run. He also made a marvelous catch. The papers were wild about the fleet Indian rookie. They had something exotic to crow about, and behaved in print about as demurely as the kranks behaved in the stands. He saved the next game with a ninth inning catch, and the papers were less restrained. The Spiders went to Cincinnati and St. Louis, and Saturday hit a home run in each town. Even without the hyperbole of the press, Cleveland's kranks would have been beside themselves. They organized a parade to meet the team at Union Depot.

48

2

There was a luncheon at the Stillman Hotel before the home opener. This annual affair was the only day of the year the Robison brothers gave anything away, and every reporter, hanger-on, and krank who knew anybody, was there. Men in the businessman's customary black suit smoked cigars, sampled free whiskey, and talked war and baseball. I felt vastly superior to these energetic, optimistic men because I wanted to own part of baseball, while they were sharks in the Republican sea of capital. I thought wanting to own a ball club gave me a secret, transcendent virtue.

It was Saturday, the King's day as the papers would later call the sixth day of the week, and war had been declared against Spain on Monday. We were playing Baltimore and everyone agreed the Orioles were the more worthy foe. Spain was merely a fifth-rate power which had the misfortune to own some islands close to the United States; Baltimore had won the Temple Cup. Boston had beaten them for the league championship, but in the Cup Series, where the first and second place teams met, John McGraw's swearing, spiking, umpire-baiting ruffians defeated the more talented Bostons. The Spiders were the League's second rowdiest team, which only made us hate McGraw more, as one's own sins are most despicable in another.

Frank Robison kept me at his side as he made his way through the packed ballroom. I saw my employer and the Episcopal Bishop of Cleveland, who raised a glass and predicted the war would be "glorious and short." A gaggle of politicians said the Spiders were "the toast of the League" with the "hot bat" and "fine glove" of King Saturday. Robison liked working the crowd with a lawyer in tow. He was an oily little man with dark hair, parted in the middle, and eyes like a rattlesnake. Frank kept introducing me as "Harrison, Harvard man," and I responded by being as obsequiously correct as possible, like the butler who has better manners than the master.

We made our way through the crowd, pumping hands and slapping backs. Mr. Robison was repeatedly asked, "Is he really an Indian?" "Is he really that good? I heard about Louisville." Every time Robison thumped his vest and said, "He's better. Come out to League Park and see." Sometimes he pointed to me and said, "This man saw him down in Pennsylvania."

Mr. Robison introduced me to Harry Von der Horst, owner of the Orioles. Von der Horst was a squat man with shrewd eyes who owned a brewery in Baltimore. Like his club, the brewer cultivated an air of pugnaciousness. Unlike most owners, Von der Horst made money with the Orioles. If the diamond in his tie and rings on the fingers of both hands didn't make this clear, he would certainly tell you.

"I've been hearing about your Indian, Frank," said the Oriole owner, taking a step toward Mr. Robison. "I hear he raises hell as good as he plays ball."

"That would be a lot of hell," said Robison, holding his ground.

"I say an Indian's good for half a season," said Von der Horst.

"We'll see about that," said Robison.

"I know what he did at Holy Cross," said Von der Horst, looking at me. "He turned the whole team into drunks."

A crowd formed around the two baseball barons. The Oriole owner had his entourage, and any time Frank or Stanley Robison were in public the gentlemen who liked to think of themselves as the "sporting crowd" tried to pal up to them. Frank wasn't good on his feet. He turned to me. "What do you think, Henry?"

I was intimidated by Von der Horst. He had built a very successful, very tough organization. Von der Horst had done what I wanted to do, so I admired and disliked him. "I don't believe your men go from the ballpark to church, Mr. Von der Horst."

That brought a round of laughs and a broad smile from Frank Robison.

"Wherever they go, Mr. Harrison," said Von der Horst, "it doesn't affect the way they play."

"We'll see, we'll see," said Robison.

"Mr. Harrison," said Von der Horst. "You saw this Indian in Pennsylvania and know his reputation. I'm surprised you got Frank to sign him. The man may have talent but a ballplayer's got to have character. He's got to work at the game. Take John McGraw. He plays every game as if it were his last, but off the field he's so careful, you'd think he wanted to live forever. It takes character, sir. Talent isn't enough. Your man is a question."

"The only question," I said, "is how good will he be."

"Half a season," said Von der Horst.

Robison announced that it was time to eat. We bumped our way into a dining room which had been decorated with bunting in honor of the war and the baseball season. A collection of regimental flags from the Civil War were on display in the middle of the room. These relics from that most serious war presumably helped sanctify the vulgar bellicosity that prompted the new, silly one. My father had gone to war under one of those banners and lived what in effect was his life in a matter of minutes, and I was sorry to see them used for the flapdoodle of Hearst and McKinley, but not even a war can take the edge off Opening Day.

Waiters stood by tables garnished with bowls of biscuits, dishes of piccalilli, and platters of coleslaw. The Stillman chef himself supervised the delivery of chicken from steaming chafing dishes, covered with sterling silver domes, that looked like shiny Easter eggs. I was relieved of Mr. Robison and seated at the far end of the head table between a large lady in a purple dress, whose whole being seemed to be held together by a pearl brooch at her throat, and her daughter, an attractive woman a few years younger than I. There weren't many ladies at this affair but there were more than would be at League Park. Few women ventured to baseball games.

"My name is Mrs. Burns," said the large purple lady, in a deep voice that bespoke wealth, but seemed a shade too studied to be refined. "This is my daughter Edith, who has just returned from Europe."

"I came back for the season," said Miss Burns, whose voice was husky and direct.

"You like baseball?"

"I want to see the Indian."

"I've never met a woman outside of a saloon that liked baseball," I said.

"Is that how you spend your time?" said Mrs. Burns.

"I'm the club lawyer," I said, thinking this would explain an occasional foray into the demimonde.

"What else do you do?" said Mrs. Burns, showing me she was difficult to shock but easy to disappoint. "That couldn't possibly be full-time employment"

"It's seasonal," I said, but Mrs. Burns was already looking at her daughter with an expression that seemed to indicate further investigation of the matter would be tedious.

"We're a pitcher away from the pennant," said Miss Burns, perhaps as a way of shielding me from her mother, and we discussed the team. Edith wanted to know if I went to saloons with the Spiders and I rather boastfully admitted the Indian and I were going to a notorious one that night.

"You mean the Gin Palace?"

"How do you know about the Palace?" I said, before Mrs. Burns, whose mouth was full of potato croquette, could offer a comment.

"I'm a krank," said Edith, "and I read the newspapers."

I decided I liked her. I had seen her across the lobby and thought she looked familiar. Miss Burns wore a brown dress with embroidered "leg of mutton" sleeves that were darker than her wavy brown hair and very brown eyes. She had a straight nose, perhaps a trifle big, an earnest mouth, and big hands. Hands aren't usually the first item a gentleman notices about a lady, but Miss Burns' were large. She noticed my gaze and held up her gloved left hand. We touched palms and my fingers were only slightly longer than hers. At the touch of her glove, I remembered who she was. Edith Burns had been one of the younger girls at dancing school. I remember everything about that school. Mother wanted me to learn the art of the ballroom with the sons and daughters of the best families, and I used to sit in a corner with my legs crossed, because I assumed everyone knew my clothes had been handed down from a cousin.

Even at Miss Walker's, Edith Burns had been tall for her age, and danced in an athletic rather than polite manner. She looked ready to run or hit a ball, and I thought Edith must have been raised with a gaggle of brothers, and was surprised to learn she was an only child. Miss Burns hadn't lost that quality of crisp, physical independence, even wearing mutton sleeves and French gloves. I also remembered her father died one Christmas, and I had wanted to say something, but didn't.

"Are you going to enlist?" said Mrs. Burns, who I think disliked the attention I was getting from her daughter.

"No," I said. "America will regret this war. It's wrong."

"Are you a coward?"

"I'm brave enough to eat in this company."

This remark might have ended my relations with the Burnses but Edith stepped into the breach. "Oh, a man of high morality who keeps the company of saloon women. This is another Hosea." This reference to the stern Hebrew prophet who married a harlot not only took the sting out of my words but, because Mrs. Burns didn't understand it, sealed a conspiracy of taste between Edith and me.

"This war is so much bread and circuses," said Edith. "Like baseball. But no one gets killed in a baseball game."

Mrs. Burns withdrew from the field and concentrated on the croquettes. She gave quite an exhibition of how to eat with someone you don't like. There was an exquisite haughty aplomb in the way she handled her knife and fork, looked at Edith, and regarded me with a series of small smiles that clearly said, "You may be able to amuse her, but there's no way I could accept you."

Toward the end of lunch, Edith brushed my hand, looked me in the eye, and said, "I want you to take me to League Park a week from today. I want to meet the Indian."

"I'd be delighted to take you both." That was an obvious lie but Mrs. Burns was right. I was a coward and one rude sally was enough. "I'm surprised a pair of ladies are willing to go to League Park."

"Escorted by you, I suppose we'll be fine," said Mrs. Burns. "Lawyers are good with the public."

"Mother likes baseball," said Edith. "She won't admit it. Given time, she might even like you."

Over dessert I told Edith about King Saturday's exploits in Hooper. She was very interested in the game, his character, and how well I knew him. I didn't tell her about the night before. "You know Ned Phillips?" said Miss Burns, quickly.

"Quite well. How do you know him?"

"I met him in Paris this winter," she said. "I didn't like him."

"I'm surprised. He's a great krank."

"He told me about Saturday."

"What did he say?"

"He said he'd be great. The greatest."

"He didn't mention me?"

"No."

3

The Burnses couldn't attend the afternoon's game. Mrs. Burns said they had a "pressing" engagement, but Edith said we would be "seeing each other and the Indian" in a week. She gave me a very pleasant smile.

Mr. Robison gave me a ride to League Park. His box was behind the Spider dugout. I sat next to his brother's wife, surrounded by his nephews, and men who worked for Standard Oil.

The game was delayed by politicians who lined up at home plate to make the politician's contribution to war: talk. The players returned to the dugouts to fidget while men with fat necks issued a call for volunteers. A tent was set up by third base, and a few young men, not too obviously drunk, made their way to the field where young women wearing red, white and blue escorted them to the recruiters. A band marched around the field, booming out an approximation of "The Star Spangled Banner."

Rockets burst over the park, mingling the smell of gunpowder with the odor of horses, hot peanuts, and an excited crowd. I preferred baseball to war but the kranks were impressed by both. A brigade of soldiers marched over the pitcher's mound. The crowd stomped and cheered. They were ready to crush

Spain along with Baltimore. The highlight of the festivities was a replica of our martyred battleship *Maine* mounted on a fire wagon which moved by its own power and belched smoke. As the "Maine" traversed the field, men hopped out of the grandstand and lined up at the recruiters' tent. Mrs. Stanley Robison, a stout woman with an unpleasant red face, gave me a hard elbow of encouragement, but I didn't budge.

The "Maine" steamed through the outfield. I feared the copy might explode like the original but the "ship" kept puffing, shooting off cinders, and stirring the kranks. A tuba followed the "Maine" and kept time with the smokestack.

"I wish I were a man," said Mrs. Stanley Robison.

A group of men dressed as Spaniards ran on the field. The crowd exploded in hisses and profanity. A turret of the "Maine" swung toward the Spaniards and the kranks bawled with delight. The Spaniards had heavy black mustaches, bandoleers, and paper swords. One of them wore a drooping crown. His subjects had oversized straw hats. I was afraid for a moment they might take one of the red, white and blue girls and re-enact the fabulous Richard Harding Davis account of an American woman stripped and searched by Spanish authorities, but they didn't.

The Spaniards cavorted before the "Maine's" paper guns and a politician delivered a speech about "slave Cuba." He unfurled a picture of Abraham Lincoln and the band broke into "The Battle Hymn of The Republic."

"How can anyone sit when men are preparing to die for freedom?" said Mrs. Robison.

"I think they're preparing to die for sugar prices," I said, which was politer than the other observation which came to mind — over-weight women are invariably patriotic.

The "Maine" blasted the Spaniards with a jet of water. The crowd was on its feet, whooping and cheering. The water ripped off the mustaches, removed the crown from the king, and sent his subjects sliding across the field. Under the rags and bandoleers were red, white and blue bathing costumes. The Spaniards were transformed into American acrobats who did cartwheels and cut capers while saluting the "Maine" and exhorting young men to march to the recruiting tent. A flag was snatched from the stern of the "Maine" and paraded around the tent. The band broke into a medley of patriotic songs which drowned out the politician.

Mrs. Robison gave me a last elbow but I ignored her and filled out my scorecard. The players were impatient while the field was prepared for the game. They hadn't expected the sport of war to advertise itself. No player signed on to become part of President McKinley's 200,000 who were going to brave disease, incompetence, and the military mind, to make America a world power.

I settled back and the crowd began to chant, "Injun!" "Injun!" "Injun!"

4

John McGraw leapt out of the Oriole dugout wearing a war bonnet with a tail of feathers that touched the ground. He danced on one foot yelling, "An Indian's bad luck!" as Umpire O'Reagan waved him back and the crowd hissed obscenities.

The kranks were angry with McGraw's feathers and dance, even though there were at least a hundred war bonnets in the stands and dozens of painted faces in the bleachers. I don't know how Saturday felt about this derisive theater. As I got to know him, I thought the Indian element of his character was given too much importance and decided a more sophisticated reading of this difficult, sometimes mercurial, sometimes brooding man, was to view him as a man, with a man's complexities, rather than as an Indian. I'm no longer sure.

Frank Robison's nephews gave the best rendition of the Plains Indian vibrato warwhoop in our section. That King Saturday had never heard this controlled western shriek until he played in front of white audiences failed to deter his most vocal rooters. Saturday's forefathers hunted in the Maine woods and speared whales in the open sea; they didn't ride ponies and howl over the prairie, but kranks, despite their ability to remember the most arcane baseball matters, are poor anthropologists. A stern look from Frank Robison, and sterner words from their father, quieted the boys.

The Spiders took the field and the whoops and shouts became a momentous cheer. King Saturday ran out to right field and some of the kranks stood up. As in Hooper, and as the press reported in Louisville, St. Louis, and Cincinnati, Saturday acknowledged no one. He ran with enormous, gliding strides, and his black hair sparkled under his red cap in the April sun. The crowd had much to cheer about. They hadn't seen Saturday, so they were all anticipation. The Indian had dwelt in their imaginations. All fans wait for a great player, the best player, the one who will be as good as the player they are in their dreams. We need the best. We want the man who by his singular ability validates the wasted time and green hours baseball has taken from us.

Cleveland's kranks had much to expect. Word had come from the East for those who knew of college ball, and louder reports had just come from the League's western outposts. There was a feeling of something big out there, something great, something coming to Cleveland to bring us the title, and redeem our lost, green baseball hours. If he failed, the kranks could always whoop, scream, and wear feathers. There was one thing in the man's favor. Saturday had been clocked at ten seconds flat for a hundred yards, which meant he was one of the fastest men on earth.

I watched our pitcher warm up. It's been ten years since that afternoon and I haven't seen anyone better than Cy Young. The kranks could whoop for the Indian and curse John McGraw, but the game comes down to pitching, and Cy Young was the best. He was the one farm boy in America as good as the rest wanted to be. It wasn't only velocity. Inning after inning Young could steam pitches over the corners: low, then high, inside, then out, and woe to the batsman with a weakness because that's where the pitch was coming with men on base. Cy Young had the arm of a god and the memory of an elephant. He picked on a man's faults like the Archangel on the Day of Judgment. He could make a slugger look like a busher, flailing at that high inside spot where vanity meets fear.

The first Oriole up lined out. John McGraw was next and the kranks hooted their displeasure. O'Reagan took his place behind home plate. The other umpire, a white haired gentleman, was at second. Mugsy McGraw was an advocate of "scientific hitting," as opposed to "manly slugging." He would try to cozen his way on base by slapping the ball through the infield, chopping it over someone's head, finagling a walk, or stepping in front of a pitch.

The Mug stepped out and said something to O'Reagan. He was trying to distract Cy Young, but when he got back in the box, Cy zipped one under his wrists and O'Reagan called it a strike. I could hear McGraw's, "The hell it was!" where I was sitting. The Oriole dugout crackled with profanity. O'Reagan called the next one a ball, and the Spider dugout erupted into what the papers used to call a "fourcabulary lexicon."

Young reared back and delivered a fast pitch that seemed to hop as McGraw swung at it. Mr. Robison smiled and gave me the thumbs up sign. Cy threw another fast one and McGraw struck out. The Mug glared at O'Reagan on his way to the dugout. The next fellow popped up.

I could feel the excitement as the Spiders came off the field. King Saturday was the lead-off hitter, and even kranks in the most expensive seats whistled, stomped, and produced that infernal vibrato. Their dream was about to face live pitching.

The Indian strolled to the plate. He looked at third base coach Frank Ember, eyed Oriole pitcher Doc McJames, and settled in. That first at-bat in Cleveland was the only time I ever thought the whoops, painted faces, and vibrato might bother him, but if they did, he didn't show it, and I must have mistaken my own taut feelings for his.

Saturday hit lefty. The best hitters always do. Lefties have a natural advantage because a right-hand pitcher's curveball breaks toward them, instead of away. Lefties also have such elegant, level swings. A reporter called Saturday's swing "level poetry." He crouched slightly, seemed to relax as McJames wound up, then the bat straightened up as those strong, quick wrists took over, and he fouled one straight back, out of the park.

McJames was a lean right-hander with a nasty fast pitch. He threw two low and then tried the inside corner. Saturday lashed a base hit into right. This brought back the chant of "Injun!" "Injun!" and Oriole manager Hanlon made a trip to the mound. McJames vigorously shook his head as if denying the noise affected him. He fanned the next batter, but King Saturday stole second. The throw wasn't close. McJames struck out another batter, which brought up Jess Burkett, the best hitter in our lineup.

Saturday edged off second. McJames looked him back and was roundly booed. This happened several times, and between the Indian's quickness and the crowd's ferocity, McJames lost his edge. He got a strike on Burkett, and then Jess lined a homer into the overflow crowd in right.

The score was 2-0 when the Orioles came up in the seventh. Shadows were beginning to lengthen and only three Orioles had reached base. The Baltimores had heckled and ranted all afternoon but Young had been unhittable. Wee Willie Keeler, the quick Oriole outfielder who was only slightly taller than the poet John Keats, led off the seventh with a walk.

McGraw stepped up shouting, "We've got you now! You're all through, Young!"

Everyone expected the Mug to bunt, but he crossed us up and hit a skimmer down the third base line. Keeler was around second before left fielder Burkett touched the ball. The throw came home. Keeler stopped at third and McGraw went to second.

The Orioles threw towels in the air. McGraw was irrepressible at second. He taunted Young with antics that resembled a carnival hootchi-coo. Cy peered at McGraw over his shoulder. Joe Kelley was up. Cy fired one shoulder-high and Kelley chased it for a strike.

Young tried another high one and Kelley lined it to left. If this drive had been to right, King Saturday would have had it on one hop and held McGraw at third. The Indian already had a reputation. News of a man's arm travels as fast as gossip. Burkett got the ball on two hops.

Keeler scored. O'Reagan came up the line. The other umpire, the white haired gentleman, tripped over second base. O'Reagan momentarily took his eye off McGraw and McGraw cut in front of third and headed home, easily beating Burkett's throw.

The Spiders, led by manager Tebeau, stormed home plate. O'Reagan was surrounded and shoved as tomatoes and cabbages flew out of the stands. The crowd was on the verge of riot as Tebeau took charge with wild, theatrical gestures. He pointed at third, pointed at McGraw, pointed to heaven, picked up a cabbage and threw it on the ground, and finally threw down his hat. Patsy put on a good show. If anyone struck O'Reagan, or the kranks came on the field, Cleveland would forfeit. On the other hand, McGraw's trick required a big enough demonstration to guarantee Cleveland the next close call. Patsy implored and even went down on his knee, but O'Reagan stood imperiously on home plate. His dignity was marred only by a lemon which came close to the side of his head.

None of the policemen in the grandstand offered to go to O'Reagan's assistance. They did an excellent job of seeing that neither man nor vegetable came near the Robisons or the politicians and businessmen occupying the box seats, but the umpire stood alone.

There was a fifteen minute delay while the field cleared and an old man with a pail picked up cabbages and bottles. The Spiders retreated to their bench and the Orioles wisely stayed at theirs, though McGraw appeared on the top step, with his hand over his heart.

I feared the delay might erode Cy Young's concentration. I should have known better. He found a new rhythm and dispensed with the next three batters.

The game was still tied in the bottom of the ninth when King Saturday led off. The ball was almost black. Balls weren't replaced when they were dirty or nicked in the last century, and this one had been in play since Burkett's homer in the first inning.

Saturday lethargically took two strikes and Frank Robison looked over at me with a baleful expression. We all turn optimist or pessimist under pressure, and Robison became Calvanistic in the late innings. Frank may have thought Saturday was paying the crowd back for the chants and warwhoops, or maybe he remembered Van der Horst's reservations. Saturday didn't look at his teammates or Frank Ember who yelled from the coach's spot at third. A krank beat a drum which seemed to lull the Indian into deeper indifference.

Doc McJames fingered the dirty, nicked ball and delivered a curve.

The problem with a curve, that marvelously devious pitch, is sometimes it doesn't curve. Sometimes, instead of dropping, it flattens into a slow, inviting arc. This one hesitated, and

Saturday belted it into right center. There was no catching this liner. It was hit harder than Burkett's homer. After a vicious hop, the ball bounced into the crowd and was ruled a double.

Manager Tebeau came out in a rage. Even though it had been agreed that any ball bouncing into the overflow crowd was a double, Saturday had already rounded second and had to go back.

Patsy stomped away. The drum beat louder. The kranks hollered and shook their fists as if the fate of the world rested on the man at second base. McJames got a new ball. He spat on it, rubbed it, and looked as if he wanted to bite it, to scuff the shiny, hittable newness off this white ball.

With a runner on second, strategy dictated bunting him to third. McGraw edged in. Shortstop McKean was up. Saturday took an enormous lead. John McGraw was a wonder to behold. He was all energy and concentration at third. The Mug pounded his glove and yelled at McKean to lay one down.

McKean bunted right back to the pitcher. McGraw hopped back to third like a madman. McJames threw and McGraw caught the ball as he dove. The throw was in time but the Indian slid around the tag with a tremendous dust-raising hook slide. McGraw pounded Saturday's thigh with the ball in his fist but O'Reagan called him safe. Mugsy threw the ball down and wanted to fight. He shoved Saturday but couldn't dislodge him from the base.

"Get your hands off him!" shouted Frank Ember. McGraw started to go for Ember but the coach took a discreet step backward.

"Play ball or forfeit!" yelled O'Reagan. McGraw turned away and cursed. He was furious, not only at the call, but at his inability to rile the Indian.

The Orioles were in trouble. The fastest man in the League, and maybe on earth, was at third with nobody out. McKean was on first and Bobby Wallace was up.

McJames tried to calm himself. This was his moment of truth. He looked at center field and went to work. Doc worked the count full and wiped his brow. The crowd was making a racket, punctuated by a drum, worthy of an asylum.

Doc went right at Wallace and struck him out. McJames strutted off the mound and reclimbed it with determination.

With one out, the winning run could still score on a fly ball. The outfielders moved closer. I wanted a fly. The throw to the plate is the most dramatic play in baseball. An outfielder paces his turf all afternoon and then the game comes down to his ability to catch and throw. There are no distractions in the outfield, no elbows or fists, just the intimate solitude of open space.

Jess Burkett was up. McJames needed another strikeout, but Burkett was a difficult man to fan. He was such a good hitter that bunting was no certainty. It was, however, the most obvious way to score the run, so Doc threw high and hard. McGraw charged from third, the first baseman was coming, and McJames was up like a cat after he delivered the ball. Jess bunted foul. Bunting was risky. If one of those charging Irishmen got the ball and threw home, there would be a mighty collision between Saturday and catcher Robinson.

Burkett didn't bunt. He ignored the Irish charge and hit a fly to center. Joe Kelley came in a step. All eyes were on Kelley to see if he would hitch or rush the throw. Frank yelled at Saturday. Instead of watching the ball, I forced myself to watch the Indian.

There was no way McGraw would let the game develop the way the rules intended. This was 1898! The United States had entered the ruleless fray of great powers! Rules were only for those powerless enough to have to obey them. Kelley put his whole body into the throw. Saturday tagged up. John McGraw grabbed the Indian's belt. I started to shout. Frank started to throw a punch. The fastest man on earth was going to be out because the most devious man was holding his belt.

The curses, shouts, Frank Ember's punch, and my anger at the unfairness of life, turned into a torrential holler. King Saturday took off like a July rocket and McGraw stood on the bag with a belt in his hands.

Catcher Wilbert Robinson was so surprised, he didn't even trip Saturday as the Indian scored the winning run.

5

There was always a line between the players and me, and this line could not be crossed except at their invitation. The near riot in the clubhouse after Saturday hoodwinked McGraw was one of those times. The men shouted, poured beer on each other, and dragged the unsuspecting under the single shower head. Anyone — management, press or stranger — was welcome fodder for the celebration. I knew how rare these moments were and intended to enjoy this one.

"He knew the bastard's tricks!" "He cut his belt!" "He cut his goddamn belt!" Men shouted and beat their lockers. They sang an obscene song to the tune of "A Hot Time In The Old Town Tonight," and I decided to join the fracas and share a wet moment of camaraderie, and even imagined telling Edith about it, but Frank Ember grabbed my arm and pushed me toward my office.

What I called an office was a small room almost completely filled with a rubdown table, which served as a desk until needed by the trainer. Frank closed the door and said, "Can I talk to you?" He was still wearing his uniform. The jersey was unbuttoned and soaked with beer. He'd removed his high-topped black spike shoes but not his stockings.

"Of course."

"You're a lawyer, ain't you?" Frank sat on the rubdown table and slapped it as though the Indian were stretched out and needed his muscular legs loosened up. I was surprised. The men didn't associate with me because I drew up their contracts, and the Robisons weren't generous.

"I want a divorce." Frank looked at his hands. His broken fingers and permanently bent left wrist were a testament to the time when ballplayers didn't wear gloves. Frank had started when wearing a glove invited comparisons to a lady's muff. He had a tough, lined face, and gray eyes. Frank was what ballplayers call the old school. Baseball was his life and there was a certain shrewd, stoical suffering as he got farther away from his ability to play the game.

"Can you help me?"

"Maybe," I said.

Frank looked me over. "I want somebody I can trust. Since I don't trust nobody, I want someone I can keep an eye on."

I smiled and he laughed. I want to think Frank liked me, but maybe he just needed a lawyer. We were certainly a strange pair: a half-dressed third base coach whose beer-soaked uniform smelled of the exertions of the afternoon, and a dandified lawyer in a brown wool suit, pin-striped shirt and freshly starched band collar, who smelled of cologne. We were both nervous. Frank didn't like talking about himself, and I wanted him to like me.

"My wife Harriet. She changed . . . She changed."

Frank tried to smile. He slapped the table and tried to laugh, as though his troubles were just the normal and universal difficulties men have with women. I thought I knew about love, having been in love once, deeply in love — or deeply obsessed — by the perfume and dark curl at the back of the neck of a lady from South Carolina. When her family discovered I was poor and a Yankee, the matter ended in a flurry of accusations that each party had thoroughly misrepresented him and herself. I used my wound as a shield to attract and protect myself from other women: I had loved and lost, and therefore had license to be a rake — I was in love with something gone, hence perfect, so other women couldn't compete with it. I went softly in the bitterness of my soul, as the Bible says. I was pretending.

Frank wasn't. I watched his calloused, broken fingers — he seemed to try to hide them while he talked. It made me uneasy. I hadn't expected a man I remembered as the rock of a tough Boston infield to come in my office and make his voice husky to cover emotion.

"She won't let me touch her." Frank gripped the table. He must have wondered if I were asking myself how anyone would want to be touched by those hands. "It's the religion, Henry. Harriet found the Lord."

A bottle broke in the lockerroom, and the clubhouse rocked with a tune I didn't recognize that fit the words, "We got McGraw right in the wrong end!" I heard later the song accompanied a shower King Saturday gave Stanley Robison.

Frank told me his wife had become a fanatic and sort of celebrity. I tried to look him in the eye, and not at the swollen ends of his fingers, the crooked joints, and left thumb which was missing a nail. Harriet had started a church. It wasn't far from the Gin Palace, where the Spiders drank. This was no accident. Harriet wanted to reform the team, particularly the Indian.

"She'll preach tonight, Henry. Preaches every Saturday night. To fight sin in its lair, she says." Frank spat.

"I'm not religious," I said.

"I don't know about religion," said Frank. "But I know about Harriet. She's gettin' rich."

He made me promise not to tell anyone what he'd said and we shook hands.

6

King Saturday, Frank Ember and I took a cab to the Gin Palace, which was in the Flats, on the east side of the Cuyahoga River. We waited for a drawbridge, rode down Independence Street through the warehouse and factory district, and stopped in front of a large red building on an unpaved street. The Palace had no sign but boasted an enormous facade that made the building look four stories high when it was only two. This faded crimson edifice could be seen across the river. The Palace front doors were flanked by fat white pillars, half a story high, which had never supported anything but the pretensions of the original owner. I stepped out of the cab and shaded my eyes. The setting sun filled the second floor windows with reflected gold. A purple curtain flapped out a corner window and a woman's white face and whiter body briefly met the red blaze of the river sunset, and then disappeared.

We went through a set of dull oak doors which had four small windows at eye level. One was broken. "Patsy Tebeau," said Frank. "Lucky he didn't take his hand off." We stepped aside as a gentleman came barging out and we faced a bar that seemed to extend for a city block. "Longest in the world," said Frank, and we saw ourselves in the mirrors behind the bar. Saturday looked dramatically bigger as the image of his tight-fitting blue suit passed behind six bartenders in red vests, who poured shots of whiskey and glasses of beer for the early evening crowd.

Green lamps hung over the bar and a few lights sputtered in brass sconces. I had difficulty seeing. There was a large chandelier over the dance floor, but this twelve-tiered reminder of the Palace's better days wasn't lit. Frank and I took a booth but Saturday didn't sit until he'd explored that entire cavernous place and the balcony which ringed it. This balcony reminded me of Shakespeare's Globe where the new profession of theater was performed on stage while some of the older ones were practiced on the upper levels.

"You're among friends," said Frank, pointing to Jimmy McAleer and Patsy Tebeau at the bar. "The lads will be gettin' oiled tonight."

I began to see the customers more clearly. They weren't the sort one cared to look in the eye. I hadn't been to the Palace before. It wasn't a place to go without an ally. I recognized a gambler called Jake McBuck, who would have been arrested if he came in the Spider lockerroom. McBuck was so lean his brown coat hung loosely from his shoulders. He had a long, slightly hooked nose, and his oddly Lincolnesque face was so smooth, the man must have applied his razor to it more than once a day. McBuck tipped his hat to several fellows wearing brown tattersall coats, and red and white spats. These gentlemen exchanged jaunty salutes, whistled for waitresses, and pinched them when they came by.

"Look at this." Frank pulled a nasty looking black rubber item out of his coat. "She's come in handy a few times." He handed me a blackjack. I struck my palm with it, winced, and gave it back.

A waitress came over and said, "Evenin', Frank." Like the other women who circulated among tables and booths, hustled trays out of swinging doors and dodged the pinches of the sports by the bar, she wore a white blouse and red bloomers. The blouse was cut low enough to reveal a gentle curve as her bosom disappeared into a ruffle. I was excited. I couldn't play baseball but wanted to try my hand at the other game the men took seriously. I'd never felt at ease in the world of Edith Burns and her mother, or the more stunning world of Ned Phillips — the world of wealth and a sense of unlimited possibility — so

72

I wanted to travel in this one. I wanted to share the dangerous freedom of ballplayers and sports. I couldn't belong here either but, like a hero of old, wanted to experience the nether world before accepting a more mundane fate.

"Give us three rare steaks, Rose, and two pitchers of beer," said Frank.

"Anything you say." Rose winked at me and sauntered off.

"She likes you," said Frank.

The crowd was growing. Lou Criger and our second baseman, Cupid Childs, came in. They were followed by shortstop McKean and Jess Burkett. The ballplayers waved to Frank. McKean gave me an indulgent smile. "They like the Spiders here," said Frank. "Good for business."

I watched women glide by. They were almost beautiful in the semi-darkness. There wasn't enough light to see the worn look their profession so quickly gives. The saloon women, like the ballplayers, had only their youth to trade on. I found this exciting.

"The lads should stay away from McBuck," said Frank. "Jake's always looking to put the fix on. Listen, Henry, see the guy with McBuck?" A stocky fellow in a derby lit a cigar. "That's Burke. He's always looking for a fight. Stay away from him."

Burke was as solid as McBuck was lean. He had a pockmarked face, thick red neck, and a tattoo on his right hand of a woman with a sword through her belly. Burke tipped his hat to Patsy Tebeau, who did not return the salute. Burke had big pink ears. The right one stuck out farther than the left and he moved his head in such a way that those cartilaginous wings almost wiggled; then he scowled, as if threatening to beat the pulp out of anyone who noticed. Several gentlemen with McBuck also looked like they might take exception to a man from Harvard and not, as Edith later pointed out, because they'd gone to Yale.

Rose returned with our steaks on wooden platters, and another woman brought beer. Both women smiled at me and I noticed how young they were. Frank insisted on paying and gestured to King Saturday who stood at the bar with three shots of whiskey and a glass of beer in front of him. Saturday shook his head, "tossed off" the whiskey and "chased" it with beer while Jimmy McAleer and Patsy Tebeau applauded.

"Start without him," said Frank, and attacked his steak. His crooked hands moved as quickly as if he were scooping up a bunt. We weren't alone long. Saturday waved away a man with mutton chop whiskers and pink spats who offered to buy more whiskey, then joined us. The Indian went at his steak as voraciously as Frank but had better table manners.

We ate next to a wall covered with theatrical and sporting mementos. Frank was under a faded announcement of a performance by Mr. Booth and a ball thrown by King Kelly. "The other King," said Frank. "You can bet he was in here." I was close to a dusty sample of the old rectangular home plate, and a Players League cap, a reminder of the baseball rebellion of 1890, when players formed their own league and fought the National League for a year before being crushed by Albert Spalding. A close inspection of a grimy picture revealed a likeness of John Montgomery Ward, the leader of the rebellion. Frank saw me admiring Ward, and said, "He came in here. This was an outlaw place. No scab or Spalding man dared show his face."

"Who were the Players?" said Saturday.

"In 1890 we revolted," said Frank. "Started our own league. Owned stock in our teams. They beat us. They crucified us."

Saturday looked at Frank closely. "I want to own a club." I saw that shrewd look I'd seen in Hooper. "The owner always wins." He looked at me.

"The League has to let you in," I said.

"Lawyers can get you in."

"It costs money," I said.

"I can get money," said Saturday.

I would have asked how, and though he wouldn't have told me, I would like to have asked anyway, because that question, and the others which followed as hell follows death in John's vision of the Apocalypse, trouble me now; but we were interrupted by a woman's voice, and Annie Gears walked into our lives.

"Like the fat one, do you?"

She must have seen me eyeing a picture of a slatternly Rheinmaiden in a gilt frame or one of several daguerreotypes of an obscure, bosomy actress.

"We've got some big ones here." Annie stood with her hands on her hips and laughed. Her hair was as black as the Indian's and it glistened the way his did, but her skin was as smooth and white as his could look dark and rough.

"Where'd you get this swell, Frank?"

"That's Harry the club lawyer," said Frank.

"He's my little brother," said Saturday, and they looked at each other.

If the Gin Palace were a theater, I needed only that look to see I wasn't the leading man. They looked for a moment, and then her round, ruddy face, with its too-full mouth and strong chin, broke into a marvelous smile. He smiled too, one of the few times I saw him smile, and his angular, ominous face turned handsome, resolving for a moment its contradictions.

I don't believe in love at first sight. Falling in love with a stranger is perilously close to falling in love with oneself — that pretty face is Narcissus' pool — and love waiting to happen is a consummation of the ego. I don't know if Saturday fell in love in one fateful glance, but there was no question she was going to be his. Did she fall in love with one look on an April evening? I doubt it. Like every krank in town, she knew who he was, and like every saloon woman, she preferred having one man to many. That she loved him later, I have no doubt.

I was ready to fall in love with Annie Gears. I was ready to love a saloon woman as another way of fending off the present with the impossible: my wound and shield, Narcissus' pool. Edith said I was fascinated with Annie because she was King Saturday's woman. I said I needed Annie to protect me from Edith, but I'm getting ahead of myself. The heart is a labyrinth but whether there's a hero or a monster at its center, I can't say. Perhaps I was fascinated with Annie because of Saturday, but her charms certainly spoke for themselves. She had a self-deprecating laugh and an awesome figure. If ladies' faces can launch ships, that shape could sink them. Miss Gears wasn't wearing bloomers but a dark, flounced skirt with a large black belt and silver buckle. Her blue blouse was cut so low, I don't believe I'd ever seen more without paying for the privilege.

Frank Ember broke the silence. "Harry's helping me with my divorce."

"Your wife's been leading her flock by here" said Annie.

"She's trying to recruit sinners for the Lord. Harriet's something, Frank. She's selling electrical contraptions at her church."

"She's saving souls with electricity," said Frank.

"They execute men with it in some states," said Saturday.

7

Saturday and Annie went off by themselves. Frank shook his head and said, "She's new. Burke wanted to run her but she said no. Either she found a man or she was in trouble."

"She likes Saturday," I said.

"Looks that way."

The band began to play "Onward Christian Soldiers." I wondered why the music had changed and Frank said, "Harriet." I listened and heard the sound of women's voices. The patrons were apparently used to this change of musical venue. Some mockingly sang the hymn, others ignored it, but no one was surprised.

"Let's take a look," said Frank. I got up, and the beer I'd drunk hit me. Frank laughed and said, "You're ready for Harriet." We made our way out as the band played a jaunty "Onward." The women's voices were quite loud by the door. They may have been trying to drown out the piano which made the hymn sound like "Camptown Races" by adding a subversive tempo. I looked back and saw Annie talking to Saturday under a green light shade. His blue suit looked radiantly gaudy and her darker blue skirt and blouse and silver buckle seemed to melt into an immense blue light. Frank pushed open the doors, and we were serenaded from within and without.

I was surprised by the size of the crowd. My first impression was that a symphony orchestra was about to burn down the Gin Palace. A little woman in a golden robe led a choir of younger women who raised and lowered torches in the twilight. The golden lady saw us, turned around, and by the most imperceptible movement of a turned-up nose, I knew it was Harriet. She energetically led her flock, which wasn't an orchestra, though a bald Negro beat a bass drum, young men in shabby black coats shook tambourines, and an obese gentleman pumped a battered accordion. Behind the choir were more young men in more shabby coats. They apparently were Harriet's apostles but their sleeves, which were either too long or too short, gave them the appearance of reverent scarecrows.

Frank and I moved carefully around the choir, past the apostles, and joined the crowd. There were old people, a bright sprinkling of women, pomaded blacks glistening at the prospect of religion, bearded immigrants who had their hands in the pockets of long coats, stout women grimly looking to the next world for what they hadn't found in this one, women poor in everything but children, and children scrubbed rather than fed, who fidgeted and peaked around broadcloth and calico to catch a glimpse of the golden pastor.

Frank and I weren't the only gentlemen whose breath might offend the Lord, but we were the best dressed. Frank wore a new dun yellow suit and black bow tie, and I wondered if he had dressed up for his wife. His off-yellow, nattily cut suit seemed to subtly mock her golden ambience, but I was probably the only person who noticed it. My neat wool was as out of place outside the Gin Palace as in.

"This is a place of death!" cried Harriet. I thought she'd warm up with sin but Harriet went for the throat. "These men and their soul-less women will surely die!"

The sun had set and the Palace no longer glowed red and gold, but the second floor windows, decorated with purple and orange curtains, were either lit by soft yellow light or suggestively dark. I'm sure the faithful were righteously titillated by the thought of what might be happening in front of their very noses.

"They lust! They sin!" Harriet waved a golden arm which seemed to encompass the city across the water as well as the old building with its high red facade. "Gamblers! Harlots! One day you will face God's holy fire!"

Harriet turned to her audience with a scowl which implied that even looking at the Palace required tremendous effort. Harriet looked young, even girlish. She had short blond hair, a little nose, and didn't look at all like a woman ready to rant about the Second Death. Her face was lit with the ecstasy of damning sin. Frank nudged me, and said, "She gets a crowd, don't she?" He seemed to regard his wife with cynical admiration. I'm afraid I have no more use for lady preachers than did Dr. Johnson.

The choir burst into a fervid "Onward." They swung their torches from side to side and I was about to make a remark about the walls of Jericho, but Frank's admiration had changed to a look of loss. I guessed that as many times as he'd observed the transformation of his wife into a golden crowd-pleaser, he still didn't quite believe it. I was struck by Harriet's energy, and by that repressed but persistent sensuality I've seen in others who decry the flesh. Her hair was cropped remarkably like that of Joan of Arc as pictured on the frontispiece of Mark Twain's biography. I would have mentioned this but Frank was lost in thought. His hands were gripped tightly behind his back.

Harriet strutted in front of the Palace, and her golden robe fluttered after her. She turned quickly, as if frightened, and led the crowd in prayer. I watched while the flock prayed. Harriet was impressive. It wasn't easy for a woman to make a career for herself, but Harriet had found one which neither required youth nor prematurely aged its practitioners. Unlike Frank, who loved a game he was too old to play, and unlike me, who knew what he wanted but saw no way to get it, the woman had a calling.

"Sin Palace!" yelled Harriet, spreading her arms like golden wings. The crowd drew together, shoulder to shoulder. "Sinners will burn!" Harriet extended her golden arms as if trying to pull the reprobates out of the second story windows. "This is lust! This is hell!"

I wondered if someone might appear at a window to refute that notion but the Palace was still, except for the rich strains of the piano. A passer-by might have thought a golden pagan with an amateur band and a strange collection of women was railing at an old building with chipped pillars and mismatched curtains, but the faithful huddled and murmured as if they saw the jaws of death. Three second floor windows were lit by soft yellow light, and the windows in the doors did glow with an insistent orange concupiscence, but I wondered how long Harriet could sustain the feeling that hell was at hand.

"There is a particular sinner here," said Harriet.

Frank shook his head as if he knew what were coming. The drum beats came more softly.

"Indian!" shouted Harriet. She turned to the Palace. It was dark and the windows reflected the torches. "An Indian has joined the Cleveland ballclub! They say he could save the club. I say he'll save nothing! These men in their ignorance choose flesh! They make a god of a sinner!" Harriet made a sweeping gesture and I almost looked to see if the Cuyahoga had parted.

She went down on one knee and in a soft but hoarse voice said, "Come to the Light, Indian. Do not flee the Sabbath."

I don't know how many of the faithful were kranks, but the indictment of a specific sinner stirred the crowd as much as the word "flesh." A shudder passed through the ladies and the apostles shook their heads. Frank spat.

"Woe to Babylon!" Harriet got up. "Woe to the land shadowing with wings. Woe to men tempted into lust, for when lust hath conceived, it bringeth forth sin, and sin bringeth death."

This scriptural hodge-podge brought cries and clapping. The choir burst into a spirited and spontaneous "Onward." Harriet walked in a little golden circle, as if staggering under the weight of what she'd said. Frank elbowed me and said, "You should see them when she straps an anti-sin belt on the fellow playing the drum." Before I had time to appreciate that idea, there was a gasp. The drum stopped.

King Saturday stood in a window over a pillar. He was lit from behind and framed by purple curtains. The Indian wasn't wearing a shirt and his torso looked like a Roman breast plate. Some of the choir covered their eyes, others stifled shrieks, and a slender woman appeared to faint.

Harriet raised her arms and cried, "Come to the Light!"

Saturday took a step toward the window and laughed a deep, loud, mocking and strangely lyrical laugh. He looked at us for

80

a moment and then closed the curtains. The crowd was already moving before he disappeared.

"He will surely die!" shouted Harriet.

8

Frank got a bottle and we went to the river. We sat on a pier and drank. A lake steamer tooted and the iron trusses of Jackson Bridge rose into the night. Frank didn't want to talk, so I admired the stone arch of the bridge, which seemed to march across the water, the towers of the drawbridge, and the lonely gaslit catwalk.

"It's funny, Harry," Frank finally said. "I used to play in front of crowds and Harriet watched me. Now she gets a crowd and I watch her."

"Do you really want a divorce?"

"I do," said Frank, looking out at the bridge. "I used to love her."

After a minute, I said, "People change."

Frank offered me a cigar, which I accepted, and lit one himself. "She changed, I didn't." He kept looking at the bridge. "I still love her, Harry. That's why I want the divorce. Can't stand things the way they are."

After the pint was gone and the steamer disappeared around the bend at Dry Dock Street, Frank asked me what I thought of the Indian. "He could be another Kelly," I said, and saw Frank smile by the glow of his cigar. He tapped a silver flask in his pocket.

"They're the most exciting ballplayers I've seen," I said.

"I'll shake on that." Frank leaned over and shook my hand with a vise-like grip. "Good God, he's got an arm. Never seen one better, and I saw Hatfield. It ain't just strength. It's how quick he gets the ball and how quick he gets rid of it." Frank dotted an invisible "i" with his cigar. "Accurate too.

"Listen, Harry. Lots of guys can run and throw. This man has instinct. He's got the feel of the game."

I expected Frank to keep talking about Saturday's ability. I wanted to hear a veteran baseball man — a man I'd rooted for when I snuck into Boston from boarding school — rave about this raw talent who I felt closer to than anyone on the club, but Frank took his flask out and said, "King Kelly gave me this." He let me hold it. "Drink kept Mike from being better than even he was." He took the flask back. A lake steamer tooted above Dry Dock Street. "It's not drink with the Indian. It's something else."

"What do you mean?" I said.

"There's violence in him."

"He has pride," I said.

"It's more than pride."

"He wants to win all the time."

"At what?" said Frank.

We were quiet. I could have told him about Hooper. Frank had told me about his wife, and I wanted to tell him something in return, but it would have to be about me, not Saturday. I did tell Frank about the throwing contest. He wanted to know about the field, the crowd, wind, and exact position of each throw. If I'd seen a sign from heaven, Frank couldn't have asked more questions, then he said, "Tom Scott came up with a sore arm last summer in the Pennsylvania State League."

"I wonder how much I had to do with that," I said.

"He should have known better than to throw before a game."

We were quiet for a while. I tried not to stare at the bent forefinger and permanently straight middle finger with which Frank held his cigar. The lights of Cleveland sparkled across the water. The river was quiet and black. I looked back at the Flats but didn't see the Palace.

"He worries me, Harry." Frank stood up. The moon was over his shoulder and I saw his profile. "I've seen wild men. Mike

Kelly would drink and whore until you'd think he was dead, but when he got to the ballpark, he cared. He loved the game."

"You don't think Saturday loves it?"

"There's more to him than baseball." After a moment Frank said, "He wants too much."

"He wants to own a team," I said. "Hell, I'd like to own a team."

"You've got to have money or friends to get a team. He has neither."

"It sounds like you don't like him."

"Harry, you see a man like that once in twenty years. Liking him's not important. Keeping him out of trouble is."

I nodded. No arguing that.

"If a man wants too much, it can make him a gambler."

"You think Saturday would throw games?"

"Men have."

I was angry. Who was Frank Ember to make such a comment? I felt that uncrossable line again. I was management and they were cynical.

"If he did sell out, it would be because he's smart. I gambled once, Harry. I gambled on the Players. Put my savings in it. If I hadn't lost that money, Harriet might not have taken up preaching. We gambled out in the open. Took on the owners and the moneyed crowd in the light of day. We put our league on the field and said, 'Come on, let's go.' Like two guys who settle something in the street. Only it wasn't settled in the street. They got to our backers. I can't prove it but I'll bet Spalding bribed those bastards. That was the problem, Harry. We had the talent. We didn't have the money. You want a team, you play by the rules and the rules is money. I sat in a hotel corridor with Monty Ward at the Fifth Avenue Hotel in New York while our backers sold us out. When it got down to the knife, they didn't let us in the room. The ballplayers sat in the hall and that was that.

"If he throws games, it's 'cause he's smart." Frank threw his cigar in the river and handed me the flask. "Get drunk and forget I said anything."

9

Frank and I did get drunk. We staggered, arm in arm, pals forever, into the heart of Saturday night. The Gin Palace was crowded. Sawdust had been sprinkled on the floor, and men stood three-deep down the length of the bar. I stayed close to Frank as we worked our way to the bar.

The bottom three tiers of the chandelier were lit, which produced a smoky radiance high over the dance floor where ladies in bloomers whirled about with sports in checkered coats. I enjoyed this parody of society balls where the generations mingle, alliances are made, and marriage is for sale. The stakes were more obvious. One didn't need the subtlety of Mr. Henry James to know who was cruel or what these people wanted. In April, I was still excited by what might be called the romance of the street — and by the idea this world used up its players as fast as baseball. Men with the bulging stomachs of bankers danced with women whose breasts almost fell out of their blouses. Drunks danced with women who held them up. The women winked at each other and reached for their partners' wallets. A Negro, who must have weighed three hundred pounds, played a stand-up piano by the stairs. He bent over the keys, his round, black face almost touching the ivory, while his hands moved like lascivious spiders. Each rag was faster than the last, and when it seemed the Negro could hammer the keys no harder, he threw his head back, grinned, and played faster.

I drank a beer and shouldn't have. The long mahogany bar and the procession of mirrors behind it were on the verge of spinning. I wasn't sobered by the sight of McBuck and Burke conspiratorially playing dice in the booth where Frank, Saturday and I had eaten.

Frank stood at the bar and surveyed the crowd. After a ponderously drunken moment, I realized he was checking the ballplayers. The easiest to spot were Cupid Childs, who was pouring a stream of beer along the bar, and Jimmy McAleer, who followed this rivulet with his tongue. The beer led to the hand, and then arm, of an inordinately endowed lady named Lucy, a favorite of Patsy Tebeau's, who was sitting beside the manager. Lucy laughed as the liquid went over her hand, trickled up her arm, and wet her bare shoulder, but much to the dismay of Childs, the stein was empty before the trail reached that ruffled portion of her anatomy where nature had been so generous.

The lady giggled as the center fielder's tongue greeted her hand and worked its way up her arm. The giggle became a shudder as the appendage reached her shoulder, but the shudder became tremulous, heaving laughter when the tongue attempted a shortcut to its apparent destination, and Lucy pushed McAleer's head into her lap. This produced a tremendous cheer, led by Frank Ember, but if the center fielder intended to feign unconsciousness to remain in the lady's lap, his intentions were foiled by a fresh stein which Cupid Childs emptied on McAleer's head.

I found this hilarious and laughed until I doubled over. Frank howled and rapped his knuckles on the bar. He led the lads in another rendition of "A Hot Time In The Old Town Tonight," which Amos, the piano player, turned into a jumping rag. McAleer got to his feet, shook his head, and said, "Who soaked me?" He tried to box with an imaginary opponent, then slid slowly to the floor, and sat quietly, resting on the brass rail under the bar.

I was ready to approach a lady of the house but wanted advice. Manager Tebeau, who rarely spoke to me, was courting Lucy. Cupid Childs, who liked me better than Tebeau, had his arm around Rose, the red headed woman who'd served us dinner. I thought of staggering up to the second floor to see if some Gin Palace St. Peter might assign me a place but decided against it. I turned to Frank, but he was helping up Jimmy McAleer, while carrying on a loud conversation with Childs.

"Grab a partner, Harry!" Annie Gears gave me a rousing slap on the shoulder. She had changed into a low-cut silk dress and her face was flush from dancing. There was a suggestion of moisture on the tops of her breasts. I looked away. That, as the Bard said, was the way to madness.

"Mingle, Harry. The girls don't bite." I noticed McBuck and Burke had stopped throwing dice. They were watching me.

"You're a snob," said Annie. "And on top of it, you're afraid."

We were near the door, under a large portrait of Abraham Lincoln, that patron saint of all American occasions. The sports and drunks gave us a wide berth. I saw Saturday at the other end of the bar, and Annie said, "We're going to be friends, ain't we? You're his friend, so you can be mine."

"I'm your little brother too?"

"Why does he call you that?"

"It's not flattering."

"I don't have many friends," she said.

"I'm your friend then," I said, feeling suave. No man likes to be demoted to the sexless category of beautiful woman's friend, but we actually did become friends. There was more too, but that was ambiguous. She was always his.

"Can I trust you?"

"That's a difficult question."

"You just answered it."

"I'm not honest but I am sentimental."

"About what?"

"Friendship."

"Then we're friends," Annie said. "It's settled."

"Yes."

"Get a lady, Harry. I'll bet you're not timid with fancy girls. You're probably a masher."

"I'm always afraid." I'm sure Miss Gears knew "nice girls" didn't kiss young men until they were engaged. If she didn't, I wasn't going to tell her. A woman pays a terrible price for freedom. I was protected by the strictest Victorian hypocrisy. My past would not affect my ability to marry. Of course, I could make a mistake about a "nice girl," and find one as uninterested in the senses after marriage as she pretended to be before; but single, like a saloon woman, I was free. Drunk and rolling on a lady of the night, I used to feel like a warrior in the Islamic heaven, where the Koran says seventy-two maidens wait for each man who dies in the service of the Prophet.

"You're a liar and a snob," Annie said, regarding me, hands-on-hips, from her characteristic bemused stance. "You're here to do things they won't let you do at home."

"I thought we were friends."

"I know you fellows in fancy clothes," she said with an edge in her voice. "You come down here for a good time and go home and act like you've been in church."

"I won't deny that," I said.

"You wouldn't be seen with me outside this place."

"Of course I would."

"How about the game next Saturday? I want somebody to take me and I want it to be a friend of his."

There was no way I could say anything but yes. Besides wanting an escort, Annie was testing me. She always tested me, she tested everybody — everybody but the Indian, and he either passed some first ultimate test or represented a failure too grand to pass up. I knew I'd agreed to take the Burnses on Saturday, but couldn't back down.

"Pick me up here."

Annie walked off and I watched the Indian work his way down the bar, shaking hands and drinking whiskey by the shot. His blue coat was over his shoulder and glistened each time he passed a lamp. His white shirt was stained with sweat. I wondered if she trusted him, but I suppose it's friends, not lovers, who one initially worries about trusting.

I had no idea how to juggle the Burnses and Miss Annie Gears. I could inform the Burnses I was sick, but didn't like admitting I was so conventional. The society ladies, or at least the older one, would probably never speak to me again, which was unfortunate because Edith was intriguing. I had tried to give the impression I was at home in the demimonde: appearing with it was another matter. The thought Edith might be secretly impressed was little consolation given the possibility I might not see her again; but I knew if the situation demanded a choice, I'd side with Annie because Annie would be in company where she couldn't defend herself. I don't know how long it took to reach this chivalrous decision, but when I looked up, Burke was in front of me. He'd just appeared, like a broadcloth apparition.

"Who told you to talk to her?" His voice was raw, dockside Cleveland. Burke's pock-marked face was as red as his neck. His hat was off and oily black hair hung behind those massive ears.

"What?" I said, wavering between bluff and pathos.

"Stay away from her."

I looked for Frank but he had taken McAleer to the bathroom. Burke's pals, McBuck and a short fellow with little eyes and pudgy fists, were leaning against a booth and jerking their thumbs in my direction. We were standing in sawdust and the piano player pumped a wild rag. "Punk," said Burke. He spat in the sawdust. His pals enjoyed the performance.

"I don't like your face." Burke pulled my necktie into a hard knot. I had to use both hands to keep from choking and ripped my collar getting it loose. A couple of sports joined McBuck and the other fellow. They laughed. I think a wager was made.

"Show him, Joe."

"Fix the snotnose."

Burke laughed. I had the distinct impression if I moved, he'd hit me, probably with an open hand to show contempt.

"Punk," said Burke, and seizing me by the lapels, shoved me into the bar. I managed to stay on my feet. "Watch where you're going!" said a bartender and shoved me from behind. Burke grabbed me and pulled my face close to his. He smelled of cheap cigars and beer and his ears seemed to move. "Wearin' perfume?" he whispered. "You know what we do with guys wearin' perfume?" If my jacket hadn't been so well made, it would have ripped.

Burke spat in my face. I expected my nose to be broken in one second-splitting smack, but nothing happened. I wiped the spit off my face.

King Saturday hit Burke across the face with an open hand. There was a quick, sharp sound. Burke stood in disbelief, put his hand to his nose, and blood trickled around his fist over the tattoo. The Indian had broken his nose.

"That's my little brother," said Saturday.

"What's it to you?" said Burke, in a bloody spray.

"You tough?" said Saturday, and smacked Burke again. Burke turned sideways and pulled a knife. I reached over the bar for a bottle. At that moment, I would gladly have killed Burke, but the bartender who'd shoved me got me around the neck, and held me against the bar. "Easy, laddie" he said, "Burke's already handicapped."

The piano and then every other noise in the Gin Palace stopped. King Saturday looked at Burke with an intent but absolutely calm concentration. It was almost as if the Indian enjoyed that awful, flush moment. Burke held his nose with one hand and the knife with the other. Saturday backed slowly through the tables onto the dance floor. He moved left, keeping away from the knife, with his big hands at chest level.

Burke followed, looking wildly at his own image in the mirrors over the bar. He cursed steadily and lumbered onto the dance floor holding his nose. I heard later someone restrained Frank and Annie cried, but I only saw the fight.

Saturday moved in a circle. Burke took plodding steps and swung the knife between his legs. When they were almost under the chandelier, the Indian smiled. Burke looked puzzled. He lunged and missed. Saturday let him get closer. Burke lunged and missed by less than an inch. His nose was bleeding and there was a red trail on the dance floor. Burke lunged and Saturday's foot moved. The knife went flying. It skidded toward the piano. Burke looked at his hand and the Indian kicked him in the stomach. Burke grabbed his stomach and was kicked in the groin. Saturday retrieved the knife. Joe Burke was on his knees. The bartender let me go. I thought it was over and looked at the bleary crowd.

King Saturday cut off Burke's right ear.

Part Three

Part Three

1

I worried all week about Annie and the Burnses, but on Thursday Edith sent a note saying her mother couldn't attend, and asking if a Mr. Lyndon Blunt could accompany us. She invited me to lunch before the game. I was so relieved I would have consented to dine with the German Kaiser, and wrote that we would be escorting a friend of Mr. Saturday's, who unfortunately couldn't attend lunch. This was the only lie I told that week, but I didn't want Annie to have to make conversation over a meal with someone I didn't know.

These details are only important in retrospect. Something happened that morning that may or may not have been significant. I met Miss Burns and Mr. Blunt, who was not so well named as I hoped — Mr. Blunt ("Call me Lyndon"), being an earnest, ambitious, blond young man with a well trimmed mustache, who wanted only to serve the strongest master, that being Standard Oil, and marry the most eligible woman, that being Miss Burns. Edith asked me to meet them at Standard Oil.

I rented an open carriage and was driven through a fine bustling May morning. Parasols and new hats were everywhere and gentlemen tipped their toppers with an élan that seemed to salute the day itself. Children raced after each other with a frenzy that seemed to say catching and squeezing a friend could make summer come and stay. Trolleys full of kranks rattled east as men lucky enough to be off work headed for League Park.

Mr. Blunt was one of the lucky ones. He had started work at 5:30 in the morning and they let him out at 11 a.m. He and Edith were on the granite steps of the massive Standard building. Lyndon shook my hand with a muscular grip and insisted on showing us his office. He was one of those men who confidently tell you about himself and then expect to be thanked afterward. Edith wore a bright yellow dress with the big puffy sleeves she favored that summer. She looked fine. She didn't look pretty. Edith wasn't pretty but she had a way, possibly because of her height and ready intellect, of challenging men and commanding their attention.

Blunt wanted us to know he had an office, rather than a desk, and so we entered the cavernous room which had been the home office of the "Octopus" before the world's most successful company moved its headquarters to New York City. That high-ceilinged, vault-like place reflected the grim Baptist determination of John D. Rockefeller. Clerks with black coats, eye shades and stained fingers, sat at rows of desks, peering at columns of numbers. The books were kept in code so no one, with or without subpoena, could decipher the tricks of the empire. Heads turned as the handsome lady in yellow, Mr. Blunt, whose gray suit indicated he was of a higher order than the factotums at their desks, and I, in brown and white suit — a badge of independence — walked by. If some of the younger men hadn't looked a moment longer than proper, and if a balding fellow with a wart on his nose hadn't smiled, I would have thought we were among the dead.

I've been to the Standard many times but am always amazed by the efficient pall which hangs over the hundreds of men whose eyes have been weakened in the service of greed and whose world is a desk. No one is in a hurry but no one wastes time. No one is proud but the company is more powerful than most countries. No one is rich but the books contain the wealth of nations. The Standard seems as patient and implacable as time itself. My life, I thought, was ruled by different numbers: oil's figures manipulate, deceive, control; baseball's numbers, those wonderful columns of averages, runs, doubles, putouts and assists, are an invitation to a green world where time exists no more than in the imagination. I thought baseball made me safe; and perhaps it would have, but Saturday added another dimension, and what might have been a normal career in the business of baseball was about to accelerate.

Mr. Blunt's office was a cubicle of opaque glass with his name on the door. I asked him if it might be possible to waste a little time if one kept the door shut. He looked at me as if the notion had never crossed his mind. "We don't waste time," he said. "We are organized."

"Not so organized that we've been fed," said Edith, whose sparkling eyes betrayed a desire to do mischief in the temple of efficiency.

"I thought you'd like to see where I work," said Mr. Blunt.

"Your name's even on the door," I said.

Blunt glanced at the papers on his desk, as if something that couldn't wait might have just appeared. I looked and saw columns of numbers, and realized, as I later told Edith, that it's not only the Standard's greed which upsets me but its style. There's much greed in the world but the high chairs, black coats, and long, respectful hours frighten me. Rockefeller pioneered faceless power: dummy companies, holding companies, syndicates, trusts, a maze of hegemony where no man, not even himself, is responsible for the entity known as Standard Oil. The sanctimonious modesty of the Standard, which extends from the penny-pinching patriarch to its poorest-paid clerk, is as offensive as its power.

Blunt, noticing that Edith looked impatient and I was bored, said, "Some day this country will be run as efficiently as this company."

"I believe there's a baseball game to be played between now and then," I said.

The young man reddened slightly and said, "There's a time to put away childish things."

"Not when Philadelphia's in town," said Edith.

"You work for the team, don't you?" said Blunt.

"Yes," I said, "and I can let its virtues speak for themselves."

Blunt looked at us both and said, "The world can be divided into those who understand it and those who don't." I felt badly for Blunt; he was not making the impression he intended. I don't think he was used to people looking bored when he made pronouncements. I think he felt very young. Blunt was an inch or so shorter than I but had powerful shoulders, and told us later he'd played football, that gladiator's game, at Princeton. I repeat what he said because even the confident and imposing, blond Mr. Blunt would be touched in a way he couldn't foresee by King Saturday.

"There are those who understand and those who think they understand," said Edith who, I was learning, was a person to be reckoned with if one were in the habit of making judgments.

"The future is organization," said Blunt, "and we are the best organization on earth." He clearly believed this, and clearly hadn't intended to fire his big gun, if one can call that a big gun — I do so because he had none bigger — so early in the conversation. I hadn't planned to antagonize Edith's friend, but he was like so many men I knew — the well-tailored legions who follow power, and its polite face, success — that I found him insufferable. It's one thing to be snubbed — snobs can he artful, but I find bright young men who know how the world should be run less than amusing.

"Mr. Rockefeller is the da Vinci of business."

"Praising Rockefeller is like praising a shark because it eats all the time," I said. I'd been saving that remark, having thought of it several months before. The quip earned the enmity of one of the people in that opaque room, and, I believe, the respect of the other. I probably overrate the power of words because I enjoy them so much, but the crack did get us out of that office.

As we were leaving — Mr. Blunt walking ahead with his head turned down and his step precise, Edith behind, but not at the respectful pace the English demand of a prince's wife if she were not born a princess, and me almost waving goodbye to the men at their desks — I saw King Saturday emerge from an office in the bowels of that gray place. To this day I don't know what he was doing there, and to this day I'm not sure it wasn't important. Perhaps I'm confusing the hidden labyrinth of Standard Oil and its ability to consolidate and corrupt with the more profoundly hidden labyrinth of King Saturday.

2

On the way to League Park, Mr. Blunt asked if Miss Gears were likely to be at the Republican Ball that night at the Stillman Hotel. I had forgotten this august annual affair, which my mother used to insist I attend, as if it were some super dancing school, and where, presumably, I might still meet the right people. Everyone, as they used to say, went to the Republican Ball.

"I doubt it, Blunt," I said, preferring to be at the Gin Palace meeting the wrong people.

"A pity," said Edith. "I may have to dance every dance with Lyndon."

This began to change my mind. There was a definite rivalry with Blunt. He was even rooting for Philadelphia, and I knew I could go to the Stillman with Frank Robison, who never missed an opportunity to show himself in public.

"What about Miss Gears?" said Blunt. "Do I know anyone who knows her?" He was ready to pounce. A climber like Blunt always senses when a man can be embarrassed.

"Perhaps Miss Gears is a Democrat," said Edith, who watched King Saturday throwing in right field with Jimmy McAleer.

We were behind the Spider dugout in the best seats. There was no bunting, and fewer men in expensive suits, but the crowd was almost as big as Opening Day. This was a baseball game, not a civic occasion. "How's he going to do?" Edith asked several times, which was the question the whole town was asking. How would Saturday do against the Phillies' Ed Delahanty, the best player in baseball?

The Indian was all potential that May afternoon. He was a rookie sensation — the most exciting baseball event: a new star, and possibly the best player any of us had ever seen. Harriet Ember was right. He was a sort of baseball god. A krank waits like a Jew for his Messiah. We all have one man who redeems sunburned hours, nights spent over columns of numbers, winters of waiting, and years of frustration. We wait for the man we would like to have been. We wait for the one who makes our baseball days a book of life, rather than a chronicle of wasted time.

Delahanty was not only the best, he was also from Cleveland. Ed held court on the steps of the visiting dugout with reporters, well-wishers, and relatives. A gray-haired lady presented him with a yellow bouquet while a young woman wearing a hat topped with red roses leaned over and kissed him. Big Ed had hit over .400 twice and once hit nineteen home runs. Few men hit for average and power. There are fellows who can do one or the other, but the player who can do both is the rich man who enters heaven.

Saturday came in from right and talked to Frank Ember by first base. He looked big in the sunshine and his hair seemed incredibly black under his Spiders cap. Kranks called to him but Saturday paid no attention. I would have said something but didn't want to be ignored in front of Edith. Blunt watched the Indian closely. He also looked good in the bright afternoon with his yellow hair neatly parted in the middle, and supremely trim mustache. Edith sat between us.

"Where is Miss Gears?" said Blunt. "Who's escorting her?" The man from Princeton had become very proper since failing to impress us with his office. "Have I met her? Where did she go to school?"

"Spare us the frippery," said Edith, and Blunt turned so red he put his hand to his face, as if shielding his eyes from the sun.

100

My worries about Annie were groundless. I was concerned with the impression I made on Edith and even Blunt, and failed to appreciate how well she could take care of herself. A murmur ran through our part of the crowd. Heads turned. The skinny fellow in a white apron who hadn't stopped shouting, "Caps!" "Souvenirs!" (which were miniature tomahawks), was quiet. Ben, a rotund vendor who sold hot chestnuts, rested the metal box that was supported by a leather strap around his neck, on his knee, and stared. Frank Robison looked up from the politician whose hairy ear he had for the afternoon. Blunt took his eyes off Edith. Annie made her entrance.

If ever a woman could rival a beautiful day, it was Annie Gears. She wore a red and black dress which went to the neck and looked like fire. A row of pearl buttons marched down the bodice, leading the eye over her bosom. Red taffeta fit snugly to her waist and then exploded in dozens of red and black folds which flowed to the ground. Annie wore no gloves and carried no parasol. Her dark hair was swept up under a hat I can only compare to an August sunset when the sun is the color of blood. On the left side of her neck was a blue feather.

She moved carefully toward our box, checking the crowd and smiling. Annie was happy. She was in love. She had spent a week with the Indian, and happiness shone through her beauty in a way it never did again. I suspect every man in that corner of League Park remembers her as distinctly as I do.

After one glance, Blunt tried to ignore the spectacle which had the crowd's attention, and attempted to show Edith he preferred her company. "Must be a ballplayer's woman. Maybe more than one ballplayer's woman." Edith, undaunted by Blunt, looked at Annie and smiled.

"Harry," called Annie, and I was on my feet, the one man in the section summoned by the fiery vision. She looked at my brown and white striped suit — the only one I owned other than the white — and said, "You look fine!" loud enough for several rows to hear. It was the nicest thing ever said to me in public. Arm-in-arm, the brown and white lawyer, well-shaven and sparkling in his own right, and that flash of red and black walked to the railing beside the dugout. A lady sighed and several gents whistled. I was interested in the effect we had on Edith and Blunt. I looked just right and Annie looked better.

King Saturday and Frank Ember joined us. Annie leaned over the railing and kissed Saturday. A cheer went up. They were a hero and his lady, and the sporting public, no easy critic, approved. It was their finest moment. I prefer to remember us all as we were that afternoon the Spiders met Philadelphia. That I prefer a pose, an image, a dazzling surface to the depths we would soon be forced to see in each other, tells as much about me as I care to reveal.

"Are you going to beat Big Ed?" said Annie.

"Bet on it," said Saturday.

Much to my surprise, we were joined by Edith and Mr. Blunt. Edith went right up to Saturday and introduced herself. "I think you'll do very well today," she said. Saturday looked at Edith and then broke into one of those smiles that resolved the contradiction of his aggressive and mystical face into a hand-some man. They were almost eye to eye — Edith in her yellow pique suit with embroidered buttons and high white collar. Saturday, his freshly polished black high top shoes gleaming in the sun and white uniform making his skin look darker — stood by the railing, and they looked at each other. It was one of those brief, full looks a man and woman who've just met give each other. I wouldn't have noticed but for Blunt. The umpires, the Phillies, and half the crowd were looking at us. I looked at Blunt to see my triumph, and saw a mixture of surprise and fear.

3

The Phillies' lineup was like a fighter with a good jab and an excellent knockout punch. Duffy Cooley and Elmer Flick would tease their way on base and then be knocked in by Lajoie and Delahanty. This was an effective strategy, but today the Phillies had to contend with the fluid right shoulder of Mr. Cy Young. Cooley stepped up and the games among us — Blunt and Edith, Edith and I, Annie and Blunt (once she sat down Blunt was gracious to the point of dandyism), and Saturday with us all — were eclipsed by Cleveland versus Philadelphia.

Young immediately showed Cooley and his mates, who were already spitting and limbering up the "fourcabulary," that he was razor sharp. The first two pitches were over the inside corner below the belt.

Duff stepped out, wiped his brow like a man faced with a difficult decision, and looked at the dugout. His concentration was broken. A hitter goes to the plate with his reflexes and ego. He must concentrate and react while the pitcher tries to break that concentration and upset the man's timing. Few men, maybe the Indian and Ed Delahanty, could just react. A hitter has to be ready for the fast one but can't be fooled by a curve. He has to adjust if the pitcher drops the pace and lay off balls masquerading as strikes. Most of all, like a fighter or lover, a batter needs confidence, and Duff Cooley lost his with two pitches. Young had him thinking: a dangerous pastime for a man with two strikes.

Duff rubbed dirt on his hands and got back in the box. The next pitch was low but Cooley was afraid to consign this turn at bat to the judgment of the umpire. He swung, grounded to short, and was thrown out.

Elmer Flick was up. I'd never seen Flick, and Flick had never seen Cy Young. Neither of us got much from this first meeting. Flick hit weakly to first and Patsy Tebeau put him out with his bare hand. With the "table setters" gone, the crowd settled into the confrontation of Nap Lajoie and Cy Young. This was one of those moments a krank waits for, a boy remembers, and a man savors.

Most players approach the plate with superstition and swagger. Lajoie was in the batter's box as quickly as a ten-year-old.

Nap fouled one over our heads. Annie leaned back and the feather was outlined against her white throat as the ball sailed high into the grandstand. The crowd cheered, refreshed by the flash of beauty, and then returned to the duel of batter and pitcher. Young got another strike and made a fine pitch on the outside corner. Lajoie, a solidly built right hand hitter, flicked his wrists and slashed a base hit to right. I would have stood up and cheered if Blunt hadn't. There was no other way that ball could have been hit. If Lajoie had taken his customary stride, he would have missed the pitch or dribbled it to the infield. Nap had to adjust. He expanded his style. That moment — the white dance of the ball on the corner and the quickness of those strong wrists — is the standard I measure right-hand hitters by.

Lajoie rounded first and hopped back with jubilant pride. He knew what a good pitch he'd hit.

Ed Delahanty sauntered to the plate. When Big Ed did anything in Cleveland, it was an event. The crowd erupted. Some, like Ben with his hot metal box, booed lustily, but most rose, shouted, and gestured at the man who'd once been our neighbor. I preferred Delahanty before he became such a study in his own mannerisms. It was difficult for Ed not to overact the role of himself when half the lads in America, and all the lads in his hometown, aped the way he approached the plate, touched his cap, and hunched his shoulders.

104

Big Ed strode to the plate and tipped his hat to Annie. Saluting a pretty woman was a Delahanty trademark. Annie shrugged, turned to Edith, and said, "Men are jerks."

Ed pointed his bat at Cy Young. This may have impressed kranks and intimidated rookies but was only posturing when Young's powerful shoulder and right arm swung around.

The first pitch was a ball. People yelled and jeered. The man next to Frank Robison kept shouting, "You owe me fifty bucks!" Ben booed like a fog horn. Edith politely but fervently clapped her yellow gloved hands. Annie cupped her bare hands and yelled, "Get him, Cy!"

Big Ed held the bat at the end, his fist over the knob. His batting style was unique. It was the way you were not supposed to hit. Instead of choking up like Keeler or McGraw, Ed held the bat like a club, and rather than wait for his pitch, the cardinal rule of hitting, he seemed to prefer bad balls. Delahanty thrived on pitches a foot outside, over his head, or about to bounce in the dirt. The most dangerous hitter in the game would swing at anything. I once saw Delahanty tomahawk a ball thrown right at him. This incorrigible, up-your-arse style would have been tedious if he hadn't been a great hitter. There was something wonderful about the way breaking the rules released some pent-up skill in the man. Who, that clear afternoon, could have known Cleveland's idol would die only five seasons later by jumping, falling, or being pushed off a bridge over Niagara Falls?

Cy Young waited. He understood the ritual of Delahanty batting in Cleveland. The idolaters and detractors calmed down, and we awaited the collision of that handle-wielded bat and a fast pitch.

Young cut one loose that hopped as it went by Delahanty's eyes with a frightening blur. This was a challenge Ed could not ignore and he swung from the heels, missed, and spun around like a demented windmill. The grandstand exploded in glee, except for Blunt, who shook his blond head.

"That's as far as he got with me," said Annie.

Delahanty was unfazed. The gargantuan miss did not affect his concentration. Ed could look foolish one pitch and make the pitcher look worse on the next. Cy Young wound up and Lajoie took off for second. I couldn't tell whether Nap was stealing or if Philadelphia was working a hit-and-run. The question was academic. Delahanty missed or ignored the sign and the pitch whizzed by. Lou Criger jumped up and made a perfect throw. Lajoie slid into the tag.

The inning was over. Big Ed haughtily pitched his bat away and headed for the outfield.

"Great throw," said Annie.

"Do you know them all?" said Edith.

"Personally," said Annie.

"Do you like ballplayers?"

"Most of them are asses."

"And Saturday?"

"He's different," said Annie.

Philadelphia's pitcher, Wiley Piatt, was a rookie. I watched him warm up and saw he had a strong arm. Being new, Piatt would probably try to overpower the Spiders to make up for lack of finesse. Power isn't as interesting as craft, but watching a rookie find the limit of his talent can be absorbing. I laughed, thinking I had power on one side and craft on the other. I looked at Annie, and then Edith. Each suspected I had made a private joke at her expense. I denied it, saying Piatt wouldn't last five innings. Blunt leapt to the rookie's defense and bet me a five-dollar gold piece Piatt would not only finish but win the contest.

"I know my team," said Blunt.

"You'd better let me hold your money," said Annie, "'cause you're gonna lose it."

Blunt produced a blue crushed velvet wallet that looked like it might belong to an opera singer and handed Annie a shiny gold piece. She put the coin in the front of her dress with the ease of a nun making the sign of the cross, and Blunt was shocked.

The Phillies ran to their positions and I watched Lajoie. In his first year, Nap played outfield and first, the least difficult infield position. He had switched to second and I wanted to see him play it.

Saturday led off and received a whooping, foot-stomping, tomahawk-waving ovation. At least three kranks had drums, which beat in unison, as if signaling that we were on the verge of a savage uprising. The Indian approached the plate with an easy stride but his eyes never left Piatt's face. The rookie was noticeably relieved when the umpire shouted, "Play ball!"

The first two pitches missed by wide margins. Piatt faced the prospect of walking an extraordinarily fast man. Piatt looked down. I nudged Annie and said, "Fastball or curve?" "Fast one," she said. "He's too nervous not to throw as hard as he can." Piatt did choose the fast pitch, and to his credit, it wasn't a wild fling at the middle of the plate but a tailing riser that bore in on the Indian.

Saturday scorched a grounder between first and second. Even with Lajoie playing a step to his left, this burner looked like a sure hit. Right fielder Flick came in but Nap dove and knocked the ball down with his glove. He grabbed it, got to his knees, and threw Saturday out by a step.

There was silence and then a tremendous cheer. The crowd couldn't help it. Nap Lajoie had just made a great play. Patsy Tebeau started to complain and stopped. King Saturday looked at Lajoie and trotted to the dugout.

"That's the best play I ever saw a second baseman make," said Annie.

"Nap's the best young player in the League," said Blunt, with satisfaction.

"Wait until the game's over," I said.

There was no score when Delahanty came up in the fifth. Ed had grounded out in his delayed appearance in the second. He took a surprisingly restrained swing and missed. Young tried another high fast one and Ed hammered it. Center fielder McAleer broke in and before Jimmy could reverse his field, the ball was over his head. He turned and ran as the ball caromed off the base of the fence. Delahanty rounded first in full stride and roared around second. Shortstop McKean made a terrific relay to hold Ed at third. Delahanty tipped his cap to cheers and catcalls. A red-whiskered gentleman, within earshot of the Robisons, loudly cursed the day the Spiders let him get away.

Philadelphia wasted no time. The next man laid down a bunt and Delahanty scored easily.

"That won't hold up," said Annie.

She was right. Piatt got wild the next inning. Two walks, back-to-back doubles, a long fly that moved both runners, and a single produced four runs. The Phillies' lone run was all they got. Cy Young found his groove. Each pitch dissected a different portion of the plate and set up the hitter for something he didn't get. The Phillies hit grounders, popped up, struggled with pitches that couldn't be hit, and stared in frustration at called strikes. Blunt spent much of the afternoon with his chin in his hand. Annie became demure as the outcome was less in doubt, except for occasionally cupping her hands and yelling through them. Edith, on the other hand, was less content. She watched Saturday carefully. After the seventh, Edith turned to Annie and said, "He's going to do something in his last at-bat."

"Maybe," said Annie.

I watched Edith watch Saturday. She was a fine balance of lady-like control and boisterous skepticism. My mother, who had an opinion of everybody who ever attended dancing school, ball, or college with me, said Edith was spoiled, which was mother's way of saying rich, but neither concept accounted for her independence and intelligence.

"Yes,"said Edith. "He will outdo Delahanty."

"I'm out of gold pieces," said Blunt, "but I'll bet you the last dance at the Republican Ball."

"Fine," said Edith.

Annie looked at Blunt, then Edith, then me. I could see she thought they had drawn a circle from which she was excluded. "Are you going to that ball?" she asked, and I tossed off an answer I thought clever. "Not if Saturday outdoes Delahanty." Edith smiled and Blunt squeezed his chin. Annie held her head higher. I had completed the circle. I wasn't on her side, but as she said later, how could I have been?

"Would you like to go?"

Annie said nothing.

The Indian was restless in the outfield. He moved with every pitch and followed the ball the way he'd eyed Piatt. Saturday was into the rhythm of the game. "He's riled," said Edith. Annie had no comment nor did she appear to be studying one man more than another.

Saturday led off the eighth. Piatt, except for one inning, had pitched well. The rookie looked tired but was throwing well. The color and texture of the ball worked in his favor. Piatt was using the same sphere Delahanty whacked off the center field fence.

"This is it," I said.

108

Saturday took a ball and strike but there was nothing casual about the way he surveyed them. Piatt was too impressed with the strike and threw the same pitch, a low curve. The Indian was ready.

The ball jumped off the bat. This occurs too rapidly for the eye, so the mind takes in details: the apocalyptic crack of the bat, the jerk of the pitcher's head, an outfielder looking up, the whole world turning to the fence. This ball, like Delahanty's, started low. Duff Cooley was off with the sound of the bat, but Flick in right didn't move. He stood in his tracks, hypnotized by the blur coming at his head. For an instant, it seemed that white rocket would decapitate him. Flick didn't move. He didn't lift his glove. The line drive immobilized Flick the way snakes are supposed to immobilize their prey. A gasp started in the collective throat, but the ball went over Flick's head and kept climbing. It seemed to pick up speed as it approached the fence. Flick didn't turn around. I think he was surprised to be alive. The ball flew over the Johann Hoff Malt Extract sign ("All Others Are Worthless") and began to unravel.

King Saturday made a colossal turn at first, pivoting with an explosion of speed. He must have known it was a homer but ran with an exuberance which almost made him leave the ground. The Indian cruised around second, joyfully touched third, and continued home full of childlike admiration for himself. McKean and Burkett were waiting with handshakes. The dugout was up and kranks stomped, shouted, and slapped each others' backs.

Annie flipped Blunt's gold piece to me and didn't say a word.

4

The ballroom of the Stillman Hotel had been turned into a red, white and blue Babylon. Bunting hung from walls, the railing of the grand staircase, the dais, a half dozen potted palms, and festooned over each doorway, even the entrance to the kitchen. The national colors had been applied to everything but the Republicans themselves, who wore black suits with heavy gold watches and fobs over their bellies. The order of the evening was blue or red cravats tied in neat bows which rode over shirt fronts so voluminous it seemed each man had the winds of success in his bosom. This was an evening when the greasy black of politicians, worn at the elbows and shiny in the seat, could glide with the finest cloth and whitest shirt fronts. Men who tout, front and climb, got to mingle with power. I heard more than one pillar of the party remark, "So this is the public," and the public, or that part of it which was useful and had a greasy suit, was here.

The ladies outdid themselves. Not restricted to black and encouraged to sparkle, we were treated to society women done up as nurses, cavalry officers (no one had then heard of the Rough Riders — a name Colonel Roosevelt appropriated from Buffalo Bill's Congress Of Rough Riders Of The World), foot soldiers, even sailors, as well as puffy, pearled, shawled matrons. A red-headed woman, a bit past her prime, had come as the Statue Of Liberty, and like the one in New York, attracted crowds, as her bust, though covered with a red, white and blue foulard, was, like Liberty herself, greatly admired.

Blunt was meeting the "right" people and shaking the plump hands of politicians who couldn't bow low enough to Rockefeller. Lyndon was in the grasp of an enormous gentleman who hadn't taken off his top coat, when Edith slipped away. "I thought you'd come," she said. "You like me better than you let on." I laughed. Edith wore crimson and I wondered if Annie had inspired her. Edith's satin gown had dark red lace on the bodice and sleeves. Her hat, which featured ostrich and peacock feathers, made her look six feet tall. I had to admire the way this handsome but not pretty woman announced her presence.

Edith took my arm and we surveyed the conclave of Ohio's rulers. The original theme for the ball, she told me, had been the Republican National Convention. Ladies were to have carried placards, tables would have borne the names of states, and the orchestra would have worn straw hats and seersucker jackets and marched around as bands do on the convention floor. "That would only have been mildly ghastly," she said. "Now we have men playing soldier." The orchestra was dressed like U.S. Cavalry, and each man wore a "campaign" hat, those wide brimmed, floppy hats the British made popular with their unpopular war in South Africa. Some real soldiers were in attendance too.

"Speaking of ghastliness," I said, "what about that?" A photograph a story high of Ohio's first and favorite son, President McKinley, dominated the ballroom. It rose behind the dais and those dense eyebrows looked demonic. The President's face seemed insidiously clever: what passed for a twinkle in smaller portraits was a veritable map of innuendo and design.

"He's a kind man," said Edith. "He visits mother whenever he's in Cleveland."

A brave man, I thought. "This war is an embarrassment. We'll get an empire and be no better than a damned European country."

"What did you expect?" said Edith. "We no longer have a frontier. The army needs something to do."

112

"First Indians, now the world?"

"Speaking of Indians, I want to thank you for the game today."

"He's amazing," I said.

"He's wonderful."

"You seem smitten with him?"

"Not as much as you are."

This remark censored a comment I would have made about the look which had passed between Edith and Saturday. "You look slick," she said, and I became self-conscious. I was wearing a black coat, gray striped trousers, and had a stick with a pearl and gold handle which had belonged to my father.

"It's difficult to say whether you look more like a mortician or a United States Senator," said Edith.

I laughed.

"Are you in love with her?" she said.

"Who?" I said, off guard again.

"With Annie. Even Lyndon was taken with her."

"Who isn't in love with Annie?".

"She thinks a good deal of you too."

"Only as a friend."

"And this greatly insults you?"

"It's the worst position to be put in by a woman."

"Men are incorrigibly vain."

"She loves Saturday."

"That makes her more attractive."

"How?"

Edith looked at me full face. Her brown hair was neatly combed up in two waves under her plumed hat. The feathers reminded me of Annie. "If you fail, you have an excuse."

"I won't try."

"Because you're afraid of him?"

"Because he's my friend," I said, and excused myself to go to the punch bowl. I was irritated. Of course, the notion of *success intime* with Miss Gears crossed my mind, probably every fifteen minutes, but that was private, and I preferred to think I wouldn't try because I was a gentleman and friend, rather than afraid, which of course I was. And there was more too. A woman who attracts two friends means more to each than she ever could alone. I was irritated, Edith knew this. With a smile of triumph, she took the floor with Blunt, who had tired of waiting to meet former Mayor Tom Johnson. Edith and Blunt did a brisk fox trot.

The punch bowl, a gleaming piece of silver the size of a bath tub, contained a three-tiered nickel-plated fountain capped by a copper eagle which bubbled a yellow liquid over a slab of ice carved in the shape of the state of Ohio. Slices of orange, lime and lemon rinds, and something that looked to be as large as the head of John the Baptist which turned out to be a coconut, and enough ice to constitute a danger to navigation, circled the Buckeye state. Lads fortifying themselves for the dance floor, gentlemen escaping their wives, and men lacing themselves at the Grand Old Party's expense, waited in four ragged lines while four black men in white aprons served with four gold ladles.

"Henry!"

I turned around and found my mother preparing to have a glass of punch.

"I knew I would find you by the punch bowl."

"Mother, you look wonderful." She did. Once a year the lady put on a dark blue velvet dress, the red and blue sash that went from shoulder to waist and was worn only by widows or family of the war dead, and paraded through an evening. This was her night to walk the battlements and remind the world of a man who never grew old, and remind the world that some never forget.

"You look terrible. Ballplayers must drink as much as clergymen."

"They're a righteous bunch."

"Why haven't you been to see me?"

"I've been looking for a wife."

"At the Gin Palace?"

Mother's wit and information were not usually so acute. "You've found me out."

"I wish you'd find a respectable job and associate with better women. And not Edith Burns. I didn't know you'd remade her acquaintance. She's not your type, Henry. Her mother is an awful woman. I've disliked Augusta since we were six and she told me I was fat. There's fast money in that family, Henry. Fast money goes as quickly as it comes."

"Edith is a krank."

"Baseball attracts riffraff."

114

Our conversation became a catalogue of young ladies present. Mother was a fund of information. Half a dozen women I thought were prizes of the season were "engaged," "practically at the altar," or "in a rush to the nearest church." The most lecherous fortune hunter couldn't have had such fresh intelligence. "If you don't settle down, none of them will have you, not even Edith Burns." I enjoy gossip, and in mother's case, it's practically an art form, but gossip is usually a harbinger of self-pity and complaint. "You're the last of your line, Henry. There aren't any of us left. Name your first son after your father." Mother looked at me with those clear gray eyes which were fixed so squarely on the past, squeezed my hand, and said, "Mix."

Edith and Blunt were dancing again. They were a handsome pair. Blunt wore a black suit with gray vest and black and silver striped tie. He was dressed precisely right, with a touch of panache in the cravat. Blunt looked charming, although the effect did seem too deliberate. He held Edith at a respectful distance and led her with a sure but generous hand. Blunt was making his intentions known and his intentions were honorable. He could lead her properly for the rest of her life. Here was a man who knew how to dress, how to dance, and who was incapable of a false or improper move. Edith was laughing. I couldn't tell if Blunt had said something funny, or if she were laughing at the idea of being led. The sight of her large red glove on his dark shoulder infuriated me.

I turned to the dais where the Republican Ladies of Cleveland had placed a cake eight feet long in the shape of the island of Cuba. This soon-to-be spoil of war lay under McKinley, who looked about to devour it. "Cuba" was topped with a sugary red, white and blue frosting, and covered with every conceivable fruit, as if to whet the President's appetite. The "island" was surrounded by blue ice, and riding on this frozen "Caribbean" was a squadron of ice ships, all melting, that resembled our Atlantic fleet. I always enjoy a gathering of Republicans. The party of Lincoln has its high-collared gentry, radiant daughters, grandams, and practitioners of the arts of this world from those who wear diamond earrings to those wearing diamond stick pins. I was surrounded by things to eat, drink and marry. Corpulent men with red faces and big cigars went by puffing like dreadnoughts. They eyed young women with less subtlety than McKinley eyed "Cuba." I saw Jake McBuck at the punch bowl. The satin lapels of his black suit were so shiny they looked like matches had been struck on them. McBuck winked at me. Frank Robison thumped my back and said, "Keep an eye on that Indian." Some of the guests thought the President might be here but "preparations for war," we were told, kept him in Washington. The crowd had to settle for Senator Mark Hanna: kingmaker, iron millionaire, and most influential Republican. That stout man with his round face and quick eyes stood in a corner, where he could eye the picture of his protégé, while a crowd which rivaled that by the punch bowl and included Blunt, formed around him.

"I don't suppose you dance?" Edith was flushed from her exertion on the floor. Her face was almost the color of her hat.

"I'm still sober."

"Where would men be without alcohol?"

"Rooted to the ground like trees."

"I'll bet you dance at the Gin Palace."

"I'm not sober at the Gin Palace."

"I suspect you're not a lot of things at the Gin Palace. Men aren't just vain, they're hypocrites."

"Men are afraid of women," I said. "They're afraid of women who are their equals, and most afraid of equals they are attracted to." I was surprised I said this, so I laughed.

Edith looked at me keenly. Her pink face, large nose, large pores — her skin was not beautiful — and big jaw, struck me as pretty when animated by skepticism. "You are part honesty and part craft, but I can't tell which is which."

While Blunt waited to be presented to Senator Hanna, his neatly parted blond hair and athletic good looks standing out from bald heads and stooped shoulders, Edith led me up the bunting-draped grand staircase. I asked where we were going and she raised a gloved finger to her lips. We went high above the floor where the cream and dregs of Cleveland waltzed — though not with each other — past two young men judiciously eyeing what they weren't part of, a stout young woman who kept looking at one of the men, and a red faced older lady, quite out of breath, whose wire spectacles, large front teeth, and self-important way of manipulating a Japanese fan, reminded me of Theodore Roosevelt.

116

We turned in a door framed by white pilasters that went from wainscot to ceiling, and found ourselves in a little room decorated "Turkish Cozy Corner" style. This ornate closet contained a sofa smothered with purple, yellow, and orange pillows — all fringed with gold, two captain's chairs, a lacquered table with bronze leaves scrolled up and down its legs, and a chandelier I had to step around. Veils and tapestries obscured the corners and blurred the distinction between ceiling and wall. We were in a shapeless, cloth room that could have been a Bedouin merchant's tent. The floor was covered by a red carpet thick enough to sleep on. The tapestries and veils were decorated with swastikas, signs from the zodiac, and wheels-within-wheels which seemed to move when looked at longer than a moment, and were, no doubt, symbolic portals to some Persian heaven and hell. The most garish object in that crowded room, a cabinet decorated with Moorish arches and crescents, turned out to be a sewing machine.

Edith sat on the sofa. Her crimson dress was surrounded by swastikas and gold tassels. "Sit down," she said. Edith took my hand in her large gloved hand. Her grip was strong. I was afraid not to meet her gaze. Edith pulled me to her and kissed me on the mouth. I was shocked. Young ladies did not kiss unless they were engaged. I pulled back, saying, "I didn't know we were on such intimate terms," which was meant to sound sophisticated but came out like a school boy, so I tried to kiss her to cover my embarrassment. She pushed me away.

"That wasn't an invitation."

"What the deuce was it?"

Edith looked at me kindly. Her eyes looked large and black in that dim, crowded room. She had taken off her hat and it rested on a striped pillow like a trained bird. Edith was more desirable than I had ever seen her. "A statement," she said.

"A most ambiguous statement."

"A statement that I'm as free as you are."

"And as rash too," I said.

She put her arms around my neck and I felt her solid body and a powerful warmth. I smelled her and it was a complicated smell: a trace of perfume, a trace of perspiration, a trace of something I didn't recognize. The room seemed very small. I was awed with disapproval and admiration: a sweet, private mixture. She was bold and I was attractive. She had kissed me.

We had a secret. I congratulated myself on outdoing Blunt and realized Edith was trembling. Her eyes were full of tears.

"What's the matter?"

"Please leave."

I got up, utterly intimidated by what seemed a deep mystery. I stood among rugs and veils, overwhelmed with how much I liked Edith, and by a feeling that her vitality was trapped in a contrived, foolish little room. I returned to the ball, wondering if my vanity wasn't everything she despised.

5

I was in for a bigger surprise than a kiss. I returned to the punch bowl to test the hypothesis that alcohol deepens one's understanding of the opposite sex, and noticed Edith dancing with a man in uniform. This was no surprise as a small but visible number of military men were treating ladies to the chivalrous side of the martial nature. They were at the other end of the room, by the red, white and blue festooned entrance to the kitchen, yet I was disturbed by the blue silhouette guiding the crimson lady. His waltz was grotesquely familiar. The feeling was so strong, I had the sensation of having been here before, then realized it was Ned.

Edith saw me, murmured in Ned's ear, and he waved. When the dance ended, as they came toward me, Ned exchanged pleasantries with Jake McBuck. Ned was wearing an Army uniform with a captain's gold shoulder bars. A sword hung neatly at his side. I'd never seen him look more creased or more natural. As he escorted Edith through the dancers, their arms linked, I wondered what still linked us. Ned moved with an ease I'd never seen. He was confident. Ned had always been confident but there had been the slightest trace of effort, the slightest trace of the thespian. His hair was cut short and his aquiline nose looked stronger. His face was sunburned and he didn't raise an eyebrow — not even at that bubbling three-tiered, eagle-capped fountain, "Cuba," or McKinley. I believe Ned Phillips had found what he'd been waiting for. In his heart of heart, as novelists say, he no longer felt superfluous.

"Hello, Henry," said Ned, offering a tanned hand and military grip.

"You're as white as a ghost," said Edith, which was funny because she should have paled at seeing me.

"I've seen the ghost of a friend," I said.

"A friend of mine," said Ned, looking at me, then Edith, "is always a friend." He stood very straight. Ned cut a fine figure in uniform. "You're doing better, Henry. This lady is enough to turn any man's head."

I waited for him to undercut that remark with a sarcastic smile, but he didn't. Ned, who had been so careful to pierce my opinion of every woman, and who could make one feel permission had to be asked to take anything seriously, seemed to like Edith.

"I'd like you to meet someone, Henry," he said.

This was the penultimate time I saw Ned Phillips, and I almost knew it. In the same way I felt I'd been here before, I felt I'd be here again: not recognizing Ned and saying goodbye. How much of our story — I mean the story of Edith, Saturday, Annie, and myself — did he author? Or was he, and the rest of us, already caught in a design the Indian set in motion that would scatter us over the hemisphere? I stood white-faced amidst the Republicans of Cleveland, wondering what the hell Ned wanted.

"Will you excuse us?" he said to Edith.

"That's not a question," she said.

"Henry could make it one."

"I'll go," I said.

"Your friend's better looking than you are, Mr. Phillips."

"It's his saving grace," said Ned, as he guided me toward the stairs. "We will be with you shortly."

"Business is rarely short," said Edith.

"But it is," said Ned, "business."

We left Edith to Blunt, who returned from the punch bowl, as Ned and I went up the stairs. Ned led me back to the "Turkish Cozy Corner" where two beefy men in threadbare evening dress stood at either side of the door, each in front of a pilaster.

I wondered if I might be meeting Senator Hanna, but the "kingmaker" wasn't likely to squirrel himself away with rugs and veils. We went in and Ned closed the door.

The little room, which had seemed mysterious as well as vulgar, was now taken up by an excited little man puffing on a cigar which left a blue cloud that hung in opaque rings around the lamp.

"Mr. Vernon," said Ned, "this is Henry Harrison. Henry, this is John Vernon, the Under Secretary of State, and Harvard '77."

"Eliot House," said Vernon, in a quick voice which implied the Under Secretary had just answered my first question. Vernon probably had good reason, beyond his one-time place of residence, to be pleased. His superior, Secretary Hay, was in England enjoying the company of Henry James, whose answer to American life is to live abroad; Vernon was in control of "State."

"How do you do, Henry?" The little man was pacing, which was difficult in that room. He pushed the lamp as if it were a punching bag, and its fringe jiggled. I couldn't imagine what sort of business the Under Secretary could transact in a closet. Vernon had deep-set eyes and a heavy black mustache. A broad nose saved him from looking weaselish, as his closely cropped hair was brushed straight back. Vernon's profile looked dramatically aggressive on first glance, but like a face in an advertisement for cheap cigars on the second.

"We live in remarkable times, Henry." Vernon puffed. The cigar glowed beside the lamp. "The word 'destiny' has a certain ring to it, doesn't it?" He eyed a green and blue veil where eight octagons appeared to move in opposite directions.

The Under Secretary must have been a Roosevelt man. T.R. came to Harvard my senior year, and in that booming, squeaky voice said the same thing, before informing the audience that "fighting races, like the Anglo-Saxon," had an "obligation to rule."

I stood by the door. Ned sat in the captain's chair. Vernon circled the lamp so he could look me in the eye.

"Destiny led us from one ocean to another. The hour comes again."

I was afraid to speak. Words might break the spell, and this little man, like the Sorcerer's Apprentice, could spend the rest of the evening with a mop.

"Have you considered it, Henry?"

"Sir?"

"Destiny."

"No."

"It's more than the final standings of the League," Vernon was so delighted at his joke he laughed out loud and then burst into a fit of coughing that shook his small but solid frame. Ned smiled at both joke and cough.

"What can I do for destiny?" I said.

The Under Secretary brandished a handkerchief like a flag of surrender. "You could begin by appreciating it." Vernon looked me over and seemed to mentally step down from a podium. He looked at Ned who was watching me. Ned had one leg crossed over the other and occasionally touched the tips of his fingers in the gesture children call "spider on a mirror." His captain's bars seemed detached from his uniform and appeared to hover in the smoke.

"Am I boring you?" said Vernon.

"Excuse me?" I said.

"You don't believe in destiny?"

"I'm better with the standings of the League."

"I sympathize" The Under Secretary reached out and took the lapel of my jacket between two fingers as if checking the fabric. "Notions like destiny and history are for fools." He released my lapel. "The affairs of nations have nothing to do with ideas. The affairs of nations, like the affairs of men, are petty, stupid, trivial, and played by rules no more interesting than force. But Henry, these trivialities, like those which make up our lives, are the substance of the world. I want you to go to Cuba."

"Cuba?"

"It's an island, south of here." Vernon was delighted with the remark but didn't cough. Ned laughed.

"As a spy?"

"Let me be direct," The Under Secretary gave the lamp a shove. He was on the balls of his feet. "You know what the result of this war will be as well as I and Mr. Hearst do." He moved closer. Half his face was in shadow. His thumbs were hooked through the belt loops in his trousers, and the red point of his cigar was by his waist. Vernon struck the pose of a statesman bored with his insight into the affairs of men. Ned kept his eyes on me.

"We will conquer the island in a month or two. Before the baseball season is over, in fact. The question is, what do we do with it? Do we give it away? Do we keep it? America is bashful. Our European friends are not so bashful. I want to know what certain Cubans think. I need to communicate, shall we say, outside normal channels. I need someone outside government. I need," Vernon hesitated, "one of us."

Ned leaned back in the captain's chair, arms folded across his chest. "This could mean a career at State, Henry."

Was this the long awaited invitation? Was I being offered a place in the world Ned had chosen — some mixture of intrigue, politics and power? Were Ned and the Under Secretary part of an inner circle — a clandestine inner circle — that carried out the will of those who actually rule like Mark Hanna, while the public is fed affable McKinley and sugar "Cubas?" Was this Ned's way of forgiving me? Was I valuable now because we weren't friends?

"I can't," I said.

"You what?" said Vernon.

"I can't."

"Captain Phillips?" said Vernon, looking at Ned for the first time.

"Henry," said Ned, in a voice I can only describe as kind. "An offer like this can not be made twice. I don't want you to regret what you do in this room tonight."

"I have a job. I can't go to Cuba."

"A job?" said Vernon.

"I work for the Spiders."

"You prefer that to serving your country?"

"It sounded like serving you."

"It might," said the Under Secretary puffing on his cigar, "be dangerous."

"Do you want my advice?" I said.

"Not particularly." Vernon was off his toes.

"I suggest." I stood up straight. "That if you wish to know the disposition of the people of Cuba, hold an election."

"The election was two years ago," said Vernon. "The winner was McKinley. Goodbye, Ned, I've got to be in Washington. Henry, Boston is the better team."

The Under Secretary rapped twice on the door and left. Ned didn't move. His arms were crossed on his blue chest. His eyes looked gray in the smoky room. "You could have had a career in Washington. That's what I want myself. We would have seen each other."

"I am not a spy."

"I wanted to do something for you" Ned unfolded his arms and rested an elbow on a purple pillow. "Vernon's right, you know. Despite his rhetoric and awful cigars, America is moving overseas. There's been a lot of talk about the closing of the frontier. Even you were concerned with it once. Do you remember waiting in Radcliffe Yard for those two sisters from Providence, after we'd read Turner's article? You thought there was something to it. Henry, I'll tell you where the frontier has gone. It's gone to Cuba, to the Philippines, to China itself. The British sun is setting, ours is rising. This country won't be without a frontier long."

"The frontier has gone to the ballpark," I thought this remark trumped him. It was another crack I'd been saving.

Ned shrugged and said, "You always confuse the symbolic with the actual."

"I don't care much for the actual."

Ned looked at his shoulders, "I may see some of it soon."

"You take the war, I'll take the Indian."

"King Saturday?" said Ned, looking up at me through the smoke, his sunburned face surrounded by red, yellow, purple and puce octagons that seemed to move in a background of blue and green. "No one can have the Indian. He's on his own road. Do you think Saturday can get you a team? Do you think he's your friend? He's wild, Henry. Wild. Crazy. Drunk. Fill in your own word. He's not in control of himself. There's something eating that Indian. I don't know what it is or I'd tell you. How secure is your position with the Spiders? It's as secure as Saturday. When he goes, you go. He almost got you sacked last summer."

I leaned against a blue veil by the door and said, "I'm not leaving Cleveland."

"There's more to life than baseball, and there's more to baseball than King Saturday."

I said nothing.

124

6

Rumors circulated that an important person had been at the Stillman and left. I heard Hay's name, but enough people knew he was out of the country to incline the common tongue to Roosevelt, Vice President Hobart, or General Shafter, the three hundred pound Commander-in-Chief, though the General's presence would be hard to keep secret. The lady whose teeth and imperious fan reminded me of T.R. said the President had been here "but was so pressed for time" he could see only "one man in a guarded room," and that man was Mark Hanna or someone from Standard Oil. "McKinley wants to know if he should annex Cuba."

The men of Cleveland were drunk enough to dance. The floor was crowded and the banners shook as the tempo rose from jaunty fox trot to brisk waltz to practically ribald rag. Young men snatched up ladies, stout husbands gave in to stouter wives, old men gallantly stumbled around with aging ladies, and even sardonic college wags, like the two we passed on the stairs, risked their vanity on the dance floor.

Had Ned and I still been friends, we would have camped by the punch bowl and enjoyed this tremendously. I wanted to talk to Edith, who would certainly have something amusing to say about the metamorphosis of Republicans to Hottentots, but Edith was dancing with Blunt, and enjoying it. They swung each other with restrained license; the crimson hem of her dress made wild circles while the dark tails of his coat made smaller ones. Ned and the threadbare thugs who caused so much speculation had gone. I congratulated myself on turning down Ned and the Under Secretary. I had another loyalty and their proposal had the odor of decaying friendship. I had once tried to be part of Ned's fantasy of wealth and wanted no part of his fantasy of power. If the war wasn't to be believed in at the level of bullets, it wasn't to be believed for top hats and starched collars.

"Henry?"

Edith joined me at the punch bowl. She was flushed again and her eyes were slightly glazed. One sensed that beneath the lady's puffy uniform, was an athlete's body.

"Where's Blunt?"

"Can we talk?" Her hat made her look like a crimson giant. Men moved away as if they felt a woman that tall should be given a wide berth. Edith's gloved hand went completely around a silver cup which she emptied in two swallows. "I saw Ned Phillips before he left. Ned was very disappointed. He thinks he'll never see you again."

"He may not."

"Ned said you were offered something that could have changed your life, but you didn't take it. He feels responsible for you."

"I was offered the chance to be a factotum in the State Department. It would have ruined my life."

"I also turned someone down," said Edith. We sat in a row of folding chairs which lined the wall opposite the orchestra. "Lyndon asked me to marry him."

"Had you kissed him?"

Edith looked at me angrily, then laughed. Her eyes became bright with mischief. "I wouldn't kiss a man who wanted to marry me."

"Only those you wish to play with?"

She looked at McKinley and the happy, dancing Republicans. Ladies' skirts rustled and flew, revealing leather ankles and starched petticoats. "I made him very unhappy."

"He'll try again. Blunt thinks he'll win you because you respect determination as much as he does. He thinks it's the masculine virtue."

"You've given Lyndon a great deal of thought."

"I've been around football players my entire life."

Edith gazed at the orchestra. They played a fierce rag and their floppy, green hats tilted wildly, jiggled on their khaki backs, or were deposited beside tapping feet. "I don't like hurting people. It makes me feel lonely."

"It's lonely being free."

"There are many kinds of loneliness," said Edith, watching the crowd. "There's loneliness for the dead. You know about that, don't you? There's loneliness with someone you've known your whole life whose selfishness makes you lonely, and your selfishness makes them lonely too." She paused and looked at her hands. "Then there's the loneliness of wanting someone you can't have. And there's always the loneliness of hurting someone."

I touched Edith's hand and said, "I wouldn't have thought you felt this way."

"I wouldn't have thought you'd understand."

We didn't say anything for a minute. The orchestra played rags. I'm glad they didn't play a sentimental waltz because I would have felt like an ass. Finally I said, "You only talk this way because we don't know each other. Like telling secrets to a stranger."

"I told you because we're friends."

"Yet another lady who needs a friend," I said.

"You're more like a stranger than a friend."

We didn't speak again and the rags got wilder, providing a ribald counterpoint to our silence. "I'd be unhappy if I weren't talking to you," I said. Edith smiled. "I am unhappy," she said, but her smile was warm. We looked for Blunt to see if he were consoling himself on the dance floor, but couldn't find him. I told Edith I'd introduce Blunt to my mother who could guide his course through the eligible ladies of the season.

"Lyndon's gone home to be miserable," said Edith.

"He's probably outside talking to someone important," I said.

Edith watched the dancers, many of whom she had known since childhood. She asked what I did when unhappy, besides talk, and I said, "Open a bottle of scotch and read batting and fielding averages."

"You're a romantic."

"What's more comforting than batting averages and put-outs?"

"I prefer to watch," said Edith. "I even like to play. I am not a scholar."

"Then you miss the game of looking for the past."

"Looking for it or living in it?"

"When you're unhappy, the difference is small." I waited, then said, "I've always been such a krank, starting at boarding school where there was ample unhappiness and many hours" — Edith smiled, she liked that phrase — "so that looking into baseball's past is like looking into my own."

"Like listening to music," she said, "and reliving part of your life."

"Yes, but this music is better."

"I think you're one of those men who value what you've lost more than what you have. You're afraid of life."

She may have been right. Neither one of us was old enough to be afraid of the past. Nothing was hidden that night the Republicans danced and Lyndon Blunt sulked away to seek his own counsel about obtaining the hand of Miss Edith Burns.

"Sometimes I feel I live life to remember it."

"You want to be safe," said Edith.

"That's part of it," I said, "but baseball becomes your past. *Spalding* and *Reach's Guides* unlock lost hours. When I see a list of home run leaders for 1884, I remember how I felt when the Chicago men hit all those homers. We were in dancing school. On Euclid Avenue. And I got shyer and shyer as I realized I didn't belong, and more embarrassed about my clothes which had been worn to that school by a cousin. Home runs were my consolation. They were a thirteen-year-old's idea of success. Remember Lake Front Park? The right field fence was 215 feet away and balls that had been doubles the year before were homers. Ned Williamson had 27. Don't you love marks that may never be broken?"

"Do you mean home runs or pain?"

"One enjoys the former and gets used to the latter."

"Billy Hamilton scored 192 runs the summer before I went to Smith," said Edith. "I wish college had been as exciting."

128

"You measure your life by baseball?"

"Sometimes, but I don't want to go back."

"The past shouldn't depress a krank," I said. "The resonance grows as the seasons pile into lists. There's a wonderful continuity between those years, this year, and the years to come."

"I prefer the present," said Edith.

This conversation could have gone on indefinitely, as I like talking about the past, and Edith's wideset brown eyes seemed to be getting bigger, but there was a disturbance at the far end of the ballroom. Two massive oak doors which opened to the lobby were being forced against the wishes of a half dozen uniformed employees of the hotel.

"Someone's trying to get in!" yelled a woman.

"They may be anarchists!"

"Or Democrats."

"They may throw bombs!"

A gang of Republicans put their well-tailored shoulders to the doors. Coattails flew and ladies shrieked as gentlemen fortified by drink rushed to help. A mob began to form by the doors. A bald gentleman next to us pulled out a silver watch and said, "It's too early for this." Two ward bosses, whose coats were stretched tightly over their backs, spread their arms, and urged the ladies to stay calm and keep back. The senior doorman, a stern gent in a neat red uniform, yelled, "Stop! It isn't done!" but the combatants were enjoying themselves. The doors were forced open a foot and we heard curses and huffing.

The Republicans groaned and pushed back.

"Are they colored?" said the woman with the Japanese fan, as she walked briskly away, showing her wide front teeth.

"Where's the Police Commissioner?" said several older men simultaneously.

"This is dreadful," said Miss Liberty, who stationed herself in the middle of the floor, and brandished her torch like a club. With her bosom thrust forward and ample foulard trumpeting the national colors, the lady looked more like a target than a bastion, but she was undaunted. Many women went up the stairs or found other exits.

The Republicans at the doors, sensing that a good time was brewing, put their shoulders to the oak and cheered. They got both doors shut, but after two surges, each accompanied by hooting and profanity from both sides, the doors swung open and a wedge of Cleveland Spiders burst in. King Saturday, white shirt open to the navel, and Patsy Tebeau, waving a labelless whiskey bottle, led the way shouting, "We're the best in the League!" Jimmy McAleer, wearing an Indian headdress that reached the floor, screamed like he was about to take scalps. Frank, in dun yellow suit sans hat, whooped and shouted. Ed McKean, whose derby was at an angle that suggested the shortstop might have come to recruit women for the streets, propelled Frank with a hand on each shoulder. Lou Criger waved a clenched fist and a bottle. The ballplayers piled into the ballroom with the delight of boys ruining a Sunday school picnic.

"Hail the President!" shouted Tebeau.

The horde waved and shouted at the supersized visage at the end of the ballroom. Edith and I were a hundred feet from the doors. She laughed and said, "Your friends are here." The Republicans, realizing who the intruders were, began to slap their backs and shake hands. This did not curb the exodus of ladies, who, seeing their champions join the barbarians, disappeared behind stout protectors, up the stairs, and even into the kitchen. Edith and Miss Liberty were the only women on the floor.

"Hail Republicans!" yelled Tebeau.

"Where's our lawyer?" shouted Saturday, and the Spiders pushed their way by men who wanted to talk, shake, and thump. The players and their admirers, some of whom tried to cling to them as children will after a game, struggled across the floor like a many-legged beast. The orchestra, safe in their numbers, broke into "A Hot Time In the Old Town Tonight." The animal came at us — singing, hooting, waving. It encountered Miss Liberty, who shouted, "Halt!" but was swallowed by the waving and stomping beast. Her torch appeared in Ed McKean's hand and the foulard in Jimmy McAleer's mouth. Her crown rested briefly on Saturday's head, then Tebeau's, but I lost track of the crown and Liberty, as Frank yelled, "There's our lawyer!" and they came at me. Jimmy McAleer yelled, "We're his guests!"

Saturday shielded Edith as the lads hoisted me on their shoulders, swatted my back, and howled the most raucous version of "A Hot Time!" I've heard. I was over the world — up with the red, white and blue — over the Republican world: up, it seemed, with the crystal, McKinley, and the ladies' eyes, struggling for balance. The chandeliers sparkled wildly as I was tossed from shoulder to shoulder. Now the mob had a victim, people laughed and ladies appeared in doors — I saw my mother on the stairs, she was smiling — and the procession headed for the punch bowl. The Spiders, Republicans, and I bumped across the floor as the band murdered a Sousa march, making its military air fit for a bordello. Miss Liberty shrieked and I was serenaded with cries of "Hang him!" "Elect him!" "Drown him!"

They spun me around and I saw Edith, tall and crimson, next to Saturday. I saw doormen in red uniforms, cooks in white, waiters in black, and ladies wearing red and green jewels. I saw the stairs which were like a ladder of ladies, so many had rushed there. I saw clerks from Standard Oil, the shiny black shoulders of politicians, the glittering fobs of portly men, a sneering Jake McBuck, the envious face of a college wag, and heard the laughter of women. Irritated respectable faces looked away, anxious sober faces looked up, and a few worried men looked around, catching their own faces on others who must have sensed their position in this Republican world was as precarious as mine on drunken shoulders. I rode Tebeau until we reached the punch bowl and they threw me in.

Patsy and Frank pulled me out. We headed for the Gin Palace.

7

Manager Tebeau stood on the bar wearing McAleer's Indian headdress and ordered a "set of whiskeys." The same husky barkeep who pinioned my arms when Saturday fought Burke, filled five shot glasses. Patsy had somehow gotten my father's gold and pearl handled walking stick and pointed at me, the whiskey, and then the crowd. A half dozen Spiders, the evening's complement of ladies, and two constables who'd dropped in for refreshment, cheered the sight of the Spider manager standing on the bar and waving a stick.

"Drink up, Harrison!" cried Tebeau. "Walk the bar and she's yours!"

The crowd cheered. The "she" was Lucy, the large woman who even by the standards of the day was an embarrassment of riches. Victorian modesty was mocked by abundance. Deeds were hidden and words hushed but the female body announced itself with bulk. Lucy had thighs like a bull. I wondered why Tebeau should be so generous.

Childs and Criger hoisted me onto the bar. Patsy jumped off: headdress streaming, stick waving. I put down three shots, looked at the eager crowd, and the Palace began to move. I tried to concentrate by fixing my eyes on the rectangular home plate but the room wouldn't stay still. I hoped to negotiate the bar before the alcohol set my stomach on fire. Patsy waved the lady in question to the far end of the bar. The green lamps which hung from the ceiling lit my way with white circles of light.

"Walk it and get your prize!" yelled Frank.

"He's staggering already," said Cupid Childs.

"He'll make it," said Jimmy McAleer, and men began to bet. The lady waved me on. She wore pink bloomers and a voluminous blouse. Tebeau waved the stick like a sword. The band played an appropriately disrespectful tune and money was thrown in derbies and Stetsons. I looked for the Indian. I wanted him to see me initiated into a Gin Palace Saturday night, but didn't see him. I took an unsteady step as Frank yelled, "Come on, lad!" and almost fell as I saw myself in the mirror behind the bar. I was lean and wet, alone in the glass, over a sea of hot faces, derbies and décolletage. I took one unsure step, then another.

"Walk, lawyer!"

"Run!"

"Look what's waiting for you!"

A laughing phalanx of bartenders wagered on one side while Spiders, ladies, and cussing gents with wet mustaches, made bets on the other. The bar was slippery and the customers didn't remove their glasses and mugs, though they were liberal with admonitions about what would happen if I knocked them over. The wall lights in their brass sconces looked like torches being raised and lowered. The band made its instruments shriek, then rumble as I lost my balance, lurching perilously close to ice buckets and kegs on my left, then slipping to a dizzying glimpse of ruffles and men's eyes on the right.

A garter went by my head and I decided I would never make it at a dancing master's pace. The room began to swirl and I had to run or fall, and imitating the determination I once saw Mike Kelly — whose photograph was lost in the cigar-dotted darkness — show on a triple — took off for the end of the bar. Glasses went over, hands tried to trip me, other hands pulled them back: men cursed, ladies laughed high, rippling, raucous laughs, and I ran. I think a woman bared or held up heavy breasts, but many tellings may have added that detail. Ten feet from my destination I slid and went off the bar in a blaze of glory like Billy Sunday showing how he avoids the devil on stage.

134

Glasses and mugs flew, ladies were splashed, gentlemen cursed, and I found myself in Lucy's lap as Jimmy McAleer caught me and the lady squealed. A huge cheer went up and money changed hands. Lucy and I were pushed to the stairs. The Palace was reeling — the crystal tiers of the chandelier rotated as the lads shoved me and pushed and grabbed Lucy. Patsy Tebeau led the way, waving my father's stick. Cupid Childs shouted indelicate advice. Lou Criger had hold of Jake McBuck's lapels and got odds on an equally indelicate matter. We went upstairs by a Cleveland Infants banner, a brown bat used by Pete Browning, and photographs of ladies of the stage. I saluted Abe Lincoln as we passed his profound face, and managed to focus on the actresses long enough to observe that like myself, they were poised between innocence and lust.

Annie was at the top of the stairs. She wore only a black laced corset and green silk trousers that ended in ruffles tied below the knee. Light from an open door made her shoulders, throat and face unbearably white. We stopped in front of her and I, being pleased with myself, laughed. Annie looked at me, eyes quick with anger, as she smoothed the silk at her hips, and said, "Where is he?" Then the mob pushed us down the hall and into a room which smelled of cheap perfume.

"Everybody out!" yelled Frank. "He won fair and square!"

"Let the lawyer handle his own case!"

"Good luck, Harry!"

They tramped out slapping the walls and door which Lucy closed and locked. After a few knocks and something I hope was water squirting through the keyhole, we were alone. Lucy lit two candles on the windowsill and a third on a table by a canopied bed whose curtains were drawn. The room had a view of Jackson Bridge and the city. The smell of perfume was heavy but no worse than the odor of perspiration, sausage, and stale beer that permeated the Palace. Lucy parted the curtains, one of which was torn, and I saw that her sleeping partners included a toy bear (This was before they were "Teddys" — T.R. hadn't yet invaded the nursery) wearing a Spiders cap, a woolly elephant who lacked a hind leg, and a preposterously long-eared toy donkey.

Talking wasn't possible. I grabbed, fumbled, and held on in a state of blind drunkenness. I rolled onto my back and closed my eyes to stop the room from spinning. I wondered how long

Annie would stay angry and if Edith were upset because her escort had been hustled to a whorehouse by a drunken mob. I decided she would be amused. I was too drunk to take my clothes off. They were, however, disengaged, and we rolled and giggled and the bear and donkey went over the side. I must have passed out because I opened my eyes and the candles were out, the moon up, and we were at it.

Lucy was wonderfully big. She wrapped her huge thighs around me and I grabbed her colossal buttocks. She was surprisingly firm. Her tongue went in my ear and a finger went somewhere respectable women haven't touched since Eve began talking to serpents. I didn't look at her face and thought about a black corset. I squeezed her round hard thighs and thought of green silk. Lucy massaged my rump and bit my ear. I was anesthetized by liquor and felt huge. Her breasts were each as large as a man's head, her bottom was soft, her ears were sweaty, and her legs were wet. We helped ourselves to the hot license of the dark. It wasn't love. It wasn't intimacy. It was wonderful.

I marveled at her breasts, amazed that items so big could be so firm. I was amazed by my own item, which on the scale of mankind isn't small, but had never been so hard. It was a night of bigness. Her back was big, her hands were big, her ankles were big, her appetite was enormous. I finally came and went to sleep.

Later, in the darker, more secret part of the night, in a state close to dream, I went at her again. Lucy began to move and what had been drunken license was sleep fucking sleep. Indeed, if the heart is a mansion of fabulous dimension, we were traveling in other rooms.

Lucy came slowly out of dreamy, sexual sleep, loving back with her own dream, her own men, her own electricity. We were deep in undiscovered country. Fucking is wonderful, whoring is wonderful, loving is wonderful, but nothing, nothing is as sweet as sex in the heart of sleep.

I could lie. I could say love is better but love has its anxiety, its competition and its charity. In that room with the toys I went to sleep and woke up an animal self. There was more toward dawn. I was awake and hungry to make the night last. My stomach and balls hurt. When Lucy went to sleep, I lay in the dark thinking about the drawing room on Euclid Avenue with the high ceiling and great fireplace which warmed us on the coldest days.

8

There was a trace of dawn over the river when Saturday woke me. I was out cold and thought Lucy was rousing me, but she was seeking another part of the night. "Wake up, Harry." I wanted Lucy to reappear so the Indian would see how I had spent my night, but my companions were only the long-eared donkey and King Saturday who, despite his beige pants, was almost invisible.

"I'm going to walk the catwalk of Jackson Bridge, Harry." He went to the window. I could see nothing but a bluish tinge over the dim outline of the city beyond the watery blackness. "Two hundred feet, maybe less."

"Catwalk?"

"How'd you like Lucy? Tebeau told me I could have her. I gave her to you."

"Where'd she go?"

"Hold this." Something came out of the dark and hit me in the chest. It was a billfold with a smooth but lined surface that could have been the hide of a reptile. "It's $1166."

"Jesus," I said. That was more than many of the players made in a season.

"You're my banker, Harry."

Before I could ask about the money, he was gone. That moment in the dark was the real beginning of my knowing Saturday. It began in Hooper, also in the dark, when I followed him into a tavern — and of course, it started before that in the darkness that surrounds our need for a star . . .

I was never his lawyer but I was his banker. I suppose he thought me too conventional or cowardly to steal. He called this "our money," and we were going to buy a team with it. "Our money" grew during the summer. I had the unenviable task of carrying it, keeping it, and making it available. I didn't think of this as I got up and checked the river which was somewhere under the bridge and its sparsely lit catwalk. I should have refused but I didn't. I sat in the dark next to a toy jackass and knew I wasn't a krank anymore.

All summer I carried money. I started two bank accounts and rented a safe-deposit box under false names. He never asked me where the money was; I just had to be able to get it. At first this was exciting, then I began to worry, and finally — and this is the most damning thing about the really important things we do wrong — I couldn't tell anybody. We were conspirators. I doubted we'd buy a team and thought I was probably laying the groundwork for disbarment, but I did it, and many nights that summer I carried a reptilian hide full of as much money as most men see in a year.

I stumbled into my brown suit as people swore and tramped down the hall. The reassuring cadence of wagering drowned out a squeaky male voice which kept insisting the Palace was on fire. Frank Ember burst into the room shouting, "Where is he? The son of a bitch is going to walk the damn bridge," and left.

The hall was a circus of men and ladies who would have preferred their clandestine beds. Women wrapped in sheets leaned out doorways. A round little man whose whiskers almost swallowed his nose marched along the balcony with a spittoon, saying, "Some say he will. I say he won't." I heard Tebeau yelling, "Where is the damned redskin?" Two of McBuck's cronies stood on the stairs explaining what Saturday was going to do, which was walk over the top of the bridge, on a narrow platform used for maintenance. "That don't seem too hard," said the man with the spittoon. "Or do it?"

"Not for him," said a woman with a towel wrapped around her head like a turban. She pulled a crumpled bill out of the pink robe she held at the neck.

"Put her in if you think he will. I say he won't."

The bill went in the spittoon.

"Indians ain't afraid of heights," said one of McBuck's men.

"He's an athlete," said the other.

"He's been drinkin'," said the man with the spittoon.

I rushed down the stairs, jostling the man whose face was all whiskers and two women who'd pulled coats over nightgowns. I wanted to find Annie, thinking that the two of us might stop him, but this was only an attempt to look useful in the excitement of the moment. A single green lamp threw its circle of light on a bartender, whose suspenders were on backward, who served men who leered at their whiskey, slapped down greenbacks, and discussed whether Saturday would "show." They bet on his survival with a mean, professional enthusiasm. Frank put a hand on my shoulder and tried to get me to drink from a pint bottle. He took a slug and wiped his mouth with his sleeve. "The Indian won't last the season if he's going to do this kind of damn fool thing." I nodded and felt the wallet in my breast pocket.

"Cab outside!"

There was a ghostly rush as the newly risen demimonde headed for the door. All of a sudden, no one could wait to get to the bridge. I heard several sports swear that, "If he hasn't walked by sunrise, we clean up." Customers and ladies in different phases of stupor and undress made their way downstairs, pushed by the bar and hustled out. A judge I'd met at the Republican punch bowl, sauntered by with a lady's bonnet covering his bald head. Several city councilors in more conventional dress slid by. I saw the clerk from Standard Oil whose morning drudgery had been temporarily relieved by Edith. He wasn't happy I noticed him.

"Let's get away from these bums," said Frank, pulling my arm, but we stopped when we saw Annie at the top of the stairs. A sputtering light made the leather coat Saturday had given her appear covered with stars. Annie showed neither fear nor disapproval. Her face was hard and pale and seemed to float out of the darkness by the picture of Lincoln and Pete Browning's bat as she descended. Frank walked on one side of her and I took her arm on the other, but she didn't acknowledge us.

We walked into the hour before dawn and the streets were deserted except for the Gin Palace pilgrims who retraced the steps Harriet Ember's army marched the night before. I shuddered in the pre-dawn chill, that hollow dampness which means night is already mixing with day's first gray in the eastern sky. I never welcome day's cool birth in a city. I find no beauty in a gray, metal city dawn. Without the sun, the Palace wasn't a crimson advertisement for seamy adventure but a sullen edifice. We brought up the rear of a hungover collection of sports, whores, pimps and gamblers. Several cabs went by and white arms waved; Annie paid no attention. Our procession, from its tattersall-coated sports to its women, some wrapped in sheets, drifted toward the river like phantoms. We went down East Clark Avenue, turned and lined up along Independence. The scurrying of rats in the alleys behind tanneries and warehouses made the drunken hoots, women's voices, and hoarsely shouted odds seem lonelier. A dog added a nervous and mournful bark, and Annie took my hand without, I think, even knowing it.

Bringing up the rear was the little fellow with the spittoon. He still wore a nightshirt and hopped along in a pair of boots that were too big. I hated him and the other hard cases who exchanged money. I always disliked the masculine willingness to brag and bet, but I was part of it. I used to say baseball was without sin and think the game — green as spring, harmonious as Thomas Jefferson's mind, symmetrical as the Old and New Testaments — was the best of us: Twain's river, the yeoman farmer clearing rocks from his field and prejudice from his mind; while gambling was that part of us which makes a mob and betrays friends — but that night when the Republicans danced, Ned offered, Blunt was turned down, and I was given Lucy, I was more a brother to Jake McBuck than to Frank Ember. I always felt nothing could approach the perfect feeling of newness before a game, the precision of fine play, and exhilaration of men going to their limit, and that to put a price on it, lay ego on it, approach it with sweaty palms and a quick eye was obscene; yet I was already implicated. I knew as I walked to the Cuyahoga with Frank Ember and Annie Gears that before summer was gone, I would carry money on crooked baseball.

142

There was a thrill — a small, obscene thrill — in holding money. I wasn't a spectator anymore. I wasn't a connoisseur. I wasn't in the past. I was on his outlaw side and I remembered Frank saying, "He'll throw games if he's smart." Did I carry "our money" just because I wanted a team? I wanted a team at boarding school, when I couldn't have anything else, and at Harvard when baseball was my country, but was that all? Did I carry money that corrupted something I loved only because I wanted to own it? Or did I, in my coward's way, like danger and like being like him? And what did he want? Even now I ask myself, what did he want?

The sun was behind us. The river was a reminder that the uncontrolled runs through the heart of the city. Jackson Bridge was a massive structure of iron and rock with a drawbridge in the middle. Four lights dotted the catwalk over the drawbridge. A crowd was forming on the other side too.

"Where's Saturday?" said Frank, finally addressing Annie, as if the light which showed us dark water curling around the base of the bridge made her approachable.

"He'll be here," she said.

"Why's he doing this?" said Frank.

"Money," I said.

"They're easier ways to make money," said Frank.

"Because someone said he couldn't," said Annie.

"Who?" I said.

"Me," she said.

The early light revealed small white waves in the river. Smoke rose from scattered chimneys in town. A lake steamer tooted as it came through the dawn. I saw newswagons drawn by sleepy horses start their rounds. In a few minutes early risers would begin to leave for church. A few derelicts, disturbed during the short hours the city is theirs, joined the curious as the sun crept west.

The crowd, not happy with the exchange of Saturday night for Sunday morning, began to complain and curse the Indian. "Where the hell is he?" said the man whose whiskers buried his nose. "He musta passed out and don't remember sayin' he was goin' to walk the thing."

"He's drunk."

"Would you walk it sober?"

The suggestion the Indian wouldn't come incensed the crowd. Faces looked anxiously to the sun, and then at the crawling, metal colored river, which wasn't Twain's river, but an extension of the night twisting by factories and mills. There was hatred in those faces. I saw Cupid Childs and he looked worried. Manager Tebeau hopped a cab and headed back toward the Palace. Jake McBuck strolled through the crowd, nodding, putting one hand on shoulders and keeping the other deep in the pocket of a brown mackintosh. We were never out of each other's sight. The sun was up enough to reveal stubble on chins and lines on faces no longer protected by the illusions of the Palace. They talked "sellout" and "swindle" but wanted spectacle, the thrill of a man walking near death with money on him. I felt the need in the derelicts, gamblers and whores. They wanted something to touch their essence but the stakes had to be mortal. I squeezed Annie's hand and decided baseball was one of the few improvements in the way humans amuse themselves. This mob, and the sun changed them from phantoms to unshaven, prematurely old rabble, wanted a gladiator, a prize fight, a lynching. Faces went from street to bridge to sun to street. They wanted to see him fly or fall.

"He wants the impossible," I said.

"He'll find it," said Annie.

The bridge began to go up for the steamer. A vocal minority decided the stunt was off and started to leave. Cupid Childs and Jimmy McAleer, who wore the Indian headdress which looked red and yellow in the new sun, urged people to go home. Two gentlemen in the Republican black, whose shirt fronts were open and whose cravats and watches were gone, sadly fell in behind the ballplayers. The bridge cranked up slowly. The steamer tooted long blasts that echoed off the water.

"He's welshing!"

"Goddamn Indian!"

"Let's go!"

Childs and McAleer looked tired and relieved. Annie kept looking back at the Gin Palace which still looked sullen and spectral with the sun behind it. Frank watched the river. He wasn't about to leave. I watched McBuck, whose hand stayed in his pocket and who kept moving closer. I was worried, knowing I'd hand the wallet over if threatened. Without Saturday, I couldn't even bluff. I didn't think I was in danger, which may have been a mistake, and tried to console myself thinking the next time these thrill-seekers, whores, city councilors and gamblers saw King Saturday, they'd pay fifty cents for the privilege.

A cheer went up.

The Indian was running down East Clark. Even at a distance his stride was unmistakable. He ran effortlessly. I've never seen anyone run like that, a deer perhaps, but not a man. Men strain when they run.

The cheers became shouts. The crowd realized the bridge was going up. Already a gap, an abyss, a horrifying absence of iron, the blue visible presence of nothing, separated the trestles. Saturday ran faster.

He went by us with his black eyes set on the bridge. I noticed a column of smoke rising somewhere in the Flats and then turned with the crowd to watch the man confront the rising iron. Men shouted and waved at the old fellow in the tower — Jimmy McAleer even threw down the headdress in a gesture of exasperation — but the old man pointed wildly at the steamer. The ship was too close while the lunatic hurling himself at Providence was doing so of his own will.

The Indian passed McAleer and was on the bridge. The steamer didn't toot, women didn't scream, men didn't shout. The world was suddenly quiet. Only Indian and bridge moved. Anyone could have stopped him. Anyone could have reached out. Then there was one overwhelming sound: boots on iron.

The gap widened. I don't know how big it was. King Saturday was on the rising trestle, running away from the sun.

Annie's scream pierced the morning. I was on my toes. The sun broke over the Gin Palace and the world had color. The river was a deep blue. The trestle, with its spidery catwalk, gleamed black. The city was white and dull red. Suddenly I was yelling too. I was rooting. Like any whore or gambler, I shouted and yelled.

The Indian jumped.

Part Four

1

My only promotional idea was used in the second week of June. I invited Professor Linton of Princeton to demonstrate his pitching gun, a touted marvel of science, before a game with Louisville. The invitation was not entirely motivated by a desire to advance science, though anything "scientific" played well with the public as all the newspaper ads for devices promising everything from stimulation of memory to restoration of sexual potency, could attest. Linton's "pitching machine" was actually a cannon that fired baseballs. By adjusting the charge, the gun delivered fast and slow "pitches" and by adjusting prongs attached to either side of the muzzle, a "pitch" could be made to curve in or out, or sail up or down. The Robisons liked the idea because Linton didn't want a fee, merely the opportunity to demonstrate the "gun" to people who might buy it; I suggested having hitters face the thing before a game with a poor team.

Distraction was welcome in June. After Saturday jumped Jackson Bridge, the season changed. Each of us moves to the beat of an internal clock, and his speeded up. The Indian had been in the big league less than two months yet he acted like a man running out of time. I wanted to spend a summer watching him play baseball. He wanted money.

At the Gin Palace people were afraid of him. Even the hardest element realized King Saturday was capable of anything. He told me the "jump" was part of his "plan," like destroying Fritz's tavern, but I was beginning to suspect the man was walking on the edge of himself. He was like a dervish and God knew what would happen when he stopped spinning. I saw that worried, apprehensive, appreciative look in everyone's face, especially Annie's. Saturday had a freedom I've never seen in a another human being. The carousing of his teammates seemed like schoolboy pranks.

After the "jump" he started to bet on the Spiders, and then against them. Betting was common in the League. Men often wagered on themselves, and no one was so naïve as to think a game wasn't thrown now and again, anymore than people thought "nice girls" hadn't been kissed; but I was shocked when he — I should say we because I was in on it — won eighty dollars after he dropped a ball in Brooklyn. When I saw him, I looked away, and he said, "We're going to own a team."

Until the Indian threw a game our gambling had seemed abstract and sporting. It flattered me to hold money on a man willing to wager on himself. And I wanted a team. Like most young men, I didn't want to change the world so much as my place in it. My answer to my disappointments had always been baseball — baseball — safe because it was its own world; its own country, green and separate. But Eden was for sale.

My reaction surprised me. We had a cause and were partners against a tough crowd, the League owners. I knew first-hand how hard they could be. I knew what our club made and what the men were paid. I knew the fate of rivals like the Players League, the American Association, and the Union Association. Spalding and the owners were ruthless. They destroyed competition with the gusto of Bismarck. Why not cheat men who cheated everybody? After one week in the big league, Saturday understood that professional baseball is business for those who own it and sport for those who play it. What it might be for those who watch was as irrelevant to him as the language his parents spoke was to me. As King Saturday put it: "The owners win and the players lose."

One didn't look to the Robison brothers for moral inspiration. They had helped destroy the Players and were planning to buy another League club. They planned to, and later did, send Cleveland's best players to St. Louis, when more money could be made in that city. The Robisons had no loyalty to players, Cleveland, or baseball. I repeat this only because I repeated it to myself so often in June.

Saturday figured we should start with a minor league team and fancied the Eastern League. He thought we could get one for four or five thousand dollars. Frank Ember told him a new league might challenge the National League again, since it had happened three times, and Saturday listened carefully. I didn't think anyone could beat the League, but Saturday quieted me, saying, "Free enterprise." One night he took me to the balcony of the Palace, and as we watched Amos' fingers dance over the piano, explained that when the next league challenged the National League, he would join it with his own club. "I want a club now, but no one can know I own it. No one will know my business. You will own it." All of this sounded good. In fact, it sounded wonderful.

Then he dropped the ball in Brooklyn. I wasn't there. I didn't accompany the team on the road, so I read about it in the papers. "Sure-handed right fielder loses one in the sun. Indian said to be 'tired.'" Every krank in town assumed he understood Saturday's fatigue. The papers had an elaborate system of euphemisms. "Pneumonia" meant a man had been on a bender. "Cholera" or "measles" meant venereal disease. "Tired" could mean both plus the Indian's growing reputation for irrational behavior. I, unfortunately, knew we made $80. Saturday's reputation for craziness helped. He was regarded as erratic rather than dishonest. One night, after a few whiskeys, I asked why we didn't only bet on, instead of against Cleveland. He laughed. "In Brooklyn," he said, "I lost the ball in the sun." The next day, with $35 riding against us, he struck out in the ninth with the bases loaded. This time a hard look from those black eyes precluded discussion. What's funny is even when I convinced myself he had to throw games, I didn't want to watch. For the first time in my life, I didn't want to watch baseball.

I was happy when Professor Linton arrived in Cleveland for a Saturday game with struggling Louisville. I met the tall, angular gentleman at Union Station. Linton had a full black beard laced with gray and wore a green tweed suit that included a cape. My impression was of an Old Testament prophet dressed as a British man of fashion. Linton announced that he was proud to be in the city, "Where Michaelson and Morly performed their famous experiment." This was some trick with mirrors to determine that the earth doesn't travel through a mysterious substance called ether, which, frankly, I never saw the significance of, other than as a metaphor that we are alone.

Linton insisted on wheeling his neatly packaged luggage to a cab, and we went directly to League Park. He was a vigorous man in his forties who clearly enjoyed being an ambassador from the world of science to a science-crazed public. "There will be nothing theoretical about my demonstration," the professor informed me, as we rode. "The kranks shall see their heroes pitted against Newton. And Linton," and he added with a chuckle: "First, I shall demonstrate the difficulty of hitting against my machine. No pitches will travel faster than in League play, but no one will hit them well. I shall then encourage the club to buy it, so the players may perfect their skill. The public will see that men cannot best science, but science can perfect men." As we pulled through the gates for the players' carriages, Linton said, "Science has reached the point where nature's mysteries are almost completely understood. In the twentieth century, man will perfect himself as men perfected science in this one."

Frank Robison and I escorted the brisk, tweed-clad professor onto the field while Bobby Wallace and Jimmy McAleer rolled the "pitching machine," which was actually a cannon mounted on two wheels to the pitcher's mound. I carried a leather box which contained the charges and baseballs the gun would fire. It was the only time I was on the field before a game, and I looked for Edith, who had agreed to go for a drive with me after the game. She was talking to the Indian. I didn't see Annie, and was disappointed, having grown accustomed to sitting with those two fine ladies each Saturday. Everyone from vendors to visiting players knew me as the man who escorted two marvelously dressed women each weekend.

The crowd was big, maybe four or five thousand, though I thought there were fewer young men. The Spiders were in fourth, two-and-a-half games off Boston's pace, and attendance for the League's sad southern entry would not have been so high had the papers not had the proverbial field day with the idea of Indian facing cannon. The black paper, *The Cleveland*

Gazette, suggested that it wasn't fair to make Saturday bat against a device so similar to the engines which devastated his people at Wounded Knee and other places. King diplomatically told reporters all he wanted was, "A fair shake with the gun."

We stood on the field as Mr. Robison, using the megaphone through which the lineups would be announced, told the crowd that three men from each club would face the "machine" of Professor Linton of Princeton. "The professor guarantees that every 'pitch' will be a strike, and no 'pitch' will be faster than in a League game." Linton nodded and the kranks cheered. The "pitching gun" had a barrel approximately five feet long, with a circular scope mounted near the breech, and movable prongs attached to each side of the muzzle. A brass chain hung from the breech. Lou Criger stood reluctantly at home, and Linton called out, "Let me test her before you try to catch." Lou moved quickly away from the plate. The umpires moved too. The professor made quite a show of aiming the gun at the plate. He bent from the waist like a waiter delivering an important message as he peered through the scope and carefully twisted a wheel on the left side of the gun. He opened the brown leather box and removed a shell with a highly polished brass casing. The box had three shelves, each containing shells of differing size, all brightly polished. Linton handled the shell delicately, and had the crowd oohing as he placed a very white baseball and gleaming shell in the breech and snapped it shut.

He turned to the crowd as if facing an amphitheater of scholars. "Ladies and kranks, by controlling the amount of powder in a cartridge, I can precisely determine the speed of the ball, or 'pitch.' I calculate the average League fast pitch to be approximately 78 miles per hour. Some, like those thrown by Mr. Rusie of New York, Mr. Nichols in Boston, or Mr. Cy Young, are faster. I am prepared to simulate pitches of 70 to 90 miles per hour, and I can make the ball curve in any direction." The professor produced a pair of calipers from an inside pocket and measured the width of the prongs that paralleled the muzzle. "There is nothing the mind cannot perfect, and that includes hitting. I believe this demonstration will show the need for even professionals to practice with a scientific device."

I stood on one side of the gun, and Mr. Robison was on the other. Linton talked of the difficulty in making such a "precise" machine, while the crowd became restless. I was glad the afternoon was bright with a few clouds drifting near the horizon. I didn't want Saturday to bat against a machine and not be able to see. We had a lot riding on this. Everyone had an opinion about who the best "natural" hitter was, and Saturday had made a dozen bets that he could hit the "infernal thing" better than any Spider or Louisville Colonel. Everyone at the Palace had an opinion and wanted to bet. Why a machine was the best test of "natural" ability, I'm not sure, but even Jake McBuck told me the exhibition would be "scientific," and I was holding over two hundred dollars.

An acquaintance at the Princeton Seminary had written that college players said Linton's gun was noisy and difficult to hit. To counter this, Saturday put cotton in his ears. Louisville had a deaf outfielder, William Hoy, called Dummy by the common tongue, who I thought might have an advantage, and I bet Frank a dollar Hoy would outhit Fred Clarke.

Linton stopped talking and caressed the barrel with his forefinger. Then, almost as an afterthought, he pulled the brass chain, and the gun fired. It made a frightful noise — louder than anyone expected. I started. Mr. Robison jumped. The ball rocketed over home plate, hit the base of the backstop and caromed a hundred feet in the air. The crowd was silent as a cloud of white smoke drifted into center field.

"That ball traveled at 90 miles per hour," announced Linton. He deftly pulled out a rod housed under the barrel, gave the bore a quick swab, and reloaded. The crowd was quiet. Generals have long known the effect of artillery on mobs, but I'd never seen it. The ear-splitting noise and smell of powder were not pleasant. Linton had everyone's attention, and they were awed too, especially the ballplayers, who moved away from the foul lines or nervously spat in the dugout. This shot didn't seem like much of an advertisement, if Linton wished to sell the machine as a practice device; but perhaps, as a man who made his living with his mind, he couldn't resist intimidating those who live by their bodies.

The next "pitch" had less velocity. If the average big league pitch is 78 mph, it must have been closer to 60. I though I could have hit it, if of course I'd wanted to stand in against a cannon. The lack of velocity, and some encouragement from the crowd, who slowly found its voice, got Lou Criger to catch the next "pitch," which he did, despite flinching, and then made quite a show of rubbing his hand.

Louisville's best hitter and manager, Fred Clarke, volunteered to be first. Clarke didn't take his eye off the gun from the moment he came out of the dugout, but the first "pitch" boomed right by him. Fred flinched as he backed away without swinging. "Sounded like a strike," said the umpire, and got a nervous laugh from the crowd. Clarke flinched, swung, and missed the next "pitch." The third was noticeably slower, and Fred managed not to flinch but missed it. I think Cap Clarke, as they used to call him, used all his concentration to look like he wasn't afraid.

"Harder to hit than Kid Nichols," said Clarke, as he left the box with obvious relief.

Our first batter was McAleer. Jimmy wasn't keen, looking apprehensively at Linton, then at the smoke that drifted lazily out to the center field wall, and only then at the pronged muzzle pointing at him. "I don't expect to hit it," he said, and didn't, jerking away and missing three loud "pitches." Linton hadn't made a ball curve yet, but the noise and fear had been enough to keep two good hitters from coming close. No ballplayers offered to take positions. They held back and no one coached at first or third. The "gun" and its inventor dominated the park, and I must say, seeing a barrel pointing down from the mound was an uneasy sight. I stood by King Saturday in the dugout. The field was empty save for the man in a tweed suit and a cannon.

Hoy was Louisville's second batter. Some of their men smiled, having figured that lack of hearing might be an advantage. Linton may have reached the same conclusion because he produced his calipers and adjusted the prongs. Hoy stepped in and looked fearlessly at the thing. He was a short, solid left-hand hitter who'd been in the League for ten years. Bill Hoy was a favorite of mine. Having been deaf since childhood, he read lips proficiently and had devised signals for fellow outfielders and running the bases. I always thought Hoy was smarter than his teammates, and was embarrassed that the world saw fit to call him "Dummy." Bill didn't flinch and took a good rip at the first delivery, a truly wicked curveball that dropped six inches, and missed. Linton readjusted the prongs, and a krank near the dugout yelled, "Give him something to hit. Who the hell can hit a cannon shot?" The next pitch was fast but straight, and Hoy managed to dribble a ball foul by third. He got quite an ovation for it, especially from the players.

Mr. Hoy stood coolly in, waiting for the gun in the same solitude he waited at the plate his whole career. I wondered if soundless baseball was as strange to him as the noises he made when he talked were to us? How lonely is the game without the crack of the bat, players shouting, leather slapping dirt, kranks cussing? I never saw Hoy show anything but a hard, intent pride. He straightened up as the next "pitch" roared over the inside corner, but didn't flinch. Despite the guarantee all "pitches" would be strikes, this one was close, and the crowd booed.

"No pitch is out of the strike zone!" shouted the professor.

"Ball one," cried the umpire, and received the biggest cheer of the afternoon.

"The machine is accurate," announced Linton.

"Like the first shot?" yelled Patsy Tebeau.

Linton reloaded. He did it faster now that the crowd was less sympathetic. Hoy took several practice swings as a new white ball and brass cartridge were sealed into the breach. I felt the wallet in my pocket which meant I had solitude too; I was on an island of silence with the Indian.

The prongs were adjusted, and this time Hoy got the equivalent of a curveball from a left-hand pitcher. The "pitch" broke down and away, but he went with it and hit a pop up that landed a few feet behind third. The ovation was long and loud.

Jesse Burkett was next, and the Crab, a name which suited his personality and batting crouch, was angry. Burkett wanted to bat last but that honor went to the Indian because of the newspaper clamor. Jess was assuaged with a five-dollar gold piece but dearly wanted to outdo Saturday. A man doesn't hit .400 twice without being smart, and crabby or not, Burkett knew how to handle a bat. He bunted the first "pitch," a nasty sinking delivery he couldn't have hit, neatly down the third base line, and got quite a cheer. "All right," said Linton, who probably hadn't expected anyone would bunt. "This man will get no pitch over 75 miles per hour," but proceeded to have the machine deliver a murderous variety of curves and drops Burkett didn't come near, and Jess got seven "pitches," because the umpire refused to call a strike on anything Burkett didn't

156

swing at. Linton made a great show of adjusting the prongs before each pitch. Jess threw his bat right by me into the dugout after missing a third "strike."

Young Wagner was next. Hans — they didn't call him Honus yet — was big. He played third that afternoon, and played it with a first baseman's glove, the other position he played that season. Wagner wasn't trusted at short then, being prone to make errors with those huge hands — they were as big as Saturday's — and I've always felt it took Honus a few years to become a shortstop because he didn't look like a shortstop. Wagner was so bowlegged, it appeared a ball might roll through him. If the Indian had an athlete's build, this husky Pennsylvanian had a coal miner's build. Hans was a shade under six feet and broad as an oak. He looked big-eared and awkward at rest. In motion he was uncoiling power.

Wagner stood at the plate and it seemed nothing, not even Linton's gun, could knock him down. The cannon barked and even this hard, sinewed young man flinched. Linton didn't spare the powder, and Hans saw three literal rifle shots. Wagner didn't back off and swung at them all. He dug his back foot into the ground and threw those huge fists and big shoulders at the white blur. You could see the tension in him as the man overpowered the urge to flinch and the struggle slowed him down enough so he couldn't catch up to the projectile. Hans didn't throw his bat or glare at Linton, he just walked to the dugout, dragging the bat by the head.

The crowd began to chant, "King!" "King!" "King!" as Wagner walked off the field. Saturday had been resting on one knee and hadn't talked to me or his teammates who freely offered advice. The Indian studied Linton carefully. We had $213 bet that he would hit a ball farther than anyone, and another $50 that he'd make contact more often than Burkett. I liked holding money bet on man against machine. I was also holding $55 on the game.

The Indian walked to the plate, nodded to Lou Criger, who took his hand out of his glove and grimaced, and stood in. Linton made an adjustment of the prongs and they faced each other. Saturday took no practice swings. He did this to intimidate pitchers — the implication was that his swing was so lethal he had to restrain it, even in practice. I'm not sure what psychological advantage he wanted over Linton, but you could feel the animosity between them. Linton loaded with elaborate extra care, even wiping the brass casing of the charge with a blue handkerchief, and staring at the ball the way some of our intense actors portray Hamlet holding Yorick's skull. All this, I suspect, was supposed to emphasize the drama of brain and brawn. The crowd hissed. Linton peered through the scope and held the brass chain taut. The *Gazette* had a point. There was something grotesque about a man in a suit aiming a cannon at an Indian. For a moment I had the feeling Linton was going to kill him. It didn't seem like we were in a ballpark at all. The ballpark feeling, the sense of a protected place in a sprawling city, was gone, and we could have been on the plains where an Indian and white man faced each other for that supernatural moment before the kill when they are just men, not a savage with a club and a white man with a gun.

Linton pulled the chain and the illusion of death in open space was shattered by the blast: it was man and machine again, athlete and challenge. The "pitch" was straight and Saturday nicked it, fouling it at Lou Criger's feet. The crowd cheered, not for the nick, but for the way the Indian stood in. He didn't flinch and seemed to leap at the whizzing white blur. He missed but he was game. The crowd was relieved and excited. Their professorial antagonist had an equal.

"Well done, Mr. Saturday," said Linton, as the calipers came out. He made a careful adjustment. This was his psychology, and I think it was a mistake because Saturday had been studying his moves with those prongs. Linton took his position behind the gun and held the chain with the dexterity of an executioner. I saw Saturday fight Joe Burke and I saw him jump Jackson Bridge, but what he did now surprised me more than anything I'd seen him do. He took two steps toward the gun. The Indian stood in front of the batter's box in an illegal position. Linton dropped the chain and appealed to the umpire, but Saturday yelled, "This isn't a game, pull the trigger." Linton took the chain, and shook his head as if agreeing, though disapproving of Saturday's logic. Some of the crowd gasped. Saturday's two steps seemed patently self-destructive. He was walking into the muzzle. I knew what he was doing but my heart was in my teeth. I watched Linton to make sure he didn't move the gun, and the word 'assassination' rang in my brain as the gun roared. Saturday swung with the noise, or maybe he swung as the chain was pulled. He told me later the first thing he noticed about "the damn gun" was that watching the barrel was pointless because the ball came too fast. Hitters, of course, watch a pitcher's arm, or if the man is really fast, they guess. What Saturday was doing — and I wasn't the only person who figured it out, Frank Ember and most the club saw it too — was guess curve and get up in front of the batter's box to hit the "pitch" before it broke. This was a neat trick provided it really was a curve. I tried to watch gun and batter and didn't see the execution of the swing. Frank did. He said Saturday lowered his hands and shortened his stroke to make it quicker. It's a good thing he did.

The roar, "pitch," swing, and result happened in perhaps two eye-deceiving seconds. Before we could pray or swallow, a line drive glanced off the gun, ripped off the sight, and sailed high in the air. The ball landed near third base, and my first absurd thought was: Is that a better hit than Hoy's?

Linton skipped away as the kranks exploded in shouts, claps, stomping and a volley of comment, little of which was suitable for ladies' ears. The ambassador of science picked up the twisted sight and put it in his pocket.

"Take that damn thing to the scrap heap!"

"Take yourself with it!"

"There's some a' your own damn medicine!"

The professor raised his hand. He handled himself well for a man who'd made himself so unpopular. "I have a charge here that will propel a ball one hundred miles per hour. I don't believe any man alive can hit an object traveling at that velocity. Would Mr. Saturday care to try?"

The question was answered with a thundering yes by the crowd and a nod of the head by the Indian. The apostle of science made a show worthy of a priest administering the sacrament as he cleaned the barrel, produced another charge from the neat brown leather box, and loaded the cannon. Saturday said later he hadn't known what he'd agreed to since his ears were blocked with cotton. I noticed the symmetry of the professor's challenge with the trick we'd played in Hooper, concluding that challenges made in front of crowds have an incendiary quality rivaled only by those made under the most intimate circumstances.

"One condition!" yelled Saturday, stepping toward Linton. "I set the prongs!"

The professor was on his own petard. He could have refused, I suppose, but would have belittled himself in the eyes of an already hostile crowd. The idea of a hundred mile an hour "pitch" — the idea of anything traveling a hundred miles an hour — was so preposterous any request would have been reasonable. Of course, we had no way of knowing what speed the ball would travel, but it was reasonable to assume this "pitch" was going to be faster than the previous ones, which had been frighteningly quick. Saturday didn't wait for an answer. He had the crowd behind him and unless Linton wanted to physically restrain him, the professor had to acquiesce. I didn't know how carefully Saturday had watched Linton work the prongs but I saw what he was up to. He simply moved them away from the muzzle. The Indian was guaranteeing himself a straight pitch.

Linton had recovered his composure. He was on the defensive, and the issue was whether his hundred mile an hour "pitch" was as unhittable as he thought. For the moment, as he produced the last gleaming charge from the leather box, the last trick from the magician's bag, he stood confidently erect, then bent daintily again from the waist as he placed ball and charge in the breech.

"I only wish to show what can't be done, to demonstrate that with practice and the proper use of this machine . . ." Linton spoke in a conciliatory tone, but the crowd drowned him out with catcalls and challenges. The professor stood by the gun, took the chain, and called out, "Are you ready, Mr. Saturday?"

The Indian nodded. He motioned to Lou Criger to move back and Saturday took a position a yard behind home plate. He wouldn't have been allowed to bat there in a game, but this wasn't baseball, it was "business."

Linton pulled the chain and the gun roared. I remember the noise and smoke, both greater than before. The park shook and the crack of bat meeting ball cut into the report which echoed over the empty ball field. A line drive sizzled off Saturday's blue bat, took a vicious hop at the foot of the cannon, and went through Linton's legs. It was hotly debated whether ball actually touched tweedy leg or polished shoe, but whether body in motion met body at rest, or merely whistled by, the apostle of science fell victim to Newton's best known law, and, with a distinctly audible squawk, fell on his ass.

2

Edith and I took a drive by Lake Erie after the game. I was quiet, having first failed to get her permission to travel in one of the closed black cabs that criss-cross the city like agents of fate, which seemed a more romantic conveyance for an afternoon with a young lady — and because we won our bets as the Spiders lost on a bases-loaded double by young Wagner. Saturday hadn't done anything to make us lose and hadn't done anything to help us win. I had $37 in the reptilian wallet which I would deposit on Monday in an East Side bank under the name A. Anson.

We rode in Edith's Tilbury, a splendid two-wheeled vehicle drawn by a chestnut gelding and driven by a wizened duenna of a family retainer, Robert, who treated Edith with discreet devotion. He sat hunched over the driver's seat and controlled the gelding, a big sturdy animal, with subtle flicks of the wrist, as if he were fly casting. Despite appearing to be asleep, I think Robert caught everything we said. He had a way of leaning to the left, which exposed a small, pointed, pixie-like ear, but if he reported to Mrs. Burns, Edith didn't seem concerned.

It was a beautiful late afternoon. Edith wore the yellow, puffy-sleeved dress with the white piping, and a huge vermillion hat that sported a blue and green feather. She was very happy and I took this as a compliment. I asked about Lyndon Blunt as we rolled through Wade Park, which is as fine a place for a drive as I know in any city, and Edith said, "I haven't seen him. Lyndon wrote a respectful letter saying we should always be friends. He's considering going in the army."

We passed the Case School of Applied Sciences, site of the experiment which impressed Professor Linton so, and I said, "Blunt already serves in a more disciplined army than that one. You haven't seen the last of him."

"I don't want to see him. I'll only hurt him again." Edith sat on the right side of the open carriage and held her plumed hat as a breeze came up. We rode down Euclid Avenue by the houses and fine lawns of the wealthy. I've always envied the trees of the rich. Those tall oaks and wide sycamores have a cool majesty their owners so often lack. The great avenue, I pointed out to Edith, like life itself, ends at a cemetery: the Lake View Cemetery; and Robert took us by the Garfield Memorial, a large monument to a small man (that observation got another laugh), and we passed a crowd of sightseers and school-children waiting their turn to ascend the tower of Ohio's fallen son.

Edith watched me for a moment and said, "What's wrong?"

I admired her directness and, when it was combined with concern, thought her quite attractive. I found myself liking Edith very much as we left Lake View Cemetery and headed north. "Something's going on with Saturday."

"What?" she said quickly.

"He and I are partners."

"You're friends," said Edith, holding her hat, and moving slightly toward me.

"It's more than that," I said.

"I like that you're friends. Maybe's there's more to you than I've noticed."

The carriage came over a rise and we could see Lake Erie looking very blue in the late afternoon sun. There is something absurdly wonderful about seeing the lake sparkling beyond the edges of Cleveland. It was Thoreau, I think, who called our century "restless, nervous, bustling, and trivial," and found escape by water. Edith also seemed to feel the city dweller's exhilaration at a glimpse of the place where men can't build. As we headed for the lake under a warm, fading sun, she moved

164

closer, and I thought I might be falling in love with her. I was happy to be away from League Park, away from a sullen losers' lockerroom, and especially happy to be away from Frank, who knew Saturday and I were betting. Frank never said anything about it. Had he told the Robisons, I would have been fired. Saturday was too valuable to fire.

"I'm his banker," I said. "I hold his money."

Edith looked up, obviously impressed. "He trusts you?"

"It's more that he doesn't trust anyone else."

"And is money so important to him?"

"Yes."

Edith thought about this. Robert seemed especially intent on driving. He knew when not to appear to listen, or maybe he didn't care what we said as long as I wasn't too close to Edith. As in the "Turkish Corner," I found her immensely attractive, but this time I surprised her.

"We bet," I said.

"With each other?" Edith laughed. She seemed so free, so pleased with wearing a vermillion hat and driving by the lake with a young man.

"With gamblers. We're trying to get the money to buy a team, but you mustn't tell anyone that." I leaned close to say this so Robert couldn't hear. She leaned toward me, not for intimacy but with a look that approached horror.

"Are you doing something dishonest?"

"That depends how you look at it."

Edith looked me in the eye. Her large nose was slightly red from the sun. She took off her hat and placed it between us on the seat. "Henry, I think it only depends on whether you are doing something dishonest." Edith was so sure of herself, so sure of the world and how to judge it, yet she wasn't, I firmly believe, motivated by vanity.

"Sometimes we bet against Cleveland, and sometimes we win."

"Do you mean he's throwing games?" Edith sat up, pulling away. Her eyes were sharp with disapproval and hurt.

"I think so," I said.

"I don't believe you." She looked at the lake, which now occupied the whole glittering, blue horizon. The gelding trotted briskly, we were parallel the water, passing white clapboard houses with red or blue shutters separated by sand dunes and maple trees. "What game?" she said, forcing the words out.

"He dropped a ball in Brooklyn."

"Did he tell you he dropped it intentionally?"

"No." I laughed nervously. "He said he lost it in the sun."

"Why don't you believe him?"

"Because we won eighty dollars."

"Players gamble," said Edith.

I looked at her searchingly. I didn't want to argue about Saturday, I wanted to talk about myself. "It makes me feel alone. It changes the game."

"Why do it?"

"We want to own a club. He'll never make enough money as a player to buy a club."

"There are other ways to make money than betting."

We didn't speak for a while. Robert hunched over the reins, as if preoccupied with wizened thoughts about his wizened life and role of Dickensian coachman, which insulated him from the world. The more animated Edith's and my discussion became, or the more poignantly silent, the more discreetly Robert slunk behind the gelding. His pointed, pixie ears now almost drooped, which made what I should have enjoyed as a humorous contrast to the quick ears of the gelding. I found myself studying Robert and horse because I didn't want to look at Edith, and looking at the water seemed too posed. I was at a disadvantage: I wanted to share a confidence, and it had been refused. I wanted to share a secret, but maybe I wanted to use the secret — I had imagined the conversation, even rehearsed it, which had really been rehearsing falling in love. I see now I wanted to fall in love with Edith, or Annie, or love itself. Or better, let Edith fall in love with me, by showing her a dilemma that would make her think more of me, both for being in it (a risky partnership with the Indian was impressive) and for my sensitivity to it. Another disadvantage — and I felt this so acutely my face was red — was I thought she knew I was playing at falling in love. What illusion is sweeter? What part easier to initiate and harder to sustain? What gives such an enticing glimpse of Narcissus' pool?

We stopped at a trough by a clump of lilacs. Robert watered the horse and asked if we could rest a minute. He stood by the horse, stroking and talking to it. This was almost a sign for us

166

to speak, since we had privacy. A fresh wind blew off the lake and small blue waves slid over a rocky shore a hundred feet away. Our voices couldn't have been more than whispers. We looked at each other, and the happy girl was gone. The plumed, vermillion girl who exuded freedom without a self-destructive edge, who was innocent by reason of decency, had been replaced by an older, troubled, bigger — Edith seemed larger, like something that's in your way — woman. *Woman* is the word. Girls don't wear expressions like the one Edith had by the lilacs. Her big pink face with its large nose had contradiction, and even fear, tugging at the corners of her wide, tense mouth. This wasn't the privileged glimpse of her heart I had hoped for.

"I can understand why he might gamble, and even throw games, if that's true, but I don't understand why you're doing it."

"We want a team. We want players to be treated better. Someday maybe we'll break the National League monopoly."

"There are good intentions behind every selfish act, aren't there?"

"I do it because we're friends."

"I never thought you were dishonest." Edith turned away. "Irritating, yes, but not dishonest," she said, bitterly. "What excuse do you have? What bit of cynical cleverness excuses you? Something Wilde said?"

A breeze from Lake Erie rustled the lilac bushes. Two sailboats had come about and were heading back to port. After a long moment, she said, "I really am sorry. I thought differently of you. Why did you have to tell me this?"

This wasn't what I'd expected. She had rejected my secret which meant she rejected me. I wanted the upper hand so I lied about what a minute before I'd wanted to be true. I tried the young man's master stroke. Like a tennis player who swings wildly and wins the point, I said, "I'm in love with you."

Edith was caught off-guard. She apparently had enough vanity not to suspect the statement had been fired to cover a hasty retreat. She looked sadly at me and said, "The works of the flesh are manifest."

"But I am," I said. "And it has nothing to do with respecting you."

"Should I be pleased?"

"I didn't say I liked you."

Edith leaned toward me and kissed me. I was so surprised, I actually couldn't think of anything to say.

"I don't like you too," she said.

On the way home, as twilight fell and the gelding trotted, we held hands. I held Edith's large hand and didn't speak. I was sealed in all the happy delusion a man holding a lady's hand can feel. I imagined all sorts of unspoken intimacy. I thought riding in a carriage with a tall woman who had taken to wearing plumes, and loved baseball, was fine. I imagined she was both deeply attracted to me, and deeply involved as a friend, and couldn't decide which pleasure was sweeter. I used to tell Ned, after we had offended young ladies of breeding — which was often — that their reactions were "veiled attraction," and the intensity of their disapproval was a measure of lust; so I told myself Edith's reticence was desire.

Robert drove along the shore, then back to Lake View Cemetery, where the world looked ghostly and marble in the twilight, and one could imagine the living and dead communing at such an hour in the easy fading light. I remember the evening. A column of gnats swarmed like a gigantic plume at the gates of the cemetery. I sat back and thought being married might not be so bad. Here was an educated, rich (what young man hasn't once allowed himself the thought that marrying a wealthy woman would finally provide an outward sign of his inward worth?) independent woman who liked baseball. That we sparred verbally, that she'd kissed me twice for reasons she didn't seem able to fathom, only added to her mystery. Life with Edith could be as smooth as this Tilbury ride through the pleasantest part of Cleveland. The motion of the carriage was hypnotic. The warmth of her hand — so full, I thought, of desire and understanding — was like a drug. The smell of lilacs and grass in the subdued radiance of evening made me think I could live quite happily without the sweat and sawdust of the Gin Palace, and the bitterness of bought baseball. Maybe I was in love. I thought I'd won Edith with my wit. Like most self-centered people, I believed if I really liked someone, they had to like me in return.

We rolled down Euclid Avenue and Edith hadn't spoken. I began to take pride in the appointment of the Tilbury. The black seats gave off a subtle odor of fine leather. The lanterns which hung on either side of Robert had been carefully but not ostentatiously polished. The horse was in superb shape. Robert one might come to like with time. Mrs. Burns might choose to live abroad. I looked at Edith's brown hair, so nicely combed up into a relaxed version of the style of the day, and wondered what all that hair would look like lying free over her shoulders. Edith had been staring at the street and increasingly domestic scenery so intently, I thought she wanted the evening to last forever.

"Will you marry me?" I said.

Edith didn't look at me right away but slowly removed her hand. "Henry, I'm in love with someone else."

Had it been revealed Edith were a man, I couldn't have been more shocked. "Someone else?" I said, as if asking for clarification.

"Can't you tell?" Her face was softer now, no longer afraid or contradictory. "You don't know?"

"I thought perhaps you were in love with me." I tried to say this with the crafty insouciance I associate with the English, but it came out with the petulance of wounded ego.

"You don't know?" she repeated.

Then, all of a sudden, with the quick and all-encompassing rip of jealousy, I was sure I knew. At first I just saw — I should say felt, one doesn't see the green passion, one tastes and feels it — a well-bred shade, a phantom from the right places — places where I sat by the door and hoped no one recognized me because no one did — where I was as uncomfortable as you can only be when young and the idea of eternity makes sense. From those places, from those shadows, from time forgotten except by me, came a man, a phantom with a history, a pedigree, a chronology, that led to this moment in a Tilbury with the subtle smell of fine leather.

"No," I said. "I don't know."

"You must," she said.

I couldn't say the word but I thought I knew. It was Ned. Somehow Ned was, and had to be, and had always been, the executioner of my dreams. Who but an ex-best friend could return like something from the dead, to fill an evening in a carriage with the smell of leather and lilacs with horror? Have you ever been told your lover, your wife, your intended, loves someone else? It distends the world. Things, ordinary things, lose their shape. The world bends. Time bends. Time doesn't stop — it begins. You realize you never lived in time but in some fairyland where the clocks went round their happy course until this hour came and the world bent back on itself. The world now has at its center an unbearably heavy event that bends time around it. When you're jealous, there is no present: only the past and only the future. It had to be Ned. The coachman's ears were no longer pixie-ish but moldy, with hairs like wires coming out of them. His ears looked like they had been underground. Robert was no longer an idiosyncratic Dickensian retainer but a full blown fiend. The Tilbury had a funereal blur . . .

"This is the second time I've seen you turn white."

"Is it?" I said, angrily, realizing Ned had been the source each time.

"Henry," she said. "I don't know what to say. I didn't know you felt this way. I'm not sure you really do feel this way. Perhaps it's your pride."

"Perhaps it is," I said bitterly.

Where this conversation would have gone, I shall never know: whether I would have come home with my shield instead of on it, or only walked in another bitterness, I will never know because the rest of the world's tranquility, or at least that part of the world strolling at twilight in Wade Park, was shattered by a horrendous barking sound. In June of 1898 I hadn't yet heard that raucous insistent racket that would be the very signature of the new century. An automobile roared up behind us. A horse drawing a cab in front of us whinnied and violently shook its head while the driver pulled for control. The gelding reared up but Robert, rising a foot from the seat, kept him steady. The machine pulled even with us. It was lower than the Tilbury, and the driver, who wore goggles and whose hair streamed behind him, was suspended in a seat between the rear wheels at an angle that suggested the acceleration generated by this frightful invention was more than a human being could bear. He waved. An enormous hand reached up and tapped my palm.

It was the Indian.

3

I don't think I ever saw Saturday play crooked ball. It seems obvious now that he chose to play straight at home and occasionally dump a game away, but I didn't see the pattern right away. The Spiders went to New York toward the end of June. I had $1,067 in our clandestine accounts which made me feel important and scared. I relished the sense of beating the Robisons and Al Spalding and the gang that ran the game, but I was sure something would go wrong. As I told Edith, I'm not a moral person, but I am superstitious. By the end of June, my mother remarked that I'd lost weight and looked older. "You look worse than a clergyman," she told me. "It must be Edith Burns."

She was partially right. I didn't see Edith after our fateful trip to the lake. I was embarrassed that I had conned myself into thinking she was in love with me, while conning myself into thinking I'd wanted to marry a woman I knew so little. I was very angry that my vanity had been revealed. I'd thought someone I had tried so hard to impress had to be impressed with me. What hurt was what we had in common. She was cynical. She liked baseball. Edith could joke about the prophet Hosea and her hands were as big as mine. Her strong arms, slightly horsy face, and general bigness seemed achingly attractive. Why didn't she like me? Then there was Ned. The poet

Blake speaks of "arrows of desire," but arrows of jealousy cut deeper. They take the flesh off the bone. That I would have to step aside for Ned seemed so natural I continually cursed myself for stupidity. Hating Ned was like hating Albert Spalding. His victories seemed inevitable. Maybe wanting to marry Edith was my last attempt to be Ned and enter his circle. Hating a friend made crooked baseball seem inevitable.

I had no business asking Edith Burns to marry me. It was one thing to flirt with her, irritate her, and escort her into the masculine world of League Park, quite another to marry her. I told myself I didn't want to marry anyone. Marriage is a labyrinth that requires one to slay his own beast, and I hadn't done that. I was a free man, beast and all, and did what I wanted at the Gin Palace. Mother told me I was leading a "secondhand life with men playing a boys' game," and pointedly wondered, each time I saw her, when I was going to get a real job and get married. I didn't tell her I had been refused by Edith. She would have thought less of me.

I was jealous. I was furiously jealous. I went to bed jealous and woke up jealous. Many nights I didn't sleep and others I woke in the dark seeing his face. I often thought of Saturday making Ned waltz and took vicious pleasure in it. I denied Edith had hurt me, denied she could, and told myself Edith was a calculating person who wanted most what she appeared to dislike. This, I decided, was a universal feminine trait. Like all women, Edith awaited her prince. I said over and over Ned was getting back at me, that he wasn't serious about Edith, but I failed to convince myself, and assumed they adored each other.

To make matters worse, Edith wrote a kind letter, possibly modeled after one Blunt sent her, saying I didn't understand anything, and though we couldn't be friends now, we would be in the future. I was touched she wrote, furious about being spurned into friendship. I was glad she acknowledged we couldn't currently be "friends," otherwise I might not have spoken to her again. The letter concluded with a strange addendum that assured me the Indian would play "straight." I had forgotten we argued about this and no longer gave a damn what Edith thought about King Saturday.

The Spiders went to New York on June 20th, the day General Shafter's army invaded Cuba. The papers had gigantic headlines announcing the deed. Only later did we learn that the "daring" invasion had been a matter of shoving men into barely seaworthy boats and throwing horses overboard. Fortunately, the Spaniards didn't oppose the landing and horses can swim.

I went to the Western Union office around the corner from the Stillman Hotel. The game started at one o'clock, and I asked Mr. Robison for the afternoon off. He knew where I was going, and later made an appearance himself. The town was excited by Saturday's first trip to New York. His popularity increased three times that season. The first was the trick he played on McGraw, the second was knocking down Professor Linton, and the third was June 20th, the Spiders' first game in Manhattan. I wasn't surprised at the crowd, which must have numbered close to two hundred, elbowing their anxious way into the telegraph office, and overflowing out into the street. Station chief Grimes manned the key himself while his assistant, a fellow named Sullivan, a few years younger than I, wrote messages on a blackboard which he hauled over the counter with great pride as the crowd oohed, cheered, or swore. Sully happily wore the uniform of his profession: white shirt, high collar, black tie — his coat was professionally draped over the back of a swivel chair — and green visor which neatly covered hair so thin and reddish blond that his face seemed framed by his skull. His passions were Mike Kelly and Sitting Bull. Pictures of both graced the green walls. Sully had been on this side of the Atlantic less than ten years and in Cleveland half that time, but was as knowledgeable as any krank in town. He got the scores first and there was always a complement of sporting men at the office waiting for out-of-town scores. Sully never bet.

I managed to get a spot near the door where the cigar smoke wasn't too thick. I congratulated myself for being on the inside of the afternoon's game. I was bitter and satisfied: I knew the Indian had bet against Cleveland. Edith was as wrong about him as she was about me. Was he going to throw the game? Could he change the outcome of a game by himself? I didn't know and didn't care. I was mad at everybody. Saturday and I were making money. We were getting even.

Our bets were getting larger and more complicated. We had $50 on the Giants, but Saturday had $25 at five-to-one that he'd hit a home run off Amos Rusie. That bet was drunken vanity as far as I was concerned, or maybe he was humoring McBuck who lost money backing Linton's machine. Rusie was the hardest thrower in the league, and kranks argued endlessly whether he, Kid Nichols, or Cy Young was the best. To my thinking, Rusie threw the hardest, Young had the best control, and Nichols played for the best team. In terms of who looked most frightening from the stands, the nod certainly went to Rusie. He wasn't called the "Hoosier Thunderbolt" because of a godlike intellect. I had two bets saying Saturday wouldn't strike out.

I came to the dim, packed Western Union office angry, but when I saw the kranks and sporting men — fellows who'd ducked work for the afternoon or closed their shops, bartenders from the Palace who'd gotten up early, even the wart-nosed Standard clerk who'd left the oil empire for lunch — the drive to win and be with winners came back and so did numb, wary misgivings about betting. My satisfaction at knowing Saturday was crooked in a crooked world, was replaced by something less easily defined. The clean pleasure of baseball in the afternoon was this smoky, murmuring room. Jake McBuck puffed on a thin cigar, and Burke, who now wore a derby indoors and out, chewed a short, fat one at the counter, surrounded by a dozen Gin Palace cronies. Jake always knew who was in a room. He acknowledged me with a tilt of the head. Burke didn't look. He stood at the counter with his one ear pointed at the crowd and his derby tilted at a rakish angle that advertised the remaining ear. Burke was seen in profile so often he was called "Egyptian," after the ancients' odd two-dimensional painting. His one visible eye moved back and forth over the room and rested on me several times.

Almost everyone had a wager on the game. The Giants weren't the best club, but New York was the biggest city, and Clevelanders wanted to do well there. No matter how good the Spiders were, we always felt like the poor kids playing the rich kids when the club went to the Polo Grounds. I stood by the door hoping that if Mr. Robison dropped by he wouldn't notice how many sports knew me. The Palace crowd wasn't friendly, but they knew I held money for the Indian, and wanted to know which way it was bet. "Hi, Sport," said J.D. Donlan, the bartender who held my arms the night Saturday cut Burke's ear off. J.D. smiled and poked me in the ribs, like we were old friends. I'd spent a lot of time at the Palace in the last two months.

"You bet New York," he said.

"How do you know?" I said quietly, hoping to stay in the shadows with Donlan, who weighed two hundred pounds, and whose biceps made his red sleeve-garters expand over the white folds of his shirt.

"Good move. Rusie can take us. You've got other bets too."

"J.D.," I said, leaning toward him, "I've got so many bets I don't know what they all are."

"I'll lay odds you know them cold," said McBuck, who appeared behind me. His clean shaven face was chalky white in the smoky room. Burke stayed by the counter. If he'd come over I would have left. "You bet the Indian would homer," said McBuck. "Five-to-one. You bet the Giants at fifty. You've got twenty at two-to-one the Spiders score three runs, and twenty-even they won't. You've also got two ten-dollar bets Saturday won't strike out."

"Thank you, Mr. McBuck. I'd forgotten the three-run bets."

Men gathered around us and listened. I didn't like this notoriety. There could be consequences for being a lightning rod as to how the Spiders would play. "How's he feelin'?" I was asked by three men wearing overcoats despite the warmth of the room. "Fine," I said, sitting on a windowsill. I wanted to imagine the game in anonymity, but for the same reason I could drink at the Palace I couldn't sit alone and conjure an image of the Polo Grounds so full kranks would be behind ropes in the outfield and in the trees on the hills behind the stands. To sit alone and get news of a ball game would be the rarest of pleasures. I was flanked by McBuck who slouched against the wall — Jake preferred corners and alleys — and Donlan who leaned against the door frame. The high-ceilinged room was hot and a slight breeze came through the door. Two oak-blade fans turned lethargically in the smoke that rose through sunbeams coming in the transom.

At five minutes to one, Sully scribbled on his slate and the crowd muttered in anticipation. He held up the thing like a teacher showing the multiplication tables. "Weather fine in N.Y." The news stimulated a round of betting. They bet on everything. Would Saturday strike out, would Rusie fan five in the first five innings, would the Spiders get a hit in the first inning? A man in a heavy mackintosh who never took his hands out of pockets, bet it would rain in New York before the game ended. Someone shouted, "He'll hit one," and people began to bet whether Saturday would homer off Rusie. "He bet he would, didn't he?" a fat guy yelled in my ear. A wave of anticipation bordering on anarchy swept the room. Jake McBuck took on all comers. God knows how many bets he got in the five minutes before the game. Enthusiasm for the Indian was wild. He was Cleveland for those five minutes. He was us. He was every man in that room who'd wanted to be a ballplayer. He was the best part of us — the part that didn't have to be at work at eight in the morning and hold a job where we would never be boss. I was surprised. Hard-bitten sports and seasoned kranks acted like schoolboys. Did they really think Saturday could do anything? Men cheered, bet, and held their money over their heads like boys outside a peep show. I was asked a dozen times if Saturday hadn't bet he'd hit one himself. For five minutes the men in that room believed in magic.

"Did he bet he wouldn't?" someone shouted, and more money flew out of pockets, hands shook, and additional wagers were concluded with jerks of the head. "What inning?" McBuck said. "What pitch? How 'bout the first pitch?" Jake didn't stop talking. He turned each situation three or four ways. I was amazed. Jake hedged every bet. He had so many options, he couldn't lose too dearly. McBuck could remember numbers like a tobacco auctioneer. Jake had the best memory in Cleveland, with the possible exception of Sully.

"First pitch!" yelled the Irishman, and the wagering cooled to a determined murmur. The game was on, Cleveland had invaded Gotham, and everyone in that room felt like we were about to strut down Broadway. "Four-to-one Saturday don't homer," said McBuck. "Seven-to-one he don't homer the first at bat. Eleven-to-one he don't homer on the first pitch." I felt I was in a group of children. They had their shibboleths, their rituals, their hope. The feeling was wonderful. Childlike exhilaration rose in that crowd where men had pistols under their vests and knives in their boots. If betting is the poor man's Wall Street, the kranks and sports rode a pre-game boom. Did it matter that most of them would lose? Was money important in those wild few minutes? I wasn't going to bet. I'd bet enough, but as Sully raised his slate with crisp yellow letters informing us that the Cleveland leadoff man, rookie Sunset Jimmy Burke had struck out, and a weasel-eyed little man who had a forest of hair growing out of his nostrils, loudly wanted to take on anyone who thought Rusie won't get "that redskin" in his first at bat, my dander rose, and I pulled out a ten-dollar gold piece.

"Five-to-one he gets a hit!" I shouted.

The little man skipped in my direction. "Three-to-one!" he yelled.

"Four-to-one," I said, handing my gold piece to J.D., who grabbed the little man by the arm.

"Nobody hits Rusie." The man's eyes seemed to grow closer together. "Nobody."

"Put up or shut up," said Donlan, not releasing his grip. "OK" said the man, tapping his vest pocket. The betting got louder as Sully hoisted the message, "Childs grounds to short." "He's up. He's up," everyone said, and I tried to imagine King Saturday stepping in against the hardest thrower of the decade at the horseshoe oval of the Polo Grounds. The Indian had come to the big city to face their best, and we all had money on it. I've never bet since that season. Saturday was the only man I bet with or for or against. I admit betting puts the game on another level. Your flesh crawls and your shirt gets wet. It's you up there in a way it isn't when your money's not on the line, but in another way, your imagination isn't there. Betting makes you a grown-up. It's what those of us who no longer live in our imaginations do. I won't put it down. Most of what I have came from betting.

Men began to shout as we figured the Indian was facing Rusie under the sun, five hundred miles away. "He'll do it," Donlan said. "He'll do it," said the Episcopal Bishop of Cleveland. "He'll do it," said half the room. "He'll do it!" "He'll do it!" "He'll do it!" African Bushmen couldn't make such a racket on behalf of their gods. Businessmen, thieves, sports, pimps, bums, and the bishop, chanted with the collective magic of communal rooting. For a moment we were one. Whether it was betting — the poor man's way of reaching for money he can't make, or the spectator's way of reaching for the athlete he can't be — we were all, for five minutes, willing to walk with the god of chance — and the excitement was something I had only felt in the company of women. Were we reaching for childhood? Was that frenzy an end and drug in itself? What do we really want when we bet? Money? Oblivion? To rise and fall like Satan through the morning?

Sully held up the slate: "Saturday at bat," was written in his neat foreign script. He turned to Grimes, a florid, bald man, with ears the size of dimes pressed close to his head, who was bent over the quickly ticking "sounder." Grimes said something, and in what seemed like one skipping motion, Sully wrote, tapped the picture of Sitting Bull, and hoisted the slate which read, "Saturday homers." Sully shouted but all I heard was "Sotorr . . ." and the message was lost in the wildest cheering I've ever been part of. Those men, who came from all Cleveland's classes and shades of professional life, went berserk. Beer was everywhere. Money was everywhere. Wet bills and froth flew around our heads. The weasel-like little man was turned upside-down and his pockets emptied. He had a lot of money on him and it was a good thing. McBuck was cool, calmly taking money out of a large purple wallet and distributing it to winners who waved it over their heads, shouted "Indian!" "Indian!", slapped my back, pummeled each other, or danced wildly with that most elusive and invisible partner, success.

For a few minutes we believed the Indian could do anything and he would do it for us. For the first time in weeks I didn't think about Ned and Edith. McBuck handed me $165; J.D. made sure I got money from the now half-naked weasel. Men bet and shouted the rest of the afternoon, and I won and lost, took money and paid up, but nothing will ever be like that first inning. The Indian had gone to New York and homered off Amos Rusie on the first pitch. Let Gotham take note and wonder: the miraculous inhabits the Midwest.

Buckets of beer kept appearing with jovial regularity and the afternoon was a blur. I noticed Saturday made an error that led to a Giant run in the bottom of the first. He gave Cleveland a run and he took it away, but I lost my fear of McBuck and Burke along with greed and jealousy. I knew Saturday could never do anything like this again. You only come to New York for the first time once. Rusie struck King out three successive times but no one cared. The Spiders won 7-2. McBuck ran out of money paying off and gave IOUs. His face was white as a corpse. Burke stayed very close to him, prominently displaying the bulge under his vest. His pock-marked face and ear were bright red. They didn't have to tell me they'd been crossed and someone was going to pay for it. I stuck close to Donlan. He, like most of the sporting crowd, thought Saturday was magic. They wouldn't have let anyone touch me. I walked out of the Western Union office with $120, and for the last time, in the nimbus of a god.

4

Three days later I was on a train east with Annie Gears and fell in love with her. She told me things I'd never heard before, and I didn't know how to react, except to fall, desperately and secretly, in love.

At four in the afternoon Frank Robison called me into his office. He let me work a full day before our audience. I was nervous. Robison had made what I recollected as a hazy appearance at the Western Union office, and I thought our gambling had caught up with me. I assumed if he suspected Saturday was betting against Cleveland, he would fire me and trade the Indian. I had worked late the previous two nights, avoiding the Gin Palace and trying to be a model employee, but I was over my head. With Saturday out of town, I wasn't safe at the Palace or comfortable at the ballpark.

Mr. Robison's office wasn't big. A large wall clock behind a flat desk made an oak halo behind Frank Robison's head. He liked to give the impression time was at his beck and call. The Spider boss had perfected a wary slouch that suggested he was about to turn around and quiet the damn clock, but he never did, which was his way of telling anyone in the office they weren't important enough to warrant the interruption. Players hated the clock. Robison would make an offer and wring his hands while time appeared to run out on his generosity.

"Your friend left the team."

I waited for a question about gambling but it didn't come. I must have looked surprised. He said, "You didn't know?" I shook my head. "Get him. We need him in Boston. Don't let this be like Pennsylvania."

The clock ticked off a few heavy seconds and I left, having no idea where Saturday was, or how to find him. I decided to ask Annie and went home to try to figure a way of reaching her without seeing McBuck or Burke.

A two-wheeled cab was waiting across the street from my lodgings, and as I stepped out of a muddy hack, Annie Gears descended from the cab. I recognized her by that aura which surrounds a woman we think about, and can recognize anywhere, even in the dark. I couldn't see her face. Annie walked quickly while the cab stayed at the curb. "Harry!" she said, running as she got closer. "Harry!" Annie wore a dark green dress and hat. I'd never seen her so unflamboyant, yet there was a sisterly beauty in her unprepossessing haste. "I've got to find him!" She grabbed my arm and we went inside.

In a dark hallway by the dull brass mailboxes, Annie held me by both hands and said, "Where is he? The club's in Philadelphia. Let's go." The late afternoon sun came through the transom, making the brass glow and back-lighting Annie. She was determined and serious, like a woman who's just gotten out of church. And she needed me.

"Saturday jumped the club," I said, afraid I was holding her hands too tightly.

"Then he's in Maine."

"How do you know?"

"He'll be in Boston," said Annie. "He bet too much on Boston."

"How do you know he's in Maine?"

"Come with me, Harry."

"I'm supposed to get him back."

"Burke," she said, pulling away and looking down. This needy, downplayed Annie Gears was unbearably beautiful.

"What about Burke?"

"I'll tell you on the train."

"Is Burke going to kill him?"

"There's a 5:11 to New York," Annie said quietly. "Wear this." She slipped a wedding ring on my finger.

We caught the *Pennsylvania Limited Vestibule Train* which would get to New York at 9:45 the next morning but we would change at Syracuse. Annie had one leather suitcase, I threw a suit and two shirts in a carpetbag, and we took her cab to the station. I was excited by Annie's presence. I thought I had it figured out. Burke was going to kill Saturday for crossing McBuck in New York, and Annie wasn't safe at the Palace. On the train Annie said Saturday had told her if he ever went away, he would go to Maine. I believed the Indian had said this; I didn't believe he'd do it.

We each took a sleeping compartment. The fiction of our marriage didn't extend to sharing a bed. We ate a good meal and sat in a green drawing-room car in a smoky corner. Annie behaved very much like a wife. Her green velvet dress with black brocade, green veil and green hat allowed her to blend into the car like a deer in a forest. Annie wore no feather and demurely kept those quick, bright eyes down, listening to me with the trained rapture that wives fabricate when their husbands hold forth on religion or politics. Anyone would have thought the lady was an affectionate, slightly bored wife, who still found that the *boudoir* compensated for a talkative husband. I talked because Annie was quiet and because I was nervous. I hoped Saturday would come back to protect her.

Like most men who find themselves traveling in the company of pretty women, I told Annie the story of my life, with the editorializing and modifications one makes under such circumstances. "My life is baseball and people who went away," I said. "Baseball and my father." I told Annie the sort of thing one only tells a woman or a stranger. My father, I said, was a blue-eyed stranger whose gaze was always on the horizon. "He was a man who was elsewhere. Maybe he thought about Antietam. Maybe he lived his life in one day. Maybe he thought of his parents and their family. They had more money than we did, a lot more. His father was a Classics professor at Case, who married well and compensated by making bad investments. Maybe my father remembered a house full of children and surprises and good things to eat. Harrison fortunes vanished into the stock market around '77. That's the way I tell it anyway."

I told Annie about Antietam. I had read everything I could find about the battle because I had a tired and gentle father, while my friends had men who crackled with the electricity of capital, and periodically bought bigger houses. I had a dream of a man on his belly in the mud of a cornfield on the "bloodiest day in American history," as books call it. "Who was that man?" Annie looked up. People always look up if you say you don't know your father. They think it strange but under that initial puzzlement is the larger puzzlement that most of us don't know this person, not in the way he knows us anyway, though perhaps everyone's father wasn't as distant as mine. (Isn't this what drives Hamlet mad? That his father and mother were different than he thought? The Ghost demanding what is better left to God and Gertrude enjoying that couch of incest?) "He was younger than I am now, by eight years. Was he afraid?" Did he cry in the mud, hoping it would pass and he could go home, wounded and proud, forever justified in being what he would be, which was a man losing his grasp on life, ever more dependent on his wife, sometimes reaching out to his only child? Was this man like me, who would have cursed, prayed, run, and hoped for a wound in the heel so he could be Achilles the rest of his life to admiring ladies and envious gentleman? I spent so much time, the later part of many nights and early parts of many mornings, making up his biography and exaggerating the wealth of the family. "A fine family," mother says. "Good family." She certainly genuflected before the coat of arms in the front hall and never failed to mention those distant, distant Harrison cousins who went to the White House. More than once I saw her given a blunt lesson in genealogy by less distant relations of the hero of Tippecanoe and recent President. I told Annie that and she liked it. The best way to charm a woman is talk family. Women care about family and privilege, even imagined privilege, and even women who work in saloons. It's their Civil War. If you wish to charm a woman, tell a family pretension and puncture it. Women understand these yearnings and the distinction of connections *sans* money, and manners which they think means treating their sex well.

"When did your father die?" Annie asked, looking up from the blue fleur-de-lis pattern in the worn green carpet.

"In '87. Almost twenty-five years to the day of the battle."

She said nothing, returning, as Mr. Henry James would say, to the figure in the carpet. I knew what she was thinking. Twenty-five years? What did he do in between? Was he an invalid? Did he hold a job? He held unimpressive jobs in unimpressive companies. There were years when he didn't work. There were years he was sick. Was it wounds? I attributed everything to the bloodiest day but Mother often said it was an excuse for a dreamer with a small, but painful part in history. "Lots of men fought," she says.

"Did he like baseball?" said Annie, as something undomestic flashed in her dark eyes.

"He loved it. Once, when I was away at school, at Thayer Academy — they made me go east. They thought it proper. Mother's father went to Harvard where she was determined that I go, so I went away to prep school — for the last two years of his life. Until I went to work for the Spiders, I was always doing something she wanted."

"Did he want you to go away?"

"He never wanted anything. He never raised his voice."

Annie started to speak but stopped.

"I wanted to go," I said, which was one of those realizations that appear before we can censor them. "I was part of it. I had complicity. I was embarrassed he didn't work. I was embarrassed by Mother's pretensions, though as soon as I got ten miles out of Cleveland, I was as full of them as she. Lonely as I was, I wanted to go. There were boys at Thayer who accepted my explanation of my family, and they became friends. Maybe they harbored their own suspicions about their people. They were the best fellows — Good God, if you aren't cynical about who you're supposed to be, you're an idiot. But to the ones who didn't like the distant relation to Tippecanoe, or the cynicism, and wanted to know, 'Exactly what does your father do?' I would say, 'It's what he did.' 'And what exactly did he do?' 'He fought to make men free.' I learned that a lot of men were in the Union Army, but not everyone fought."

"Not in the cornfield," said Annie.

"No." We were quiet and I lit a cigar. I like putting a wall of smoke between myself and the world, which was ably represented by a persistent train boy, who wanted the world to buy inferior cigars and infernal red candy — I gave him a dime to stay away — and two couples who had absolutely nothing to say to each other ("Married," said Annie), and several drum-mers speaking loudly of their wares. If either Annie or I had looked, however briefly, in their direction, we would have spent the rest of the evening in the company of free enterprise's most ubiquitous class.

"One day my father arrived at Thayer. It was one of the few times he left Cleveland. He lied to the headmaster and we went into Boston to see the White Stockings play the Red Stockings. He wanted to see Mike Kelly with me. We loved Kelly. He was the most exciting player, maybe the most exciting ever. Until Saturday. Kelly hit a triple, and flew into third base head first. It was the most wonderful day of my life. To see your hero hit a triple. It was everything. It meant greatness existed. I suppose it meant my father existed too. Then he went back to Cleve-land. He came east for the sole purpose of taking me to that game. We told everyone we'd been to a funeral."

Annie put her head next to mine. We might have been mistaken for newlyweds. Whether she liked me, felt sorry for me, or knew the drummers would practice their brand of democracy if we didn't look preoccupied, I don't know. "You must have loved him," she said.

"I miss him."

We rode for the better part of an hour without speaking. I don't know what Annie was feeling but I know I pretended she loved me. I pretended I could take care of her, and find Saturday and make everything right. Of course, I knew she couldn't ever be mine, but it was nice to pretend. I pretend more than most. I had my arm around a green lady in a green room whose tilted, green, embossed walls made a ceiling like the burial chamber of the Great Pyramid. High, small windows let us see speeding, cloudy darkness. I thought of something I memorized at Thayer: "Now Gawain goes riding in lonely lands, his life saved by grace."

5

We dozed, drank whiskey and soda, and neither of us left for our sleeping compartments. Annie woke me with a squeeze of the hand and we were alone. A crescent moon played along the silver band of the Erie Canal behind the reflection of the gas light on the windowpane. We were going east, to the home of America, along the waterway that made New York king of cities, by a narrow band of moonlight that brought the American mercantile adventure west where oil and steel made Cleveland and Pittsburgh boom, and Chicago a titan. We were going to Boston, bypassing New York City, a place I don't pretend to understand just because I've been to the Polo Grounds, eaten at Delmonico's, and seen the electric fire of Broadway. We rolled through New York State, once home to six Indian nations who fought white men who spoke three languages. Those Indians had to go west, assimilate, or die, except the West ran out, and they got shoes and shirts and Jesus, and their children became American — to the extent a man who buys whiskey out of the back of a saloon is American — and they died, and went to game preserves called reservations. In a man's lifetime, the canal and iron horse replaced the footpath and oxen trails, and the wilderness Mr. Jefferson thought would last a thousand years disappeared.

We were going east, seat of my deepest ambivalence, to Boston, where I spent five years in boarding school, four in college and two at the law: Boston where they look down on Clevelanders as well as Indians, where Emerson said the natives were "umpires of taste." From Boston we were going to Maine, on Annie's hunch, to look for King Saturday. What did he know of the canal and iron horse? Saturday was a Catholic, connected more to the losing history of Canada than to Tecumseh's conspiracy, that last dream of united Red Men, put down at Tippecanoe by my distant relative.

What did Saturday know of Tecumseh, Canada, or the Virgin Mary, for that matter? "What does he know about anything?" I said, as the train made its way beside the canal through what was once the territory of the Six Nations — some of whom, I told Annie, were people of pain who tortured their captives and desired pain to show they could stand it.

After a while she said, "He knows money."

"He knows fighting," I said.

"Do you need that too? Don't you see that men who own things don't fight?"

"I have a friend who owns things. He needs to fight so badly he's in the army."

I told her about Ned, and because it was late and the car was empty and stale — even the drummers had gone, and the red-headed train boy had finally put his wares to rest — I told her I once thought Ned could make things right.

"And now?" said Annie, getting directly to the point, but I didn't want to get to the point, and said I had been seduced by the idea of Ned's money and Ned's plans. It's dangerous talking to pretty women because some of what you say may be true. Only then did I see in Annie's sleepy, unpretending eyes — her hand tightly in my hand — the obvious, unspoken reply: And now you think Saturday . . . ?

"But Ned found himself," I said. "He joined the army. He found a game and offered me a part."

"But you," said Annie, "are part of something else."

"There's more. The woman, Edith. You met her. The krank. Big hands. Handsome woman."

"Rich," said Annie.

"Very rich. Very nice. Or so I thought. I thought she was like me, too. That's the easiest mistake to make. Thinking a person is like us. It's a trick of vanity. I asked her to marry me." I laughed. "She's not stupid. There's somebody else."

"There's always somebody else," said Annie.

We rode in silence. A convoy of barges broke the silver ribbon and we went by a line of dark hulks going east behind a tug. I lit another cigar and Annie opened a window. The biting smell of coal and sharp night air rushed into the car. I watched my smoke pass out into the New York night, over land that once sustained Six Nations.

"I thought I was like King," said Annie. "I thought he would take me places."

"He will," I said.

"He won't."

"He will."

"He won't take anybody."

Our hands separated. I stopped pretending we could be in love. Our privacy was interrupted. I looked up from the blue fleur-de-lis, to the green embossed walls, along the seven dimmed bronze electric lights, to the high small windows and speeding night: the Indian's presence filled the car like a spirit. All summer I was haunted by that perfect swing, the chest like a Roman breastplate, and the calm before his explosions. He was with me in my first-floor flat with its bank books and *Spalding Guides,* in my tiny office, in the cabs that took me to the Gin Palace: only at the ballpark, when he roamed the outfield or dominated the batter's box, was I free of him. Only when he played, was he out of my imagination. I was afraid. I knew I could betray him.

The feeling, as feelings often do when we're tired, drunk, or dreaming, became that unpleasant sense of not being alone. It was something akin to those supernatural states Mr. William James analyzed as religious experience and the more cynical call hysteria. It was like a finger pointed in a dream. Why does one man betray another? It's never just a woman. Was it the only way I could be free of him?

I sat up with a start and said, "We have plans."

"You have plans," Annie said. "He has bets."

"We have money."

"It won't help."

"He loves you."

"He don't."

"He does."

"He left me. Two weeks ago."

I took both her hands to plead his case as eloquently as any phantom could wish, but Annie put her finger on my lips. "No," she said. "Burke raped me."

I was stunned, then furious. The presence in the car dissolved into the superreality of places we hear bad news. The Pullman seemed to expand and contract. My stomach did the same. I held Annie's waist.

She kept her finger firmly on my lips. "Burke did it for crossing them."

"Saturday will kill him."

"I'll tell King I let Burke do it."

I almost lost control thinking of that red pockmarked face, the huge ear, his hot rancid breath . . .

"If King kills Burke," said Annie, "I lose him forever."

"I'll kill Burke."

Annie looked at me tenderly and kissed me hard on the lips. I turned red with embarrassment. Cinders tapping the roof reminded us we got farther from Cleveland by the minute. I was so angry. Why had Saturday left her? I was angry enough at that moment to kill.

"Men like Burke don't live long," said Annie. "Don't you or King waste yourself. Thank you, Harry." She kissed me again which inflamed me enough to repeat the threat.

Annie pulled back. "I'm a whore. I'm not worth it."

"Don't say that," I said.

"You don't know them, Harry. They would have done something to you, but you wasn't at the Palace last night."

"Why did Saturday leave you?"

"There's others." Annie stared at the window.

I looked at her face in the half-light of the green car: the full bottom lip, the many shades of red, white and black that make beauty, hair so dark she could have been Spanish, small white hands, and this somber, much too somber, ability to evaluate what she had to do. Her calm made me afraid.

"Saturday will kill Burke no matter what you say," I said. "He'll do it for pride. There's nothing you can do."

"I don't want him ruined over a whore."

"You're not a whore," I said.

"What do you think I am?"

"A whore sells her soul."

"I sell what I've got. King sells games. You hold his money. You want a ballclub. I want a restaurant. A tavern. Out west. Somewhere they never heard of Annie Gears." She leaned on my shoulder and sobbed. "No one-eared son of bitch is goin' to ruin it either."

"I'll kill Burke."

"Harry," Annie said, looking at the canal which was a silver ribbon behind the shimmering reflection superimposed on the night. "It don't do to talk about killing. I've been raped before. My . . ." Annie stopped. "My father raped me when I was thirteen. It went on till I ran away. I used to think about killin' him but it didn't make me no better. Don't look so strange, Harry. Women become whores for lots of reasons. That's just one of them."

I'd heard of such things but they were as abstract as the ancient Greeks. I had no idea what to say, so I said, "I love you."

I held her but I was trembling.

6

We didn't find him in Maine. He found us.

He found us, or I should say he found Annie because I didn't speak to him on that early morning train ride, where he appeared and left like a ghost. He let us see the place he was born, which is not far from the place I put a stone, and where we met, or at least saw, the woman who raised him. Clara Neptune didn't speak and looked at us as if we weren't there. I don't know why he let us go to Maine, nor do I know why he went himself. Perhaps he wanted us to learn about him. We learned his father, Andrew Saturday, was killed in a fight with a logger who outlived Mr. Saturday by two days, though without benefit of testicles. Louis may have witnessed the fight. The logger, a walking boss from Bangor, was armed with a cap-and-ball pistol. Mr. Saturday had a hunting knife. This was in the year of our Lord, 1875.

I saw the rocky field where Louis King Phillip Saturday learned baseball: where Indian lads and a Catholic priest played with homemade gloves and twine balls, looking at trees over one shoulder and the Penobscot River over the other. Pere Jean died the year before I saw the island, and we met another priest whose cassock was stained with blood and home-made whiskey, who passed his days in the shadow of the tuberculosis which killed his predecessor. Many Indians in those gray huts were sick. I didn't see any drunk Indians but I saw sick Indians. Pere Jean had been an indefatigable little man, who insisted on living with "his Indians," even sleeping in the houses and beds where Indians had died.

The source of my information was Dr. John Cook: "Mr. Bones," the Indians called him. The doctor was an angular Yankee who shook his white head and told me he had been trying to "civilize those damn people for twenty-five years," telling them to keep their houses clean, burn the blankets of the sick, throw away the clothes of the dead, and stay away "from Old Joe Pru's whiskey." Cook didn't follow his own advice on the rainy morning he, Annie, and I went to Indian Island. The doctor was "nursing" a cold with whiskey he'd made himself. "Maine votes dry and drinks wet," he said, holding up a brown bottle with a cork stopper. "Call it self-reliance. After Emerson. Or call it the great spirit. After the Indians." The doctor kept looking at me with gray, strangely intimate, cynical eyes, and invoking those rhetorical silences New Englanders use on strangers, but Cook couldn't stay quiet long enough to induce me to fill the gaps with my business. I said I was doing a piece on Saturday for the *Plain Dealer*.

We went over to Indian Island in a boat rowed by Saturday's cousin Joe Neptune as a late arriving July sun went into the trees on the far bank of the Penobscot River. The doctor coughed, drank, and spat in the river. "You're not a reporter. Reporters don't have women that pretty with them." I said nothing, using the New England weapon against this shrewd native, whose gold rimmed spectacles, the only concession to vanity in the doctor's brown, rumpled appearance, caught the late afternoon light. I thought the doctor regarded life as something he understood but could not change. "You're looking for him," said Cook, running his hands through his stringy white hair. "It doesn't matter. Louis Saturday has been a law unto himself since the day he was born."

We crossed the west fork of the Penobscot as the dying sun made brilliant ripples downstream. Joe Neptune methodically pulled the oars and kept his deeply lined, sunburnt face on the shore. In the other fork of the river, was what the locals called the Indian boom: a whole river of logs going downstream, steered by loggers on rafts wielding pickpoles and hookeroons

— long poles with a menacing iron spike at the end — who directed thousands of logs, belonging to dozens of owners, in an intricate system that keeps track of and delivers twenty miles of floating timber to various mills. Logging was a hard business and working on the river was a hard way to make a living. Saturday's father did it, and a few men of the island, but the doctor said Indians were the exception, not the rule, on logging crews.

I was sure Saturday had been on Indian Island. I could feel it in the silence and the grim indifference of Clara Neptune. The woman was small but stood up straight. She didn't look away when I looked at her. She looked through me. Clara's house was clean and bare. A creased photograph of King standing under a large tree in a Poland Springs baseball uniform was nailed over a rusty stove which dominated the front room of that damp, cold cabin. The doctor said Clara "survived" raising Louis and ministered to two dying sons. A cousin lay in a room we didn't see. Cook paid a quick visit and returned shaking his head. We heard a deep, hoarse cough. I was sure Clara Neptune had seen Saturday. There was something in her silence that reminded me of him — something of the warrior.

The doctor coughed and drank, but didn't spit in Clara Neptune's house. He asked if King had been there and received no answer. I'm sure he hadn't expected one. Clara didn't look at Annie or me and went to the sick man in the back room. None of us wanted to stay in that damp cabin with its hacking, dying man and powerfully sullen woman. "Louis grew up in that room," said the doctor, standing in a half-open door. "Pere Jean got sick there. He stayed when Wil Neptune got sick."

We stood outside by fir trees which came right up to the cabin. In her green velvet suit and green hat, Annie looked like a goddess of the forest as the late sun made her dress a deeper green. Annie leaned over so the doctor couldn't hear and said, "King is here. I know it." There were tears in her eyes.

"Why did he come?" I said, bringing my face close to her. "Did he bring her money?"

"He would have sent you with money. He trusts you."

I don't think he did, but didn't contradict her.

The sun didn't break through the lead gray Maine sky until it was almost down, but then the island and two-forked Penobscot were bathed in the clear hard light of what the day could have been. Annie and I stood by the fir trees, murmuring like man and wife. She dried her eyes. Cook joined us and gruffly said, "He's not married. Not to anyone here." Annie didn't look at him and the doctor, perhaps embarrassed at having spoken so frankly, began to explain the Indian boom.

We could see both forks of the river. Logs and irregular patches of open water broke the silver of the late afternoon river. We saw rafts, more men with long poles, even a checker clinging to a trapeze-line suspended between island and shore. Cook earnestly explained the jargon of boom logging, pointing and spitting and trying to get Annie to look at him.

"Louis didn't want to log," said the doctor. "It's tough work. Maybe ball playing is too, but folks here don't think so. No sport would be hard for Louie. God, he could run all day. Didn't get tired. Used to run on this river when it froze over. Never wore shoes."

Joe Neptune rowed us back through bright ripples and long shadows as the last light glinted off the doctor's spectacles. We took Dr. Cook's trap to town, passing the Jordan Lumber Company and the Old Town Canoe factory. Annie said she didn't notice any Indians, and Cook said they weren't allowed in town after sundown. For some reason that infuriated me. Annie didn't like it either and we decided to leave that night. The doctor insisted on eating with us at the hotel but neither of us listened to his stories. He repeated a "stretcher" we'd heard on the train that "young Louis" had once thrown a ball from Oak Hill on Indian Island which hit the smoke stack of the Jordan Lumber Mill — the places in question are about two thousand feet apart — and the doctor became morose and drank gin. I think he wanted us to like him, and felt alone in a town where "self-reliance" wasn't supposed to come in bottles and men didn't stagger away from dinner at the MicMac Hotel.

I ignored the doctor, ate venison, and thought about Saturday running shoeless on the frozen Penobscot. I tried to think about anything rather than Annie, her father, and the men who locked doors behind her. The doctor watched her, furious I think that we might spend the night together in this very town. Annie still played at being domestic but her vibrant face was pale. Dr. Cook became less deferential and looked at her with a cynical, lecherous stare, oblivious to my irritation. Our dining companions, bearded Yankees and relaxed guests, looked contemptuously at the doctor.

All I could think of was Annie and her father, that vile man who took her into a locked room so she would follow men into locked rooms forever. I wondered if King knew. He might be one man who could know and not care: I never knew what Saturday cared about — I'm not sure he even cared about money — but he may have known hate well enough to forgive hatred. To me, in a provincial hotel dining room, with its moosehead, English hunting prints, gratuitous antlers, and leering, pathetic doctor, lost in jealousy and the limited spectacle of making a fool of himself, Annie was tragic. I kept thinking of that word, as if a word could obliterate and heal — as if that word, with its promise of doom and release, could let me stop seeing a drunken man pulling a girl, a beautiful child, by the arm, or hair, or dress . . . so I kept repeating the word and thought no more of betrayal.

Dr. Cook tapped his glass with his fork, as if he were the after-dinner speaker, and informed the room he had just learned that "A Hot Time in the Old Town Tonight," referred to "ribaldry in a canoe." Most of the diners had apparently heard this before and paid little attention, though a corpulent gentleman in a white jacket with a gravy stain on his cravat, tittered. "Bet you didn't know that?" said the doctor, and ordered another gin. He leaned forward so his chin almost touched the front of Annie's dress. "Hot time. Old Town. This hotel can be peculiar about couples."

"We're taking the late train to Boston," said Annie.

"No harm, no harm," he said. "Let her go, Harrison. Stay. I'll tell you all about Louie Saturday."

On the train Annie told me I was the only person she had ever told her "secret." We were in a Pullman Vestibuled Sleeper — one of those well advertised fine looking things that are as comfortable as a park bench when one tries to sleep. The car looked fit for the millionaires who travel to Seal and Bar Harbor, and was only mildly overheated by the steam system that replaced those awful cast iron stoves the railroads operate every day of the year. The ceiling sported a double row of mirrors so passengers could see each other at different angles, and filled the car with so much light, there was no question of sleeping until the shiny row of electric lights dimmed. Annie was tired which made her eyes rounder and robbed her face of its ruddy luster. She leaned against me and tried to sleep. I put my arm chastely around her. I wanted to protect her from what she could not be protected from: locked rooms, Burke, the lean past . . .

It never occurred to me Annie might be lying. It hadn't occurred to me such things happened, so I hadn't imagined they could be lied about. In less than a week, Annie said she made it up. I don't think she did, but I see now how much of the Indian's story, and mine, revolves around lying. I have always thought I could tell when a man is lying, but I know to a certainty, I can not tell when a woman is.

I think Annie lied about lying. Lying or not, on the trip to Boston, there were no more glimpses of my soul, no passionate hand holding, no pretending she loved me, no spirit barring and sealing paradise. I was tame.

We remained sitting. Annie didn't want to be alone and I wouldn't leave her. We slept fitfully. Sometimes Annie wept. What else could she do, caught between Saturday, Burke, Saturday's others, and her father? I was full of anger: at Burke, at the unspeakable father, at myself for knowing I wouldn't do anything to Burke, at Ned who could have Edith, at Saturday for leaving Annie. I cursed and tried to sleep — angry at the world and angrier still because I knew I'd never fight, only cheat. Trees hurled by the soot-streaked windows and danced in the phantom night silver of the mirrors.

Toward dawn, the light a blank hint over the trees, the train still in Maine, land of timber, summering millionaires, poor farmers, and violent lumberjacks, I woke half-dreaming, not sure I wasn't imagining Annie was gone, then realized she was, tried to sleep to change the dream, woke with the effort, rubbed my back, touched the pillow, and realized Saturday was there. I closed my eyes. This was no guilty premonition. The Indian was there. Beyond two sleeping couples and a snoring drummer, Annie and Saturday were whispering in the last seat. He was almost invisible in the dark but something, perhaps a gold toothpick, caught the tiniest bit of light.

I was overwhelmed by the sense this had happened before. Sometimes this feeling comes with sweet foretaste, sometimes fear. I was afraid and pretended to sleep. Saturday had followed us. I heard the words "Love" and "No." Annie cried and kissed him and touched his face. Was she telling him about Burke? Saturday comforted her. She wasn't pleading, King wasn't threatening. They seemed to understand each other perfectly. Saturday talked, Annie cried, they kissed. As the sun crept into the trees, I realized I'd seen this in Hooper. Saturday was planning. He was lying. I have no idea what he said, but I'm sure he was lying. I waited, but when Saturday got up — black suit and black hat now distinct in the early light, he opened the rear door, and went over a grilled railing into the dawn.

Annie left for Cleveland as soon as we got to Boston. "He'll play on the Fourth of July. It's almost over." She kissed me on the cheek.

I was her little brother again.

7

Monday, July 4, 1898, was hot in Boston. The South End Grounds had been a second home to me during the years when I, like Henry Adams, did my best to get educated at Harvard. I knew the neighborhood, called the Village, with its flapping laundry and Irish kranks. I lifted my share of glasses at Nuff Said McGreevy's saloon where the proprietor settled disputes with his stentorian voice and encyclopedic baseball knowledge. McGreevy was the leader of the Royal Rooters, those loud, devoted kranks, who, some eight hundred strong, march on the field, blow horns, sing, razz opponents, and create as much mayhem in the stands as the Orioles did on the field. I always enjoyed deserting the mannerly bastion of Harvard, where an Irishman was more apt to be seen with a broom than a bat, to visit the Village and its raucous Royalty. If the Brahmins found the South End Grounds and neighborhood a "filthy cabbage fen," as one of my classmates put it, let them stay on Beacon Hill and puzzle over the novels of Mr. Henry James. I never found the Irish dirtier than any other people without money. There was so little food in Ireland in the nineteenth century, its sons and daughters perhaps can be forgiven for not knowing how to cook.

The old South End Grounds had a twin-spired grandstand that suggested the Taj Mahal. The '94 fire, which Ned and I saw from the bleachers before exiting through an impromptu hole the faithful drove through a rear wall, ruined the place. The Triumvirs, as the Boston ownership were called — no classical overstatement ever embarrassed a parvenu — did not have sufficient insurance to completely rebuild, so the finest club of the decade, the finest club I've seen, played at the Congress Street Grounds where the Players League Reds played, then returned to a modestly rebuilt South End Grounds. The new Grounds didn't have the twin spires which so grandly suggested a connection between the mud of the ball field and other worlds, but New Englanders prefer transcendence without statuary.

The Beaneaters were the best. Even a Cleveland krank and tolerated Midwesterner could like that club. Boston played the game the way it ought to be played. I've never thought baseball teaches anything about life, except the strong usually beat the weak, but if there were a club which met Kant's dictum that personal actions should be judged as universal principles of conduct, that club was the Beaneaters.

With Boston there was no belt grabbing, no spitting in your face, nor fisticuffs when a simple tag would suffice. That club played baseball and beat you at baseball. They played the game in a state closely resembling what kranks dream it to be. What an infield! Fred Tenney of Brown University was the finest fielding first baseman I ever saw. Bobby Lowe bettered all but Bid McPhee at second and once hit four home runs in a single game at the Congress Street Grounds. A ridiculous feat, I admit, because a home run simplifies the game to a point where it could be a dog fight, but an interesting accomplishment as it set the boundaries of what can be done. I thought Lowe's homers were a fluke, but Ed Delahanty hit four in a game in '96, so it may happen again, though I can't see the public ever getting excited about home runs. At shortstop, Germany Long, who never stopped talking — to umpires, opposing players, himself, his mates, God; the man was a wonder of chatter — could get to more balls than any shortstop I ever saw. What the "Flying Dutchman" did after he corralled impossible skimmers, could also stagger the imagination. At third, Jimmy Collins was the best who ever played that position. Collins was as accomplished with his glove as John McGraw was with his fists. This was a great team.

I wish I could say I stood outside the red door of the visiting lockerroom thinking of the great match up between Cy Young and Kid Nichols, or the two clubs' contrasting styles of play, but I was thinking if it weren't for Annie, I wouldn't go back to Cleveland. The door swung open and Patsy Tebeau, in uniform and digging splinters out of the floor with his cleats, led the team out. He saw me and said, "I'm lettin' him play. You tell that to Robison." The players crowded out and dug a forest of splinters as they went down the runway and through two doors to the hot, bright field.

King Saturday and Frank Ember came last. Saturday was in uniform and had his arm around Frank. He stopped and Frank kept walking. "Take care of Annie, little brother." I didn't know this was the last time I would see him in a big league uniform, but, had someone told me, I wouldn't have been surprised. We were alone for less than a minute before some reporters, a trainer, and a small mob came out. "How much do we have on Boston?" he said. "Five hundred and fifty-five," I said. I was always exact about money with him. "If we win?" His eyes were big in the dark. "A hundred," I said. "Fifty more if you get two hits. Another fifty if you steal two bases. I've got ten at five-to-one you hit a home run, but we have to win."

"When I get back to Cleveland," he said as the doors to the field opened and a burst of light lit him up like a gigantic photograph, "we'll buy the Gin Palace. Annie will own part of it."

"What about Burke?" I couldn't bring myself to say he'd hurt Annie but I had to mention him.

"I'll handle Burke," said Saturday.

I wanted to ask how but the reporters, trainer, and mob swarmed out of the lockerroom accompanied by the odor of carbolic acid and sweat, I had time for one question — his hands were on my shoulders — and I could have asked if he had a deal with McBuck, or why he left Annie, or who he loved, but I was afraid he'd lie, and I'd know it, so as a gaggle of temporarily blinded Boston reporters led by Tim Murnane bumped down the ramp, followed by the vaguely wounded smell of a mid-season ballclub dressing room, I said, "Did you get any sleep last night?"

Saturday gave me one of those smiles that for a moment unified his angular, contradictory face, and disappeared into the Fourth of July.

I stood near the dugout and talked to Frank Ember while bands, color guards, politicians, and the Royal Rooters marched, drummed, tooted, and sang the "Battle Hymn of the Republic." Rockets burst over the park. Firecrackers rattled outside as if we were under attack. In Cleveland this would be only vulgar; here the self-proud mixture of immigrants, college men, and Yankees seemed ready to explode. The day was sweltering and a majorette in a cavalry uniform fainted. Several ladies in the crowd, not to be outdone and demonstrating that hysteria could be as contagious on this bright afternoon as it once was in Salem Village, swooned into the arms of nearby gentlemen. I sat near the dugout with Frank. The club, he said, was divided about Saturday. "The men don't know whether he's helpin' or hurtin'. Patsy's playin' him 'cause of the owners. The men don't trust him. Word is you and him have a thousand on Boston." I said this wasn't true. Frank didn't look at me. "Harry, don't sit by the dugout. You're no more popular 'n he is, and you ain't half as big."

A string of firecrackers went off in the bleachers and rockets rose behind the stands where Sullivan's Tower once stood. An Irishman had built a tower beyond right field and charged only a quarter to view a game from it. For a while the club and Mr. Sullivan competed to see who could build higher, but the tower had not survived the fire. Salvos of rockets whistled over the grandstand and burst over the bleachers. A fireworks demonstration worthy of a country at war was planned that evening from two barges anchored in the Charles River.

The color guards, Civil War veterans, and cavalry girls left the field, and knowledgeable kranks, of which Boston has many, concentrated on the pitchers warming up by each dugout. The last group to parade around the Grounds was the Royal Rooters, led by Nuff Said himself, that king of kranks, his hundreds, and their trumpets and bass drum. The heat didn't distract those happy, portly, red-faced kranks. They sang, sweated, and performed the Boston ritual of the most loyal.

Kid Nichols threw near first base. I watched his compact, muscular motion and tried not to think about going back to

Cleveland. Manager Tebeau was playing Saturday in left and batting him first. Everyone on the club knew we'd bet on Boston. If the Spiders lost, I was going to have to stay away from the club. I watched Nichols. I wanted to be distracted.

Kid Nichols was smaller than Cy Young. It was said he had only one pitch, his hard, hard fast one, but he actually had many. They were just all straight. Nichols threw fast pitches at different speeds. He was a master at dropping the pace. Kid disdained the curve, and since he won over thirty games for seven straight years before foul balls counted as strikes, who was to say he needed one? Bench jockeys wanted to know if Nichols could throw a curve and hoped he would because it might be easier to hit than his fast pitch. In Cleveland we said Cy Young threw harder, but I wouldn't want to swear to it. Cy had better control and threw with a fluid motion that may let him pitch forever. Kid Nichols bent more at the knee, pushed off harder, and that fast pitch came out of an explosion of shoulder and wrist.

I had a club pass which meant I could sit in an empty seat or stand where I liked. There were no empty seats so I stood shoulder to shoulder with Irishmen who complained about the heat and the "nastiness" of the Cleveland club. We were behind the seats behind home plate. If no one stood up or moved, we had a tolerable coign of vantage. The fellow next to me said, "Damned heat. This day belongs to the divil." I wiped my brow and the back of my neck. The day was as hot as any I could remember, and as far as I was concerned, my life had already gone to the "divil." I stood with a beery, patriotic crowd of derby clad Irishman perspiring into their dark suits and howling for Cleveland's skin, and decided my life was out of my control. Most of our lives are out of our control, but we don't notice or care. We live in the security of our illusions. My favorite is that intelligence affects life.

King Saturday was leading off. If Patsy had to play him, he was going to showcase him. If Saturday was going to sell the Spiders out, Tebeau was going to let him do it on the Fourth of July in front of five thousand descendants of the Puritans and sons of the old sod. Saturday had faced Nichols in May and been hitless in four at-bats. He hit the ball solidly twice but was put out. The only pitcher King was utterly baffled by was the red-headed Cincinnati kraut, Ted Breitenstein, whose curves got slower as the game wore on. There wouldn't be any curves today but no Cleveland batter was likely to see two pitches at the same speed.

Saturday walked to the plate in a spotless dark Cleveland uniform. The stands erupted with cheers and warwhoops. "Where've you been?" "Get the cavalry!" "How was the bender, Chief?" A fellow in a white suit, sitting in a crowd of seersucker and skimmer hats with crimson bands, yelled, "Curveballs aren't the only benders that keep the red man down!" This didn't go unanswered by those standing in dark suits and derbies. A stocky fellow, who later introduced himself as "Michael from Galway," rose to his full height, and said in a voice that didn't have to strain to be heard, "Lads, there's the living proof drinkin' don't hurt ye. That Indian's as fit as anyone on the field." Saturday did look strong as he got in the batter's box. He was bigger than sour Marty Bergen, the Boston catcher who two years later would murder his family with an ax and take his own life with a razor. Nichols wound up, and out of that compact delivery came a fast pitch at the hands which Saturday took for a strike. "Try swinging," said someone in the Cleveland dugout.

I was sure we were going to lose but couldn't stifle the quiver in the gut one gets when a great hitter faces a great pitcher. Nichols sent a fast pitch high and outside. The umpire, a little man who exaggerated his smallness by crouching, called it a strike. Several complaints came from our dugout but not with the vituperation one expected from Patsy and his men. I expected a high and inside pitch. Kid Nichols hadn't won thirty games seven times giving left-handed hitters pitches they could smash to right field. I took a deep breath. I didn't want to see King strike out without swinging. I could justify cheating the Robisons and Al Spalding and the gang that killed the Players League, but to see my friend, and the greatest talent I or John McGraw or Frank Ember ever saw, take three pitches while a hostile crowd howled and scoffed, would be misery.

Nichols wound up with that tight, muscular delivery, the right arm fired over the top, the ball burst toward home plate, and his right hand came down as if he would bury it in the ground. The pitch was high but clearly in the area where it could be called a strike, depending on the umpire's disposition and pitcher's reputation for accuracy. This pitch was slightly slower than the last. Nichols knew what he was doing but Saturday did too. The Indian raised his wrists, started, stopped and then with an almost circular motion clubbed the pitch on two vicious hops past Nichols. Germany Long raced toward second and got the ball in his glove. The Dutchman could almost do the impossible. He got the skimmer but, perhaps taking his nickname too literally, threw and left his feet at the same time. The throw whistled by first baseman Tenney. Saturday went to second.

The Irishmen around me were delighted. Several bottles glistened in the sun. One made its way to my hand. They decided to adopt the Indian for the afternoon. "May ye live forever!" "Don't stop drinkin', lad!" Saturday couldn't have heard them, but he looked toward our part of the grandstand.

The mark of a pitcher is how he performs when men get to second and third. Nichols looked quickly at Saturday and studied Cupid Childs. Great pitchers have great confidence, and I think a Cy Young or Kid Nichols almost likes to see an inning start with a man on second to show their stuff. Nichols focused on Childs and delivered a high, fast pitch. Childs didn't move. The pitch was quick but when catcher Bergen leapt up with strike-one in his hand, Saturday was on third. The theft was somewhere between foolhardy and superb. There was no need to steal on the first pitch but Nichols had stared at Childs a second too long. Bergen was so angry — he threw his mask on the ground and stomped and cursed — that I thought Saturday might try to steal home. Of course, the Indian could get himself tagged out and appear to play straight while being crooked. There would be no way to tell, and the thought made me uneasy.

Nichols struck out Childs on two wickedly fast pitches and Saturday stayed close to third. Kid gave Jess Burkett two high pitches and Crab topped the second, which rolled like a bunt toward third. Jimmy Collins could only get Burkett at first while Saturday scored.

The game stayed 1-0 until the sixth when King Saturday lifted a fly into the overflow crowd in right. It wasn't well hit and glided over the rope as Chick Stahl, who so recently and mysteriously took his life, watched helplessly and the crowd moaned. Nichols muttered to himself as the Indian circled the bases. I still thought Saturday might try to lose the game, but by the seventh it would be difficult. Nichols and Young hadn't wilted in the heat, and King was the only hitter who hadn't wilted in the pitching. Cy was at his best. A Beaneater didn't get to a full count until the eighth, and through eight they had only two singles. It looked like Saturday was playing straight, as Annie said he would.

In the middle of the seventh, Michael and I had gone out to left field. If something were going to happen, it was going to be in the outfield, and I was tired of the view behind home plate. We made our way through the sweaty crowd. The Royal Rooters sang a sad song and swayed side to side with the music. Many kranks had taken off their coats which made the area beyond the outfield a sea of white shirts, so batting was even more difficult. I may have had a feeling Saturday was looking at somebody I couldn't see, I'm not sure. We climbed over the left field wall, and lubricated with whiskey and sweat, pushed into the crowd on the field, and I saw a lady in vermillion wearing a great hat that made me think of a Spanish galleon. In one complete and devastating instant, I knew.

There are only one or two moments like this in a lifetime. The rush of omniscience is like seeing the face of God. You turn to stone. You cannot see. You cannot think. Your stomach drops and your legs feel like lead. You could not pick up a ticket stub. Then numbness replaces knowing.

Edith was watching the game. Or should I say she watched Saturday? She never took her eyes off him. There it was. Edith was the "others." Annie must have known but hadn't told me. It wasn't Ned. It had never been Ned. Ned had nothing to do with it.

How could I not have known? It was so clear. Edith said she was "free." Edith talked of "loneliness." Edith wanted the "present," and Annie said there was someone else. I stared at the back of Saturday's uniform which was stained with sweat. He took off his cap and his black hair glistened in the July sun. Hadn't Edith told me he would play "straight?" Hadn't he followed us in that automobile? I had ignored it all.

For the first time in weeks I didn't care about gamblers or money. I had lost everything. What would Ned say? Would he laugh? Would he say, "Didn't you see what he did to me?" Or, "I don't know much about people, but I know who not to trust."? Or maybe he wouldn't say anything. Maybe Ned and I wouldn't talk about something like this. I always carry on conversations with absent friends. It's a substitute for thinking. I drank whiskey and looked at the broad back and thick legs of King Saturday. I wasn't going to get Edith. I wasn't going to get a club. Saturday wasn't my friend. Ned wasn't my friend. And, if I didn't play my cards right, I could get killed.

I squinted into the sun watching the lady in vermillion. How could Edith think anything could work out with the magnificent, erratic man in left? The answer was Edith didn't care. She was free . . . There was a certain beauty to it. What if . . . ? I couldn't name it. This wasn't mysterious and tragic. Saturday took a woman I loved.

"You're red," said Michael. "Take this." He gave me the bottle. I didn't watch the game. I watched a lady, and a broad, sweaty back.

You don't know how much you admire someone until you are jealous of him. I stood in that July heat and wondered how I would get through the next minute, the next hour, the next night. Jealousy is solitude. Only two people in the world can break that solitude and they have other arrangements. I hoped the Indian would throw the game. I hoped he was cheating everyone. Sometime later in that dizzy, red afternoon Michael said, "Last call for Boston." I didn't care. I remember grinding a cigar stub into the ground with my right foot and squeezing my watch so hard, I couldn't believe it didn't break. Breaking my watch would have been absurdly literal. Time stops for the jealous man, but that doesn't mean he need break his watch. Jealous time goes back: always back, only back.

Even sweating on the sunbaked turf of the South End Grounds, I had to admit Edith had done nothing dishonorable. She had broken with me. She had written a letter. She hadn't mentioned Saturday, sparing our friendship and a scene. Edith had done nothing wrong. She was a lady.

As the years pass — and despite jealous men, they pass — I've heard many a krank say that Fourth of July Boston-Cleveland game was the greatest he ever witnessed, but I had no interest, except to see if Saturday threw the game.

I stared at the Cleveland left fielder as hard as anyone, save one, in that whole hot park. King's brown face looked puffy and heavy. He bent over, putting weight on his knees rather than the balls of his feet. I doubt Saturday had slept the night before. Billy Hamilton led off the Boston ninth and Cy Young wiped his brow, delivered two balls, shook off a sign, and delivered two more. This was a mistake. Sliding Billy ran the bases better than any man I've seen. Hamilton did what the game is about. He scored runs. In '94, when pitchers hadn't adjusted to the new mound distance (ten feet had been added), Billy scored 196 runs. In my opinion, this is the great record, not Hugh Duffy's .438.

Duffy was next. The man who scored the most runs in a season was followed by the man who hit for the highest average. Boston, as I said, was the best. Hamilton was a superb base stealer. He took a big lead and timed his jump like a cat. Billy wasn't as fast as '91 when he swiped 115 bases, but the instinct was there.

Young stood on the mound squeezing the ball with his right hand. Cy was trying to throw Hamilton's timing off by changing the rhythm of his delivery. The sunblind crowd came alive, hooting and taunting and demanding to know what the great Cy Young was afraid of. I doubt Cy was afraid but he was facing the best lineup in baseball. Hamilton didn't run on the first pitch, but took off on the next, as Duffy hit a skimmer to McKean at short. Against another club, we might have had a chance at that rare and beautiful thing, the double play, but Boston was hitting and running. Hamilton left with the pitch knowing Hugh Duffy would swing. Frank Selee and the Beaneaters invented that play. Other clubs let a man steal before hitting, but Boston combined the two strategies to make infielders leave their positions while ground balls skip through newly opened holes. Instead of going for a double play, McKean had to throw to first. Hamilton was on second with one out. Boston trailed by two.

Young had pitched superbly all afternoon, but pitching is a Puritan activity. One slip and hell beckons. Collins was up. Jimmy was having a good year though he would never be more respected at bat than in the field. After taking a strike and a ball, he tried to fool our third baseman Wallace with a bunt. Collins may have thought Wallace was too deep — no one played bunts better than Jimmy, so he was sensitive to how other men played them — or maybe manager Selee called it, but with the Beaneaters down two, the tactic made little sense except as a surprise. Wallace came in quickly, got the bunt with his bare hand, and threw Collins out. Billy Hamilton was more surprised than Wallace and stayed at second.

I was worried with two outs. Cy Young could end it without the Indian being tested. The Royal Rooters beat their drums, blew their trumpets, and howled. Like Napoleon's Old Guard, they wouldn't recognize defeat. I didn't want the game to end. I wanted Saturday to prove himself. A jealous man doesn't accept logic. The Indian had given Cleveland two runs, but like Othello, I had to see and keep seeing.

I was ready to panic — when the game ended, I would be totally alone — but Young surrendered an opposite-field hit to Fred Tenney. Saturday had moved in and Hamilton held at third, not risking a game-ending play at the plate. Bobby Lowe was up with men at first and third. Lowe was right-handed, and though not known for power, could be dangerous with a game on the line. Saturday moved back, and then back again — a strange move against a hitter more likely to slash a base hit than power one into the crowd, but the Indian played hunches. He moved in for Tenney and out for Lowe. Saturday was breathing hard and his entire back was wet.

"Liquor makes a man sweat," said Michael, "but it don't bother that fellow."

Patsy Tebeau trotted to the mound while spectators and players wiped their faces. The Royal Rooters kept beating, blowing, and calling Cy Young a "coward." Cy listened to Patsy, and, without paying heed to either runner, threw two excellent fast pitches to Lowe. Young might be tired but was going to finish at full strength. He challenged Lowe. Maybe Cy wanted to get out of the heat or maybe he couldn't resist the taunts of the Rooters. I thought he was setting up Lowe to drop the pace, but Cy came with another fast one. I'm sure he didn't intend it to be belt-high and over the plate.

The crack of ball off bat must have reached Harvard College. Lowe told the *Globe* he hit it "perfect." Anyone who's played knows what he meant. You hit a ball so squarely, you barely feel the contact. It's a feeling of absolute physical mastery. Bobby said he hit this one better than all but one of his homers in that game in '94. The problem, he said, was he hit it "too level."

The ball came at us on a line. Even King Saturday, with his magnificent speed, would have had no play if he hadn't moved back. The Indian was moving as Lowe swung — what kranks think is anticipation is really a fielder moving with the pitch before the ball is hit — Saturday wasn't off with the crack of the bat — he was off with the pitch. King hadn't done that all afternoon. He hadn't gauged and anticipated as he had earlier in the season. He hadn't played his position properly.

The ball came at us. Saturday came at us. I saw the muscles in his neck flare, his eyes were black bullets. With two steps he was at full speed. Two more and he left the ground like a man who isn't coming down. Saturday went over the rope. The ball went over the rope. Indian and ball flew over the crowd. Indian and ball flew over the world. Indian and ball kept going up — and then Saturday plucked the ball out of the air with his bare hand! He caught the ball in his bare hand! The kranks leapt like the Bacchae reaching for their god, Saturday disappeared beneath elbows, white shirts and straw hats. They got his glove and hat but didn't get the ball. King Saturday may not have been the greatest outfielder, and that may not have been the greatest catch, but no man ever had stronger hands.

8

Saturday had a system for receiving and paying. On my lunch hour the day after a game or road trip, gamblers met me at one of three banks. One, and only one man, went in with me. He either gave me money, which I deposited, or I withdrew money and gave it to him. I never carried more than cab fare to and from these meetings. Two days after the Fourth, or "the catch," as it was known in Cleveland, I met three men at three banks, and settled. Jake McBuck was his smooth usual poker-faced self. He paid me a hundred and fifty dollars and walked out of the bank without a word. McBuck had taken a beating and I was scared of him. The other gentlemen I paid, and felt better. I decided I wouldn't take another bet. I didn't owe Saturday anything.

The Indian didn't come back with the club. This didn't surprise me, but if he had, that wouldn't have surprised me either. What he was doing now, I assumed, he did for Edith. Frank Robison called me in, five minutes after eight o'clock, my first morning back. Mr. Robison was excited by the "catch." His small eyes followed me quickly. He was so solicitous, I thought he was going to fire me.

"Henry, the people of this city have never loved a player like they love that man. I know he has problems. Drinking?

Ballplayers drink. Women? who doesn't have problems with them? Money. I have problems with money." Robison opened a huge green ledger, wrote a check, folded it carefully, and gave it to me. "See he gets this and keeps his mouth shut. Everyone on the club will want a raise if word gets out." The check was for twenty-five hundred dollars.

A large grainy photograph of Saturday in a Spiders uniform now flanked the clock, along with the 1895 Spiders. The Indian wasn't smiling, and it was hard not to think what attracted Frank Robison to the portrait was the hard look of the ballplayer. It was as if Robison were saying, here's my real face, which I found interesting since Saturday had repeatedly sold out the club, and Robison had to know it, but that may have been part of the message.

"When he comes back, we'll keep a closer eye on him. If he stays, there'll be some Spider stock for you."

This worried me. I was sure Frank Robison couldn't be offering anything of value, and figured he wanted Saturday back because he was going to sell the club. I wasn't far wrong, as anyone familiar with the fate of the Cleveland National League baseball club knows. He was offering me stock in what was soon to be a corpse.

"Go home and get some rest, Henry. Then find him."

I went home and got drunk.

I wanted to find King Saturday. I had no idea what I would say, but I wanted to find him. The jealous man lives in two unreal times: the past, which he never stops recreating in extraordinary detail; and a future which will never happen. The past is unbearable. The jealous man can not inflict pain equal to his pain. The woman and friend have killed part of him. He can not love her the same way. He will not love another woman the same way. He will not trust friends.

The jealous man is at the center of a wheel. He is still and images of lover and friend never stop passing before his eyes. The past may not have been what he thinks, the future will not be what he imagines, but the wheel will not stop. The heart of the jealous man does not move, so he moves. He walks, drinks, finds listeners, finds friends, finds another woman.

214

I woke in the twilight as teamsters were driving their last loads through the settling dust in Spring Street. The bleary nausea of a day's drinking was a relief after the clarity of imagined embraces. Jealousy has its metaphor in that new, and I believe insidious toy, the cinema. A jealous man can stop his mind no more than a patron in a cinema can stop the show: at the theater one can shout, make a spectacle of himself, and be escorted out, but the spectator can affect the actors. Where are the gendarmes to eject one from the theater of his mind?

I hadn't been to the Gin Palace in weeks but I wanted to find Annie. I didn't care what happened to me, or so I told myself as the cab let me out in front of the chipped white pillars. I was Saturday's enemy, and the Palace was full of his enemies.

The place seemed big and gloomy. I wore a brown coat and hat and tried not to look at myself in the mirrors behind the bar. The sports liked to tip their hats and salute themselves, as if walking by bar, mirror, and truculent bartenders were to pace the world.

The Palace was a place to strut, if you dared, but I no longer dared. I went through pools of light under those green lamps, and in and out of darkness made deeper by mirrors, but saw only an unshaven man who looked like he'd given his youth away.

Frank Ember, Cupid Childs, and Jimmy McAleer were at the bar. Frank looked at his hands as he spoke. Childs and McAleer watched themselves in the mirror and eyed newcomers. None of them looked at me. I took a booth by the dance floor and sat with my back to a wall under a grimy picture of Monte Ward and a bat once wielded by King Kelly. I started when Amos slid out of the dark and sat across a table scarred with the marks of men so lonely or bored they cut their names in a table. I'd never seen Amos anywhere but at the piano, unless it was very late. He shook his head. "Bad night, Harry."

"Why?"

"Just a feelin'."

"Where's Annie?"

"She layin' low. Annie be here tonight." Amos kept his stubby hands and big rings under the table. He lowered his head and didn't show his luminescent teeth. Monte Ward's handsome face seemed to look disapprovingly at this Cleveland night. An upstairs door opened and a burst of yellow light

215

momentarily lit a faded Players League eagle. Sports and gamblers drifted in, lifted patent leather over the brass rail, and talked loudly about King Saturday's catch.

"He say take this," and I felt the butt of a pistol in my hand. "Iss loaded but de hammer's on a empty chamber. Watch yo'self."

I wanted to know where Saturday was but Amos slid off the bench and was gone. I looked at the gun. It had a smooth, white handle. I had never held a pistol before. The thing was light and finely balanced. The trigger would be easy to pull. I held the gun for a long time under the table and then looked at it again. A brass plate on the butt bore the inscription, "Be just."

The gift had a quality of fatal understanding. For two days and nights I had hated King Saturday, and he gave me a gun. Was this a challenge, or was he saying he couldn't protect me?

Two men at the bar in red-checkered coats and white spats talked about the Indian buying the Palace. The lankier one, who looked like Connie Mack, the old Pittsburgh catcher, wasn't sure who owned it. The other said Jake McBuck. J.D. Donlan, the bartender, said, "King Saturday's buyin' the place."

I didn't think Saturday wanted the Palace and wondered why he wanted people to think he did. He wanted Edith. As Annie once said, King wanted the impossible.

The crowd kept growing. The gloom of the big place with its balcony and doors, where the women took men or found privacy in drink or morphine, took on the feel of a theater. Amos played faster. Two couples were dancing. A door opened on the upper floor and the ancient chandelier sparkled. The Palace was a stage again.

Edith loves him, I told myself, and held the pistol under the table. She loves him, I kept repeating. She loves him. I stared at Pete Browning's bat and a black ball split along its seams that had been used by the Forest Cities, one of Cleveland's first professional clubs. My life had been so simple, I told myself. I had liked three people. Two were friends and to one I proposed marriage. When they met, hell followed.

I nursed a whiskey and wanted to talk to Frank about Mike Kelly and Monte Ward. I wanted drunk talk about ballplayers we used to love and drunker talk about women we used to love, but Frank still didn't look at me. Childs and McAleer looked over angrily. They thought I was getting rich selling them out. I could have told them Saturday sold everybody out — me worst of all — but what could that matter to them? I was on the Indian's side. I had made my choice.

Another door opened and the chandelier sparkled. More couples danced. Two black women — "from New Orleans," J.D. said. "Burke runs 'em." — danced with each other. They wore black and red striped gowns that fit tightly and erupted in ruffles at the wrists and hem; so as the ladies flew over the floor, they seemed to ride a red wave. The Creole ladies were thinner and more athletic than our Cleveland women. The taller and darker had a double strand of pearls that went to the floor when she bowed or threw her head back. Both women wore a dozen silver bracelets and shook them over their heads like musical instruments. The women strutted only for each other. They embraced, spun, and touched with insolent pride, as if, like dervishes, they were invulnerable while moving. Their hot eyes looked only at each other. A gent with a derby and white spats cut in but couldn't follow either lady and looked like a fool. The women danced with a teasing grace that flaunted membership in an erotic society most of the sports didn't know existed. Men at the bar stared. Several spat. The gent who looked like Connie Mack said, "Look at those bitches."

9

When the crowd got mean enough to spit at the Creole women, J.D. Donlan auctioned them off. He hit the bar with the butt of a .38 and shouted, "Who wants 'em? Who's man enough? Let's hear it!" Money was reluctantly pulled out of checkered coats, hatbands and boots. Men came down the bar and out of closed rooms. They spat in the sawdust and wiped flushed faces with pink handkerchiefs. Most of them wanted to watch, not play. The sports were intimidated. None of the ballplayers wanted to bid for those hard eyes and lean legs. Amos looked up from the piano and ripped into a lurid "Dixie." The fellow who looked like Connie Mack said, "They ain't worth spit," but his voice broke and he looked at the floor.

Judge Ryan, a hack with a soft belly from the west side, put a twenty dollar bill on the bar and said, "I want both."

"Then pay for both." A tall gentleman in a black suit put a fifty on the bar. "Double you," said the judge, and put down a hundred. Sports and regulars gawked at the bills. I stared at the gent and realized he was the man King Saturday visited at the Standard offices the day he met Edith. The judge raised the Rockefeller man twenty, and the bidding got spirited. The men evidently disliked each other, and the sports enjoyed seeing pillars of the community scrap like pimps over women. Judge

Ryan had a pudgy unevenly shaved face with soft brown eyes, and seemed to want everyone to know he could handle himself. The Standard man had a smooth handsome face but hard gray eyes. He was cool and determined not to lose. The Palace didn't often witness this sort of competition, and the sports bet and spat with glee.

The Judge slowly put down eight twenty dollar bills. The Rockefeller man crisply took two hundred dollar bills out of a thin alligator wallet, and said, "That ought to do it." The sports whistled as Judge Ryan folded with a mock tragic shrug that indicated he was but another victimized man of the people. Mr. Robert Morgan of Standard Oil escorted the two tiger-striped red ladies to the "Presidential Suite." They each smiled, and offered an arm as demurely as if they were going for a stroll.

I hadn't seen Annie or Saturday, but Burke slinked along the bar and leered at me during the auction. He shook his head knowingly, almost cocking his single ear, and went upstairs. J.D. told me, "Saturday's buyin' the Palace and Burke's in on the deal."

Even before the first strains of "Onward Christian Soldiers" word spread the Indian was outside. A mob of waitresses, pimps, sports, and Palace regulars piled into the chilly night. I don't know, if like me, they wanted distraction. The auction left a stale and nasty taste, and interrupted Saturday night — that illusion of women, whiskey, and license. Amos subverted "Onward" and a good part of the Gin Palace flock trudged through the double doors into the summer night.

I wanted to see Saturday's face — that face which haunted, gave, took, fooled . . . The night was cool for July. Harriet's crowd was big. I can judge crowds, and it was about two hundred. Harriet had brought all her artillery for her weekly assault on the mouth of hell. The large Negro with the bass drum stood at the head of column of bedraggled musicians — none had properly fitting jackets and none could stay on key. One flank was secured by young women in wheelchairs, whose white faces and smiling attention to the radiant pastor seemed horribly sad. The other flank was the white-robed chorus who raised and lowered torches in time with the music. They were alive with the ruddy pleasure of damning sin. Harriet, in her golden robe, stood like Moses before Israel, pointing a golden arm and accusatory pale finger at a man in a white shirt, standing under one of the new electric street lights.

It was King Saturday. I saw his hands and stopped hearing Harriet, her singers, or her band. There he was — shirt open to the chest, hair black-blue, almost purple in the electric glare — hands preternaturally big. He was, for me, profoundly ugly. The Indian was no longer the glistening Ajax, lost in a fury neither he nor I understood, nor was he an avenging angel come to cut off Joe Burke's ear and make the Palace safe; he wasn't the swift ballplayer defying every possible expectation — Saturday was a creature of the night: something horrible, lonely, irresistible. I hated him.

"This is no king!" yelled Harriet.

Saturday stood under the light, half in shadow, half lit. He was still. He was the dead calm center. The night had stopped around him. Neither Harriet, nor anyone else moved. It was a standoff — an exhibition: sinner and accuser — man and woman. The crowd grew.

"The hour is late, Indian!"

I didn't move. I didn't move at all. I thought I would go to him. Look at him. Make him look at me. Then . . . But I had nothing to say. I stood in a cool, torch-lit July night and realized I had nothing to say. What could I have said? The Indian had been what I wanted him to be. I didn't know who he was. Maybe Edith knew. I never had. I never would. I didn't want to see him or Harriet. They were both tricks. I looked back at the Palace. It was an old building ready to fall down. I was walking away when Annie Gears grabbed my sleeve.

I'd never seen anyone so changed. Annie wore a black crinoline dress, a cheap thing no effort had been made to improve. Her face, even what I could see by the torches, had black circles under the eyes. Her hair was roughly parted in the middle and hung in two unequal loose pieces. Annie did not care what she looked like. This struck me harder than the story about her father. She had been taking morphine.

We stayed at the edge of the crowd. I held her up. Annie didn't look at Saturday. She looked at me. Harriet yelled, "Leave us, black angel! I pray for thee no more!" I looked at Annie. Harriet held up a hand of warning. "Go not near him lest he bring Judgment." She took a step toward Saturday and he moved out of the light.

Annie and I stopped. Saturday headed into the next block and the crowd followed. We heard him say, "Hypocrite," and Harriet yell, "Who is like unto the Beast?" but we turned into an alley. The Cuyahoga was moving silently between dark factories. The city was a massive presence, shining and winking beyond the water. Harriet shouted, "Red devil!"

"He don't love me," said Annie.

"Did you know about Edith on the train?" I was angry.

We heard shouting but couldn't make it out.

"I was scared." Annie looked up. The moon made her dirty hair glow with a blue radiance neglect could not diminish. "I thought he'd married her and gone to Maine."

"You didn't tell me."

"I had to be sure."

Annie turned and I saw her fine profile.

"On the train," I said. "You saw him. You were happy."

"He said he was comin' back. He said a lot of things."

"What happened?"

"He's with her."

"Harry", said Annie. "I told King, Burke raped me. He said he couldn't do nothin'."

We were holding each other. I felt numb. I understood nothing. "It's business," I said. "Always business."

Annie looked up. The color was back in her morphine-paled cheeks and she swept the loose hair away from her face. I was afraid Saturday would circle back and take her, but Annie pulled me around a corner and up another street.

10

Annie had a room over an abandoned stable a mile from the
Palace. Unpainted steps led to an unlocked door. Neither of us
spoke. The door was secured from inside with a board lowered
into two iron hooks. Annie opened what I thought was a
window but was a door. She stood in front of the moon and
took off her black dress and black stockings and kept on a black
camisole and black lacy underwear. I left my clothes by the
door and we lay on a lumpy mattress on the floor. A single
sheet flattened straw that stuck through. We were still for a
long time. She was sweating and felt cold. I shivered. We were
like children in the dark, then Annie kissed my mouth. I gently
held those large, sweaty breasts, and kissed her soft, then hard,
heavy nipples. I ran my fingers over her white neck, shoulders,
broad back, and muscular ass. I could not believe I was touching her. Annie touched my thighs, legs and between my legs.
I felt her wetness. She put me in around the wet edge of her
underwear. Annie was very wet. We went slowly at first — as
slowly as if I would burst or she might sob or the world break
— Annie arched her back as if she were on an altar.

I didn't look at her. She didn't look at me.

We betrayed him in a filthy room by two streamer trunks, a mess of hatboxes, half a dozen pairs of shoes, and a syringe in a saucer. The moon provided a phantom light — everything was white. I could see two wagons, a rotting trace, and the back wall of a shoe factory. Perfume, which smelled like lilac trees, had been sprinkled on the mattress. It cut the stale smell of horses but did not discourage lice.

We heard the fire wagons and bells. We saw red in the sky but stayed in the little room on the narrow mattress. We didn't want to know what was burning.

At dawn we bit, sucked, scratched. She rode me. I took her every way. It was close to love. "Harry," she whispered. "Harry, Harry, Harry." We did it with supple mercy and pagan heat. I wish they knew how well we made love.

I loved Annie thinking of Annie.

Did Annie think of me?

Part Five

1

Nine people died in the Gin Palace fire, the papers said. A week later rumor had it the coroner found two victims died before their bodies burned. Both had their throats cut. One had previously lost an ear. The other was identified by dental records. I wasn't the only person surprised to learn Jake McBuck went to the dentist regularly. The coroner did not change his report; there was no investigation — not publicly anyway, and no one was indicted. This must have required influence because Judge Ryan died in the fire. Robert Morgan did not.

The papers pointed out that many more should have died but were "miraculously" diverted by a lady preacher. Harriet Ember claimed to have performed a miracle, and there was a controversy in some of the minor papers. No one mentioned King Saturday. He was gone. He had left Cleveland. I thought the Robisons stopped the investigation but now I think it must have been someone more powerful. Frank Robison wanted Saturday back. The players were glad he was gone. They felt the club wasn't as good — they meant spectacular — but wasn't as erratic. I saw Patsy Tebeau shake his head when Dude Blake missed a ball in right, and say, "At least nobody made money on it." It was hard to pay attention in August: even when Cy Young or Jack Powell pitched, Jess Burkett and Ed McKean hit, or Bobby Wallace and Cupid Childs were their reliable selves. Something was missing at League Park — something wild and unexpected. The Indian drove us crazy, dazzled us, ignored and cheated us, but we paid attention. I wasn't the only krank who felt this way. There was restlessness in the grandstand and discontent in the bleachers. Healthy or crooked, sharp or glassy-eyed, King Saturday demanded attention. When he was on the field, there was the chance we might see something we had never seen before and wouldn't see again. I felt this so clearly one afternoon when Nig Cuppy beat the Reds 3-1, and the game went exactly as it was supposed to. The fielding was good, the strategy correct with appropriate bunts and proper steals, the pitching crisp and umpiring fair, but something was missing. I sat near our dugout watching the men do their jobs with honest precision and knew Cleveland no longer had an ambassador from another world.

I spent years trying to learn what happened to King Saturday after the Gin Palace fire. I never doubted he set it, killed Burke and McBuck, and deliberately led sports and whores out of the building before the fire. What I don't know is why. Were the murders and fire more "design," as he liked to call his escapades? Was he going to buy the Palace? Or was that a trap for Burke and McBuck? Did he kill them because of Annie or over money? I do not know.

Annie left Cleveland after the fire. I'm sure she still loved Saturday; I don't know what she thought of me. I wrote Edith and got no reply. They were all gone and I was miserable.

On August 11, 1898, one year to the day I met King Saturday, a telegram arrived from Ned Phillips saying Saturday was in Cuba with a black ballclub that staged exhibitions against white soldiers. Ned hadn't seen Saturday because he had been "ill." I showed the telegram to Frank Ember and left for Cuba.

For three months I moved continuously. I have no interest in recounting the horrors of travel. They pale next to the horrors of war, which Ned saw; and they pale next to what I saw when I found King Saturday — let it suffice that I'm no more a traveler than soldier. I was ill most of the time with everything from sea sickness to influenza, but ironically — irony was my chief consolation from the moment I left Cleveland, until I returned in December, when mother said I had aged so she and I could be mistaken for contemporaries — I didn't get malaria. It could, as they say, have been worse. I saw people die of malaria, and a year later, of gun shot: what happened to me was trivial. No matter how bad the trains, how awful the food, how voracious the lice, how high the fever, how lonely, dirty, cold, or hungry, I got better, clean, fed, the fever broke, the dysentery stopped, there was a krank to talk to, women were kind, and I came home.

The Plain Dealer provided press credentials and a steam ship ticket. The paper wanted to know what happened to Saturday, and I said I could find out. I had money. Saturday left without taking anything from our accounts. I took three hundred dollars in a belt and my pearl-handled pistol. Five banks were prepared to wire money. I had been told my employment with the Spiders was ending September first. I couldn't concentrate anyway. I had to find Saturday. He had to know we were even.

Before leaving, I went to the Burnses' massive green Georgian house on Euclid Avenue. A plump but pretty maid informed me from a half-open door that Mrs. and Miss Burns had left for Europe. I smiled sadly — the best way to elicit information from a serving girl is look tragic — and learned there had been "difficulties with a young man." The woman blushed, apparently thinking the young man, the Lothario who had shaken Miss Burns, was me. I felt like a cad in a Henry James story who is told the heiress has left instructions he is not to be admitted. The heavy blond hung in the door in such a way that she could close it should I rush the citadel, but draped herself around the knob in such a naïvely bold way I didn't want to leave.

The only man who had a worse passage to Cuba was Mr. Stephen Crane, whose ship sunk. The tub I took to Havana might have been commanded by Lord Jim. The crew spent the nights in the lifeboats. It's not pleasant to be rocked in darkness on the Atlantic, especially when your bunk is below several smelly decks, but nature compensates and I got so seasick I lost my fear. Cuba was a circus. The fighting was over and the victorious army competed at cards, barter, and thievery. Our soldiers were ready to sell anything provided by the taxpayer, and swipe anything native that could be carried. All selling and stealing was accompanied by endless complaining about "thieving Cubans." Correspondents were everywhere — drinking, wagering, gossiping about Stephen Crane, making up stories of heroism for their papers, and having an all-around cynical good time in *Cuba libre*.

I lost at cards or had stolen everything but a carpetbag, the gun, money belt, and a beige shirt, jacket and pants that might have been worn by a plantation overseer. My pride was a pair of boots I won at poker while too sick to fold that reputedly belonged to Richard Harding Davis. As sick, dirty, uncomfortable, and ridiculous as I was, I didn't die. As I said, it could have been worse.

Press credentials were virtually worthless in Cuba. There were too many correspondents, and the Army couldn't make us work, so they were sluggish about feeding us. In any situation, no matter how chaotic, there is no substitute for money. Cheap as I am, I've never objected to spending for food, and while constantly complaining I had no cash, actually got the best food U.S. currency could buy. I probably saved my life by avoiding the "bully beef" the Armour Company made so much money on, which poisoned so many soldiers. Though wholly miserable, I was glad to be out of Cleveland and on the move. There was no crooked baseball, no jealous rage or bitter disappointment. After Annie, I was ready to find King. I rather enjoyed being part of the biggest gaggle of camp-followers that ever plagued an army.

Officers talked about Teddy Roosevelt, fame, reputation, and how filthy Havana Harbor was. Everyone else talked about El Indio and Lopez. El Indio was a ballplayer leading a black team that challenged soldier clubs, always white, to games played for big money. I heard about El Indio and the Superb Giants, Elite Pirates, Florida Rattlers, or a host of other outlandish names, from every English speaking krank and gambler on the island. I had no trouble finding kranks — they quickly form an ad hoc community — and the first thing the kranks talked about was El Indio and his black mates, who played the best and priciest baseball in Cuba. El Indio, I was told, was black, had tried to play the Big League as an "Indian" and was "exposed." He was "a big fellow" who could hit and throw farther than any man in the U.S Army. I didn't doubt it. The men on the Giants, Rattlers, Pirates, or whatever they called

230

themselves — (There may have been more than one such club.) — shaved their heads like Mohawk Indians, and cut loose frightful howls when they took the field. I found many a man who said he'd seen them, but couldn't find them myself. The Army forbade competition between black and white clubs, and there had been trouble, as whites didn't "cotton" (as an Alabamian put it) to being "shellacked by niggers." White clubs and spectators may not have liked the outcome, but couldn't resist the challenge. Games were played in almost any open place, at any time, even dusk, when burning palm trees, I was told, provided light. Each time I went to a deserted parade ground or church field, I only found a crowd of disappointed enlisted men. El Indio was as elusive as Lopez, the guerrilla leader. By September, both were reputed to be in the mountains.

Lopez was an effective commander who had bedeviled the Spanish, and according to the common tongue, was ready to do the same to the Americanos if they decided to stay. One widely circulated story was that the Superb Giants were winning money for Lopez and had gone to the mountains to join his band.

I had no luck getting the Army to help me find Captain Ned Phillips, but by one of those accidents that happen in wars and bad novels, ran into Tuck Krueger at the railroad station in Santiago. Lieutenant Krueger was genuinely happy to see me. He had been wounded in the arm while the Second Massachusetts was pinned down at San Juan Hill, and he was not inclined to ignore acquaintances. I was too feverish to give a damn what he thought. Tuck arranged for me to get to Ned.

A corporal from Cleveland was instructed to take me on the back of a mule. He talked baseball and mules — how much he liked one and hated the other — Corporal Hicks was a krank. Hicks knew about the black team, which he thought was called Rattlers or Indians. The corporal hadn't seen them but said their games ended in riots. He said an umpire had been shot for being "too impartial." Like all kranks, Hicks had his opinions and stories, and said "the smokes" played a game he'd never seen. "Damnedest ball you ever saw. The center fielder plays behind second base and throws runners out at first. Ever heard of that? Runners on second find a black bastard cuttin' behind them on pick-off plays. The third baseman is in left half the time, and if you bunt, the damn shortstop gets it."

I laughed. "No wonder everyone on the island wants to see these fellows."

"You only think so," said Hicks. "Who wants to get whipped by a bunch of coons?" The corporal didn't think Saturday was on the club. "I'd know if he was. Ain't he back in Cleveland?"

I held onto Hicks' belt and rain came down so hard I thought the mule would sink in the mud. The rain kept the sweat and mosquitoes off and cooled the fever I'd had for two days. The corporal didn't believe I worked for the Spiders or had ever met them. He thought I was another "lying correspondent" trying to get a story, but we talked baseball until we came to the medical tents. The rain came down straight and anything not on four feet was stuck in the mud. We passed two ambulances mired to the axle. Hicks said, "Hope they ain't goin' to surgery."

A red-faced sergeant told me Captain Phillips was sleeping and not to "bother comin' back. We've seen enough journalistic scum." This line seemed a bit literate for a ruddy ass with a .45 strapped to his hip, so I assumed I had the right Captain Phillips.

"We were classmates at Harvard," I said, aping Ned's accent. I couldn't help it. "Wait," said the sergeant, and I sat in the driving tropical rain looking at the white tents. I was hot. I won't say sick because I saw people who were sick. Ned was sick. I was just a gringo whose intestines didn't like the tropics. Water rolled off the brim of my hat in cool sheets and I felt less dizzy. I couldn't see more than fifty feet and listened to rain beat on canvas. A fat corporal ten feet away stood in muck that covered his ankles, and whipped a mule so hard he didn't notice two bulging leeches on his arm.

Sentries stood slackly at the entrances of certain tents. The hospital area was guarded, so the army of hungry children and native thieves didn't have an entirely free hand among the wounded, sick, and dying. Our own men did a more than adequate job of relieving casualties of their belongings. Rain pelted my back and I looked down at the muddy boots which had belonged to Richard Harding Davis, gentleman adventurer and correspondent *extraordinaire,* and wondered if this were the end of Ned. Ned had a touch of Dick Davis, though Davis

232

took fate by the ears while Ned waited for it, and Davis would have called his life duty while Ned called it fate, but Davis wasn't dying and Davis hadn't been a soldier.

I sat in the rain thinking I'd come a long way from the Republican Ball. Life rarely makes sense but rarely fails to be ironic. An important man in a little room offered me a glimpse at a clandestine world and a trip to Cuba. I didn't believe in the clandestine world, because I don't believe that the stage-machinery of history is in the hands of an elite. The "Turkish Corner" had its secrets — secrets I didn't understand — they weren't the secrets of history, not the history of Vernon and Ned Phillips, but my history: my secret history. Our lives have a secret history and clandestine power centers. Can we write the biographies of those we love? Edith told me about Saturday in the "Turkish Corner." She told me about herself. She showed me she wasn't afraid. I should have been afraid, but I was vain.

I told a fool, who thought he understood the wheels within wheels of power, I wouldn't got to Cuba; but there I was outside Santiago with my feet in Dick Davis' boots: wet, hot, aching in unmentionable places, and waiting to see a man I'd already said goodbye to twice. Feverish and blinded by hard rain, I saw that vanity led to Ned Phillips, and Ned Phillips led to King Saturday, who led back to Ned Phillips. I wanted destiny too, yet where Dick Davis and Ned Phillips had duty and fate, I had a circle. And irony.

I got sentimental waiting to see Ned. He had been more than a friend. Ned was an attitude, an invitation: a style. I needed him once and he was my friend. I wanted to see him. If Ned were dying, I wanted to be there. I had gotten quite emotional when the ass with the .45 told me to go in.

"You came," said a voice from an emaciated man on a cot. He was so thin he looked very tall. A cloth intended to cool his forehead had slid over his eyes and he made no effort to remove it. Ned shook with fever and chill. His teeth chattered. "Why did you come?"

I looked around the tent. A lamp on a deal table burned by the bed, and the rain beat random, noisy patterns on the tent. My attention was caught by a gold crucifix hanging over a silver-framed picture of Ned's mother. I'd never known Ned to be overtly devoted to our Lord or his mother, and this rather obvious, and if I may say so, Catholic display, made me shiver.

233

Ned was going to die. The tent was neat. Two empty cots flanked the door. A steamer trunk held a wash basin, two bottles of quinine, three spoons, and a glass. The tent was cool in the drumming rain. The lamp and crucifix were the only points of light.

"The price isn't always right, but it's always the price," said Ned.

I came up to the cot. A thin brown blanket was wrapped around the skinny, shaking man.

"Are you a soldier?" he said. The voice was more familiar now. It came from far away but it was Ned Phillips of Pittsburgh, Harvard and the United States Army, speaking through a trembling throat from what sounded like another time.

"No."

Beneath the damp cloth were deep, black rings which made his eye sockets, even covered by a cloth, stick out of his skull. Ned pulled the blanket around his neck. His nose was pinched and sharp, like a caricature of a decrepit English lord. To my horror, the tips of his fingers — no, their whole length — were a ghastly white and the nails were blue. I thought this was a trick of the tropical darkness, but it's a sign of malaria. Ned's face was deathly white. The skin over his nose and cheekbones was pulled back like the skin on a shrunken head.

"Does anyone know you've come?" he said.

"No."

"We have a deal."

"You telegraphed."

"It's the woman, isn't it? I can't get you the woman." Ned shook with a terrible spasm, which made me shudder. He held the blanket to his neck like an old woman.

"Henry," I said. His blue nails held the blanket to his throat.

"No." Ned pushed up the cloth but didn't open his eyes. It was as if they were held shut by the tightly drawn, wrinkled mask the sickness made of his face.

"I've come."

"Call yourself whatever you like, but go."

"I want Saturday."

The shaking got worse, and for an hour I couldn't understand what Ned said. The rain came in sheets and the tent door flapped. The patterns of light and dark over our heads changed like a mad kaleidoscope. I watched the roof and heard the rain

234

as Ned shook, mumbled, and in a low voice said, "Who's there? Why have you come? Who?" I waited for the sergeant but all that moved was canvas, shadow, and Ned, with his eyes shut, shaking and clutching his blanket with white and blue fingers.

When the rain slackened, the ague passed and Ned released the blanket. "Who's there?" he said quietly, and to my surprise, sat up and opened his eyes.

"Henry," he said. "Come here." Ned put out his hand and rose to hug me when I came near the cot. I had to catch him to keep him from falling. "You came," he said.

"I'm looking for Saturday."

"He's here," said Ned, lying back and closing his eyes. The rain made a quiet patter.

"He left Cleveland."

"He's here," said Ned. "For us."

"He killed two men in Cleveland."

"He came here to kill a man." Ned lay back and closed his eyes. "You're one of us, Henry. I always knew." Ned was still. The rain beat evenly on the tent. "When you get back you must see Vernon. Take this." He motioned to me, and slowly, with a painful but graceful, almost feminine delicacy, took a ring off a white and blue finger, and put it in my hand. He held my hand in his emaciated hand, and then lay still. "Vernon will help you."

I stayed with Ned all night. The rain stopped and thick Cuban heat came with the darkness. The sergeant brought a meal but Ned didn't eat; he slept. Sergeant James had a bottle of whiskey and we became friendly. James was devoted to Ned and told me Ned had distinguished himself under fire on San Juan Hill, repeatedly exposing himself to fire to pull wounded men back to our lines. "All that fighting, and not a scratch. Then one day . . ." The sergeant made a helpless gesture. He repeated what I had heard since arriving in Cuba — more men had died from Armour meat and malaria than Spanish bullets: "Many more." It was malaria — the parasite that lives in our blood — that infected Ned. He had stayed away from the "bully beef," but mosquitoes were everywhere.

Late in the evening James left. Ned talked, slept, and toward three, when the lamp burned low and a big moon was behind high clouds, became delirious. Ned went on about Saturday, Edith, me, "us," "our people." He wouldn't answer questions and didn't talk about Lopez, but I heard about Edith and the Indian. It was a long night. Ned's ramblings were subtle, contradictory, and, I believe, deliberately mysterious. He was still playing with me, or maybe he was just too sick to know the difference between what he made up and what he wanted to believe. Ned said those who "knew" had great "responsibilities."

"It's connected, Henry. The world is a web. Life makes sense. That's what you refuse to believe . . . chasing baseball . . . chasing an Indian . . . Why did he throw games? Baseball isn't a place, Henry. It isn't safe."

The lamp was low. We could barely see each other. Mrs. Phillips and the Spanish crucifix were lost in the dark.

"The world makes sense, Henry. You don't want to take sides. Baseball? When you admit the world makes sense, you take sides. People get hurt. People die. You don't like that. You want to be moral. You want to escape. You think baseball is the way."

I said nothing. Mosquitoes buzzed at the door behind a net Sergeant James had unrolled. I could have been listening to a skull. If Ned Phillips was making his last will and spiritual testament, I was going to be quiet.

"Why don't you become a clergyman? They're not all stupid. They have feelings, wonderful feelings. They hurt for the world. They pass judgment and never make decisions. They root for goodness. Women like them. A clergyman, Henry. You can comfort wives. A clergyman, Henry.

"You think you're better than Vernon and me. But you really think you're worse, that's why you say you're better."

Ned was quiet. The moon was gone and the lamp was a tiny point of light. When he spoke again, I could barely hear him.

"How long could these fools stay independent? Who will rule them? The British Empire? Germans? Clergymen? The world belongs to those who know it makes sense. Not Indians. I bought him. I paid him. He's like you, Henry. He doesn't know who he is. Only who he isn't. But I didn't buy you, Henry. Don't say I did. Don't tell Edith I did. Doesn't like me. Monte Carlo. That mother. The Indian didn't beat me . . . You were wrong. Bought him."

Ned talked on: rambling, raving, accusing, vindicating. Mosquitoes buzzed beyond the netting and the tent was still and warm. The lamp went out and Ned talked — it was more of a whisper — in the dark. He was conciliatory. He wanted to let me in on secrets, but I'd heard them before. He whispered that I'd missed his world by the War, but that wasn't a secret. He said, whispered, that I belonged in his world, that I was part of it now, Vernon would see to that — but I'd heard that too. Ned was trying to charm me, and that was very sad. I have a weakness for people who try to charm me, but I didn't want to listen. There was something much too sad in the hypnotic monotony of sick-talk through the tropical night, so I said, "Make sense of Edith, Ned. Who does she love?"

"The world makes sense," said Ned wearily. "Women never do. Think like a Frenchman. I was happy when I saw you with Edith Burns. You got her yourself, Henry. One of us. You'll learn that here. You'll tell her I bought Saturday. Tell her that. You'll tell her I tried to buy you, but I didn't. I only recognized you. I always recognized you, Henry. But you'll lie. God is my witness you'll lie. You'll lie to get Edith. You won't tell her the truth about that Indian. You won't tell her the truth about me. You may be above me and Vernon but you're not above lying. As God is my witness. You'll lie to get Edith. You're one of us but you'll lie. God is my witness."

"Who does Edith love?"

"She loves herself. The clever ones always do. A bad love affair cures them."

We couldn't see each other in the dark. "She loves Saturday," I said in a whisper.

"He's an assassin. How could she love an assassin? You don't know him, Henry. I recognized him just like I recognized you. I knew he was an assassin. Perfect assassin. Angry. Cunning. Perfect reflexes. Perfect hate."

"You don't know him," I said. "Or me. Edith loves him and he loves her."

"Then why is he here?"

"Because he killed two men."

"He's here because he's an assassin," whispered Ned.

"You didn't buy him. You only gave him money."

"Why is he here?"

"It couldn't be avoided."

We didn't speak for what seemed a long time. I thought Ned was sleeping and got up to go, but he said, "What happened between them?"

"What do you think?" I said bitterly.

"And what if it did?" said Ned patiently. He sounded so much like my father I started. "It was temporary." Ned's voice was kind. "She can't marry him. She'll marry you."

"Edith refused me."

"You asked too soon. Saturday doesn't love her. He loves the saloon woman. He told me."

"You, of all people, believe Saturday?"

"I know him, Henry. We did business."

"You don't know him and you don't know why he came to Cuba. Have you seen him? Have you talked to him? Yes, he took your money. He took your money before. Is Lopez dead? Have you seen Saturday?"

Ned said nothing. I heard the blanket move.

"You only know part of his story, Ned. You know a little of the money part and a little of the woman part. You don't know all of it. He doesn't need your money. He and I have money in five banks. Plenty of money. We will get a club. We'll get into baseball."

Ned shook. I lit the lamp. The chills and fever were back. I got him to drink quinine. It looked like death had blue fingers at Ned's throat, I thought of Falstaff's words: "Speak to me not as a death's head, Doll."

Later in that long night Ned was lucid again. He talked about the day the South End Grounds caught fire, and how the game went on for a few smoky innings before the crowd left. He joked about Nuff Said McGreevy and said we had missed our calling and should open a baseball saloon in every League town. Ned remembered the sisters from Providence and asked me to tell him the story of the night we were arrested in a whorehouse on Beacon Hill.

238

2

Two days later Lopez was killed in the Yateras mountains and I wanted to go home. I didn't want to find Saturday. If he were killing men for a State Department cabal, the fateful and unavoidable meeting I waited for was irrelevant. Perhaps I had never known the man, only the ballplayer; and baseball, as Ned said, is not a safe place. I wanted to go home and wait for spring. Saturday would find me. I had his money.

With the aid of hard U.S. currency, wrinkled and sweaty from riding over my gut, I got to Havana and stayed in a hotel near the cathedral. After locking the door and wedging a chair firmly under a crystal knob, I bathed, and slept for two days. When I woke, a note under the door said Lt. Krueger would meet me in the cathedral, at the Tomb of Columbus, at five that afternoon. I thought Tuck would tell me Ned was dead, so I morosely washed my clothes in a copper basin and dried them over the fan back of a wicker chair. I trusted no one, not even to wash a shirt. My worldly possessions were those clothes, money belt, gun, Dick Davis' boots, razor, and *The Essays of Montaigne*.

I went to the cathedral early, having some notion I would pray for my friend. Ned wouldn't have approved of being prayed for in a Catholic church, which is why I wanted to do it — I wanted the ornate tranquility of the Church of Rome, about which I am ambivalent, to mourn a friend, about whom I was ambivalent. The Havana Cathedral wasn't the dark, incense filled place I expected. The riotous atmosphere of a liberated city had spilled into the courtyard and beggars cadged Indian head pennies from wary privates, or showed scars as evidence of Spanish misrule to earnest lieutenants, and demanded silver. A country friar with a palm leaf serving as hat — the good man had clothed himself in his vow of poverty — begged alms from every man in uniform until two stout clerics in brown robes drove him from the piazza. Army and naval officers milled about the gates as if the cathedral were a museum, and stopped their chatter only for black-shawled and purple-mantillaed ladies who entered for vespers. The pious ladies of Havana were the highest class of women these men had seen in months, and they behaved accordingly. Ladies of the other class, which doesn't fear the streets, were prevalent enough, but not in the cathedral. The liberators parted for the faithful.

Priests did their somber best to be spiritual sentries, but many of the Americans had never been in a Catholic church before, and having been brought up to abhor the Scarlet Woman of Rome, gawked at the altar as if a woman had actually sat there, stared at alabaster saints in dim niches as if they were mechanical gypsies in an arcade, and queued up to see the remains of Columbus as if they were at a county fair. Since the United States had taken the last of what the Great Navigator claimed for Spain, it was rumored we might take his ashes too. I heard a brigadier tell his staff the Spanish had "planned" to remove the urn but, "We took the island too quickly." The general felt the ashes, "like the Philippines," were spoils of war; though outside of the Ringling Brothers or the university, I couldn't see who would want them.

The Havana Cathedral is not beautiful like Chartres, or a colossus like Notre Dame, but a massive structure of brown stone, darkened by age, that has a chaos of pillars, arches, and cornices, which make it look as if the Boston Public Library had been designed by Quasimodo. Its towers dominate the town while, inside, white pillars and vaulted ceilings tower over the faithful like the promise of grace. Candles in carved stalls provide the luminous peace the Roman Church offers in this world as a taste of the next. American soldiers and sailors waited in a long line to see a slab of stone which bears a likeness of the Great Navigator and conceals his ashes.

At least two hundred Americans waited in the rich twilight of the lengthening afternoon. I stood back and admired the altar. Being a Protestant, I find it hard to reconcile the splendor with which Rome celebrates God. We Protestants face God in the bare chapel of our conscience, and for us sin cannot be mitigated by beauty nor absolved by ritual. Still, I admit the altar was beautiful. A massive gold cross flanked by carved angels sat on white linen embroidered with gold thread. The chancel was lit by thousands of candles — all under the stone vault of medieval arches. This was no bare ruined choir but a portal to a celestial stage, and I was full of transcendent sorrow. I wanted to let my soul drift in luminous peace and thank the Roman Church for establishing its sanctuaries in the midst of the greatest rush for gold, conquest, and slaves the world has ever seen. Didn't individual priests decry the slaughter and pillage, even if bishops and popes always found it in their hearts to forgive the gold-laden butchers?

I was full of fine feeling. Ned Phillips came to Cuba to strut in the first act of the American imperial drama. I came for baseball. He came for power; I came for someone who was once a friend. He came to die.

I stood in a stall by a saint I think was Theresa, remembering when the world was contained in a friend and two sisters from Providence. I wanted to mourn my friend, and when we mourn friends, we mourn our youth. When we mourn our youth, we mourn people we didn't become. We don't mourn lost ideals — that would be proof we never had them — but people who never were, who never could have been. I could have wept in the cathedral twilight. I wanted to weep for my friend, and for his friends; for my friends and their friends; for a generation. Maybe it was the kneeling faithful, gawking Americans, chanting priests, candles, saints, or the ashes of the greatest tourist of all; I had tears in my eyes when something hard was stuck in my back.

"Don't let anyone get behind you, little brother."

I turned around. Saturday was wearing the white trousers and shirt of a peasant. A large white hat held across his heart, covered what was in his left hand. He had a black mustache and looked like any of the thousands I'd seen tilling fields, walking beside columns of American soldiers, or coaxing donkeys.

"Little brother, do you have a gun?"

"Yes."

"Little brother, did I betray you?"

"Yes."

"Then we will walk out of this church and you will kill me."

"No."

"Edith was yours."

"Yes."

"I betrayed you."

"Yes."

"Kill me."

"No."

We stood in the darkness. Saturday smelled of the fields. He was sweaty and dirty, like a peasant who has come into town.

"Did you come to Cuba to kill a man?" I said.

"No."

"Why did you come?"

"For money."

"To kill a man named Lopez?"

"Yes."

"Did you kill him?"

"No."

"You knew he would be killed?"

"So did you."

I hadn't thought of that. In all my profoundly sentimental thinking, I hadn't thought of that.

"Little brother, did you betray me?"

"Yes."

"With Annie?"

"Yes."

"The next time I see you, I make us even."

3

I went to Cleveland and Saturday went to Mexico. I didn't learn this until later, and only much later did I piece together what he did in Mexico, and even now must guess, imagine, and conjure what happened.

Two years ago I went to Mexico to ask about "El Indio" and heard many stories. Some of these were no doubt made up on the spot for the rich gringo and his wife, some had obviously been repeated many times, and some may not have been about Saturday, but other men who wandered in the dusty hills of northern Mexico. On the first day of October 1899, a year after my exhausting and filthy trip to Cuba, I received word from King Saturday to bring his money to Leadville, Colorado. This is what I believe happened in the intervening thirteen months:

Saturday went to Mexico. He landed at Tampico with his black cohorts, and a baseball game was played, the first seen there, or at least the first bet on. Saturday, known as El Indio — his real name was apparently as dead as McBuck and Burke — made a wild display at a bullfight — whether he fought a bull or interceded in a kill is unclear, this story is so shrouded in conjecture it could be the origin of a religion, as indeed it is — El Indio became the object of a cult in northern Mexico, or so I was told by a drunken Jesuit. Saturday attracted enough attention to draw a crowd for a game between his cohorts and some American merchant seaman. The crowd was bored by the North American pastime until someone shot a fly ball in half and El Indio caught both halves — or at least this is what is said now. El Indio and his men went north, following the railroad. When they weren't playing baseball, they sponsored cockfights — the group got its hands on some of the best birds in Mexico. Whatever the local passion — bullfighting, cock-fighting, boxing — the troop staged an exhibition that attracted crowds and money. Like Cortez, marching inland and playing rival Indians against each other, El Indio had a woman who translated, acted as guide and emissary, and scandalized those who had morals enough to be scandalized. The priests saw the dangers of this stranger, who like Cortez, came across the water with a band of resolutes, ready to plunder the country.

Stories spread El Indio was dead. I believe he started some of them, profited by them, and enjoyed them. There were spectacular appearances in bullrings after he had been pro-claimed dead by newspaper, pulpit, or police broadside. The Jesuit told me the Church was worried because this ball-playing adventurer made a cult of himself. Mexico is full of local deities but most of them do not introduce games, wager on battles of fists and birds, or appear with an entourage that began to resemble an aboriginal wedding of brothel and circus. "He was a marked man," I kept hearing. He was either dead or pursued by death. Death, like politics or baseball up north, is a Mexican obsession. "There were men who wanted to kill him." What men? As often as one asked the question, one got an answer. The priests, I was told. He was "Godless," and worse, got money that might have gone to the Church. In the little towns in the dusty hills, he was a god. His game replaced the bullfight. What might be next? The Church preaches miracles and sacrifice, and if El Indio was performing one, then he might be courting the other. "He was dangerous to men's souls," the Jesuit said. "The sooner he died, went to prison, to hell, or the United States, the better for everyone." Representatives of Church and state feared he was stirring up the peasants. There was talk that "beisbol," a gringo abstraction, devoid of bulls and obvious trappings of manhood, might in fact be the resurrection of an

244

Aztec ritual that holy and secular officials feared could become a share-the-land-movement.

I hoped to discover that he wandered in mountains and desert, alternating between philosophical insight and religious hallucination — a kind of well-tempted, ball-playing St. Anthony who came to some profound understanding, which, like Hamlet after his "sea change" in Act IV, he could not, or would not, articulate. My gringo-snooping revealed a man who was never alone. El Indio never lacked for company — male or female — publicity, sporting events, or trouble. What I found, and this I believe more than Aztec rituals and Cortez-like marches, was that someone was trying to kill him. He behaved as if he feared assassination: was never alone, arrived randomly at unexpected places, broke schedules — made them perhaps to break them, and kept his followers and public off-balance. He avoided cities. The priests were relieved when he left Mexico, but I doubt the Church tried to kill him. Not that country priests don't fear and condemn strangers who attract crowds, but I don't believe the Church has an official policy of assassinating prophets, not those who bring games, anyway. I heard some American sergeants, who had lost money in Cuba, put a price on his head. This was possible, though the non-commissioned officers I saw would have had trouble organizing a crooked card game, let alone taking on King Saturday.

Someone else may have wanted the Indian dead and who that someone was I do not know. I'm sure Saturday didn't go to Colorado by accident. Mr. Robert Morgan, who granted Mr. King Saturday an interview on the morning of the May afternoon Mr. Saturday met Miss Burns, and who was present the night of the Gin Palace holocaust, and who, to my prescient surprise (The most shocking things are like the answers to the best baseball questions — you knew the answer all along.) was in Leadville, Colorado.

Was Saturday stalked in Mexico? Who tried to kill him in Chihuahua at the Casa Robinson? It was the only time he stayed in a hotel I could find and I recognized no names on the guest list. One of his men was killed. Did that man take a bullet for El Indio? I was told he did. I was told he did not. There was another incident in Guadeloupe, near the border. The club had broken up, and one of his men, a black named

Carr, fired two shots at a man on a horse. Was Saturday that man? Was there more to this than anger over the way El Indio divided the money? A Pvt. Henry Carr, who played in an outlaw league in Texas, deserted the United States Army near Santiago and was lynched in Beaumont, Texas, in 1902. I inquired at the sheriff's office and heard, "He asked for it. Shouldn'ta' even looked at that white woman," and then, "Strangers was mixed up in it." I didn't get very far at either newspaper and left town without going back to my hotel when the editor of the *Mirror* suggested some stolen bonds might just turn up in my suitcase.

Saturday's career as a *capitán* ended when he crossed the border in September 1899. From May to September that year I found no trace of him, the club, or his men; then a baseball game was played in Guadeloupe between a black team and some of the best white players in west Texas, attracting the attention of lawmen on both sides of the border. Saturday's club, and I'm sure it was Saturday, was losing early, more money went down, and "those damn niggers," as a Texas Ranger put it, changed pitchers, "shut us down," and "come roaring back." Money changed hands and a rematch was set for the hour before dusk, but nine of the fastest horses in northern Mexico went in nine directions, and a week later an Indian, wearing the robes of a Franciscan monk, crossed the Rio Grande on a white horse, surprised a U.S. Army surveying crew, and told one of my classmates, who later built Harvard Stadium, that he once played big league ball.

As any gringo knows, if you ask questions and distribute pesos, you get stories. If the streets of America are paved with gold for the smelly immigrant from the cold reaches of the Czar's empire, the villages and dusty byways of Latin countries are rich in tales for the paying gringo. What happened to Saturday in June, July and August? His carnival disbanded or disappeared in the killing heat of the Mexican summer. Where were their women? Where was that roadshow of whores, dishonored maidens, bold wives, and rumor had it, a Cuban nun? The club reunited in September but the women were gone. By this time there were children. Were they all in the mountains where banditos have gone since the time of Cortez? Where was the child of El Indio and the woman who translated, tricked her countrymen, and kept Saturday and his men that crucial day-and-a-half step ahead of Church and soldiers? We heard a son was born in a miner's cabin in the silver hills, and stayed in Durango six weeks asking, paying, hoping. Had we found the child, my wife would have done whatever was necessary to take it.

I always asked: Did he kill anyone? Were any rabble rousers, radicals, troublemakers, heretics assassinated while he spent that long year in Mexico, in the dry north of that hard land? No, I kept hearing, no señor and señora. The one who should have died was El Indio. He was the man who frightened the priests and landowners and excited peasants. He and those men who were not exactly gringos, who spoke English and Spanish and a mixture of Negro talk that was a language of its own, but freebooted, fought, gambled and whored like gringos. El Indio. How did he survive, señora? There's your story. How could a man, whatever he was — bandito, prophet, criminal, have so many enemies in so short a time? Did you know, señor, Jesse James came once to Mexico to hide, but this Indio, he did anything but hide. Everyone knew of him. Yes, he was hard to find. Sometimes he was with those men, sometimes he wasn't. Maybe he hid and left the men to gamble and whore and make trouble. Maybe he went to the mountains or to the United States? Maybe he went alone? Maybe when we thought he was here, he was there? In Colorado. Nevada. Your West. The country where they used to say Judas took his annual vacation from hell. A wild country. Did you know Judas got a vacation? Did you know hell opens its gates? For our sakes, señor and señora, let's hope it's true. El Indio. The crazy ones are children of God. But that one wasn't loco. Poor Mexico, so far from God and so near to the United States. Poor Indio. So near to us. So far from God.

Part Six

1

I thought he would come in the spring, and I thought he would kill me, but he didn't come. Frank Robison bought the St. Louis club and our good players went west. We were left with a team that couldn't win the Eastern League. The '99 Cleveland club won 20 games and lost 134, a record of futility that I can safely say, will never be surpassed. To put those twenty wins in perspective, in eight full seasons, Cy Young never won less than 20 by himself.

I had anticipated some Robison chicanery, but nothing as cruel as this. The same stunt was pulled between Brooklyn and Baltimore, which demonstrates that only baseball in the mind is safe. The Indianless Spiders were stripped of Cy Young, manager Tebeau, Cupid Childs, McKean, Bobby Wallace, Lou Criger, Jesse Burkett of course, Jack Powell, Nig Cuppy, and even Dude Blake. By the season's end, we had said goodbye to the club too. Stanley Robison, who stayed in Cleveland to run the "team," stopped playing home games, so the once proud Spiders became the "Exiles," and then were no more. Kranks grumbled at the unfairness of the League, which is like grumbling at the unfairness of life, but during the ludicrous '99 season Cleveland wasn't the only city where writers and kranks thought the National League was too bloated, too "syndicated" (the system of one man owning two clubs), and that the League was staggering like the late Roman Empire. Something was going to happen, and I wished Saturday and I could have been part of it.

I thought about taking our money and disappearing, but I didn't want to leave my mother, or Cleveland, and I thought he'd find me anyway. I give the Indian too much credit — he didn't have supernatural powers. I waited for Saturday and I waited for Edith. No matter how deeply in love or compromised she had been, a year in Europe ought to be enough, though I was afraid Edith might obliterate her past by marrying some impoverished European charmer. I thought Edith would return for the reason I didn't go: unfinished business.

It was a long winter. I did some lawyering for the man who wanted to marry my mother, and I represented Frank Ember in his divorce. Both men finished the year unmarried. A week after Frank's divorce decree, Harriet was killed in a freak accident involving an automobile and a street car. The evangelist, a passenger in one of Alexander Winton's creations, apparently saw somebody or something and stood up, distracting her driver, and a fatal accident ensued. The faithful said it had been something "Wondrous," possibly a direct summons from the Almighty. The obituaries mentioned Harriet's "miraculous" preaching at the Gin Palace the night Judge Ryan died. Whoever Harriet saw, it wasn't her ex-husband. He was with me, insisting I take a fee for handling his case. The funeral was an orgy of righteousness, which Frank survived with his hands behind his back and the iron he showed during the ridiculous season. Had his wife's body been for sale, the affair couldn't have been more meretricious. After the funeral, he left Cleveland and did not leave a forwarding address. Like me, Frank was no longer wanted by the Robisons or anyone in the League.

The winter was a succession of cold, transparent days. I left Cleveland only to go to a memorial service for Ned at Harvard's Memorial Hall, a fine brick place built to commemorate Northerners who fell in the Civil War. Ned's mother looked almost saintly in her grief. His father, who had great plans for his son, could not control his tears. They asked me to sit with the family and I was very moved. Vernon was there, but we only spoke formally. Colonel Roosevelt delivered a restrained and dignified eulogy.

252

The wind howled bitterly off the lake in February but I found myself walking by the ruins of the Gin Palace and staring at Jackson Bridge over the frozen Cuyahoga. I thought about the past so much, it was as if my mind had become a hall of statues, all gigantic and white. I was in limbo waiting for spring but spring came and Saturday didn't. Summer came and Saturday didn't come. Spring and summer came and Edith didn't come. I kept waiting. I wasn't sure what I was waiting for — friends, enemies, death. I was very sentimental.

On October first, as luck or fate, call it what you will, would have it, I received two letters. The shorter one said, "Bring mine. Pioneer Club. Leadville, Colorado. 3 p.m. Oct. 7. We're even." The other was from Edith. It was six pages of determined, back-slanted female script. She said she loved Saturday but, "It went wrong. You told me he threw games and I hated that. I asked him to stop and he did. King stopped for me, Henry, but those men at the Gin Palace did something to Annie. He wouldn't tell me what. I can only imagine. In some way, I'm responsible. I made him break the rules of his world. He killed them, didn't he? They died in the fire and innocent people did too. He never should have left Annie.

"I knew it wouldn't work, Henry, but I did it anyway . . . I fell in love. I was selfish. It's only been a year and a summer, but that May seems so long ago. Do you remember when Cleveland had a fine club? Of course you do. You remember everything. So do I . . . I was starting to like you, Henry, really like you, but then . . . That was part of why King liked me . . . I don't suppose I have to tell you why I liked him.

"Tell me, Henry, is sin forgiven? In Rome, a priest told me, 'It is not for us to say. God judges. We can only forgive.' Do you believe that?"

Edith and her mother, the letter said, were returning at the end of the week, and would I come to dinner?

I went to Colorado.

2

Leadville sits less than a hundred miles east of the Continental Divide. I, who had recently been in the city of William and Henry James, went now to the territory of Frank and Jesse James, crossed the rocky spine of the country, and came to a town whose history is a compressed burlesque of America's. In Leadville, mine owners and miners were locked in daily struggle with little recourse to the five-hundred-year tradition of the Common Law. It was a place where Indian, Spaniard, cowboy, miner, gambler, whore, killer all took their turn, and in twenty years silver and gold transformed a village of 150 into a boomtown of thirty thousand, which the Depression of '93 had knocked down to ten thousand. There was still money in the hills, and men finding ways to get it.

From the train I saw those ways: mountains scarred by mines that strip and cut the earth, stinking smelter and mill towns where families live in tents and tin-roofed shacks and the air is so full of burning minerals it can be seen. I passed towns where silver, gold, lead, and zinc paid off in pillared and gabled houses that could have graced Euclid Avenue.

In Leadville, two hundred years of history had been condensed into twenty on a naked economic frontier. In '99 men still came looking for a fortune, but big companies owned the best land and had combined into the powerful, labor-squeezing trusts Rockefeller so effectively pioneered. Rockefeller and Guggenheim owned much of Colorado, but men still came looking for the luck of Horace Tabor, who in '77 spent seventeen dollars for a claim worth a million a year later. In 1899 they found war: armed miners faced off against hired company guns. The miners knew if they resisted too hard the governor would call in troops. They knew but they fought — for an eight-hour day, for $3.50 a day, for pride. They knew they'd lose either way. They lost their health in the mines, their money at the tables, their lives in the saloons. If a man didn't die in an accident or get killed by a company thug, he could die over a card game. The miners' lives had few charms.

The high country, however, had its charm. The mountains are spectacular and the air, when one escaped the smell of the sulfur and smelter towns, was light and heady in a way easterners never know. Evening brings gigantic shadows and a strangely exhilarating gloom as darkness covers an enormous purple sky. On the train I told myself any town where saloons outnumber churches thirty-to-one, and, "is 40 degrees nearer hell than any city in the Union," couldn't be all bad. I found a roistering, gaming, violent town set in some of the most awe-inspiring country God ever created. The place once had the distinction of hosting Mr. Oscar Wilde, a man with as good a nose for burlesque as anyone, and the Great Wit was impressed by a sign in a casino that read, "Please don't shoot the pianist; he is doing the best he can," or so Wilde reported — I have my doubts about the semi-colon — and concluded, "Bad art merits the penalty of death." It is not recorded whether Oscar meant the art of life.

On the train I heard about "the game." The Western Federation of Miners had been challenged to a football game by the mine owners' organization, the Miners Alliance. Heavy money had been bet and high-priced ringers were coming to town. The game was a distraction before a strike. The strike in '96 had been terrible. Governor McIntire sent in troops who controlled the mines while families virtually starved during a workless winter. Men suspected of union sympathy were kept in bull-pens — foul, impromptu lumber prisons that lent a name to the place where pitchers warm up, though the average krank neither knows nor cares of the word's origin. "Smart move by the Alliance," I heard on the train. So much money had been bet, that, "If the men lose, there ain't no strike. If the Alliance loses, the company might just settle. Hell of a deal." I wished they were playing baseball.

Every man on the train had a gun. I was advised not to get off at Leadville. The pistol was in my suitcase.

I stepped off a Pullman sleeper on a clear, cold afternoon and three men grabbed me. I didn't see much. They had black slouch hats pulled down to the eyes, brown coats, and bandannas over their faces. I remember a hard pair of blue eyes, spit on a red-checked bandanna, and being thrown against a Pullman sleeper car. A shotgun was put next to my ear.

"Who are you?"

"A reporter."

My coat was ripped open. My wallet and some papers were yanked out.

"Kill him."

"I ain't killin' him till I know who he is."

"Henry Harrison, *Cleveland Plain Dealer,*" I said. "Sports." My voice cracked.

"Kill him. He's from Cleveland."

"Maybe he's here for the game?"

"Do it."

"Wrong man."

My wallet was dropped at my feet and I received a crack on the head with the butt of the shotgun. Three brown coats, three black hats, and three drawn revolvers seemed to swim into the tilting afternoon. A big fellow with dirty false teeth helped me up and said, "Welcome to Leadville." I stood up, breathed the sulfurous air ten thousand feet above sea-level, and saw Mount Massive. Had my gun been in my pocket, I think I would have been killed. While rubbing my head, a man in a brown westerner's long coat walked by. He wasn't carrying a suitcase. It was Robert Morgan.

The Pioneer Club made the Gin Palace look like Monte Carlo. It had a yellow linoleum floor like a bathroom, white-washed plaster walls with occasional and impressive bullet holes, a large clock — still intact — moose, elk, and deer heads, which stuck out of the plaster sans mounts, and gave the place a surreal look, as if a herd of animals had stuck their heads through the walls expecting water and been surprised. Beneath the heads, every foot of wall was taken up by gambling machines. These things, which stood as tall as a man, had wheels, keys, and levers, which operated spinning reels that flashed playing cards, horseshoes, bells, lemons, or spiraling designs to mesmerize the feverish gambler. This mechanized vice took pennies, nickels, or customized slugs — literal coins of the realm produced by Leadville's gambling dens. These coins completed the sense of having entered a bizarre, satirical America — towns whose histories were measured in months, lives that could end over the pettiest squabble (or the most brutal labor struggle — in Colorado the two were interchangeable): a place where fortunes rose and fell in days, and lives could be compressed into a Saturday night. This was indeed the frontier, where the raw appetites that drive Boston, New York, or Cleveland, walk down the main street of town.

A Chinaman with a shaved head stood by the doors and chanted, "Women, smoke, dream," in a sing-song, insistent voice, until two bartenders, each with sleeves held by red garters, booted him into the street. The Chinaman picked himself up, spat, muttered in his ancient language, and went to the next establishment.

Inside, two hard looking, wide hipped women offered advice to miners playing slot machines. The women looked as rough and ready as the men pumping nickels and slugs into the machines. I got a beer from one of the fellows who dislodged the Chinaman, and sat near the *pièce de résistance,* a triplet slot machine that allowed a gambler to simultaneously run three games: a roulette wheel appropriately red and black; a wheel where a cowboy, a sinewy Indian, and a coyote chased each other that appeared to be a snake biting its tail at full tilt; and an ornate gold and blue model of the heavens that moved at a dignified speed. The machine was popular. Men with dirt behind their ears, blisters on their hands, unwashed shirts, black coats, who reeked of bunkhouse sweat, jostled each other to be next in line to throw fifty cents after the chance to dominate the laws of chance, American history, and the cosmos. A slightly cleaner, and better smelling class of men I took to be drummers, but learned were professional gamblers. (Mr. Henry James would be pleased to know that drummers, like proper ladies, fear the hellholes of Leadville where men don't sell — they win or lose). The machines on one wall were played by hard looking men, with bulging pockets, who frequently looked over their shoulders. They were Alliance thugs, and meaner looking than the miners, who might be missing a finger or an eye, but had the look of men who give their bodies for work. The thugs, with their scars and lumpy noses, had the look of men acquainted with fear.

I watched six men play faro, the pastime of the west. The gun was in my coat pocket. The knowledge one has a pistol is far more comforting when you are sure you won't have to use it.

Pioneer Club coins cost 12$\frac{1}{2}$ cents. I assumed this was to confuse drunken minds and impress men who dealt in ounces. I bought four. I didn't want to stay. I expected Saturday to appear in that sullen place with a hat pulled over his face, carrying a shotgun under a long brown coat. At three o'clock I noticed something familiar about a crooked pair of hands playing the triplet machine.

Frank Ember fed fifty-cent pieces — no Pioneer slugs in the *pièce de résistance* — and kept the wheels spinning as if they controlled his destiny, until the third machine delivered a landslide of coins which he collected in his hat. Frank looked up, nodded to me, and played again. No one in the Pioneer was speaking. Men eyed each other, muttered to the machines, and looked over their shoulders. I've never seen a place so tense. Frank played three more times, each accompanied by three raps on the left side of the third machine, before surrendering it to a blond thug with a cleft chin. Frank brought over two whiskeys.

"Hello, Harry. Keep your back to the wall and eyes on the door."

We sat next to each other, backs to the wall.

"Nice town," I said. "I was almost shot at the station."

"I should have met you."

"Three men were looking for somebody from Cleveland."

"They're lookin' for anybody from anywhere. All that's holding this town together is the football game. Both sides got ringers comin' in."

"I've never seen Saturday play football."

Frank watched the door.

"You know," I said, as a lean man with a dirty face slapped a machine where dice danced on green felt in a bell jar, "I always wondered why Saturday never played in college."

"Probably didn't pay enough." Frank put out a crooked hand. "You look terrible." We shook. I had been sick after Cuba and lost some hair. Frank didn't look good either. His face was as lined and cracked as his hands. He wore a black hat and his eyes had lost their irreverent sparkle. The loss of his wife and baseball had taken away the cynical humor that showed through the blisters and scars. Frank looked older than a man who once hit three doubles off Monte Ward. Ballplayers retain a hard innocence, often mistaken for arrogance — or maybe it's just a dumb hope that life can be as good as baseball, and a powerful lack of care when it isn't. This was gone. Frank Ember had been unbowed by his inability to play the game, the defeat of the Players, the wife he lost to God, celebrity, and finally death: now he looked tired.

"The money?"

I smiled. The money was around my gut, like Cuba. I had decided to use the gun if it were threatened. Someone could beat hell out of me, or the person next to me, and I wouldn't have pulled the gun, but I had decided to fight for the money. Saturday's share, including interest, was $7,706, which I had in my belt. The rest was in three Cleveland banks, all ready to wire it.

"Do you want it?"

"Outside."

We drank to the football game. Frank explained that the Western Federation of Miners' boss in Leadville, Jason "Horse" Donovan had been challenged by Jeremiah "Puff" Johns, owner of the Florida Mine and employee of John D. Rockefeller. Johns was known as "Puff" because of his diminutive size, and a reputation for promises that, as Bill Haywood of the WFM said, "disappear with the first puff of wind." Puff's Saturday night poker games were legendary. They were to mine owners what the slot machines were to miners. The WFM knew the football game was a trick, an "opiate" as our radical brethren say, to divert energy from their demand for an eight-hour day; but, as Frank said, "Leadville is a sporting town, and Donovan's a sporting man." As Puff no doubt hoped, so much money was down the game had taken precedence over the strike.

"Horse has a brother who played for Penn. Pony Donovan. Pony brought men."

I knew about Pony Donovan. He had played for Princeton, Cornell, and Penn, under a half dozen names at a half dozen weights. The miners had a good club even without Pony Donovan. They had beaten all comers, including the Alliance team in Denver.

"King's bettin' on himself. I see we collect. You see he gets his pay."

"Donovan would stiff you?" Cheating an athlete didn't jibe with my idea of the WFM.

"He ain't playin' for Donovan."

I looked at Frank. I couldn't imagine he was helping Saturday play against a union. Frank leaned over. A front tooth and his breath were bad. "Saturday was hired by Mr. Robert Morgan, and he's gettin' paid by Mr. Robert Morgan, who you know."

"I don't exactly know him."

"You're goin' to sit with him. The minute the game's over, you get $15,000 and meet us at Puff Johns' railroad car." I looked up. $15,000 was an awful lot of money for playing in a football game. If Frank thought so too, he didn't let on. "Just do it fast. This town ain't goin' to be happy after the game." He leaned toward me. "I told King not to let you do it, Harry, but Morgan asked for you. Get that money and get to the train. By the way, Annie's here. She been workin' in the Coeur d'Alenes. Hard time by the look of her. She's real happy. King sent for her. She don't want to see you, but that ain't my business."

3

I've never seen anything like the football game between the Alliance and the WFM clubs. Sport may delight and instruct, but it is not life, nor a substitute for life, anymore than athletes are prophets or scapegoats. The boundary between sport and life is as absolute as the boundary between spectator and athlete. In Leadville, that boundary was as obscured as I ever hope to see.

This wasn't Collinsville — families didn't come to town for the game. They left. The game, like the freezing muddy streets, was for gamblers, miners, and whores. Families who didn't pack a wagon and a mule, stayed in the tent city on the west side of town. The day was cloudy and cold. A cutting wind and powdery snow swirled over a rough field and newly constructed grandstand. The ground froze by dusk. This wasn't baseball. It was football, then it was war. The referee wore a six-gun and fortified himself with whiskey. Puff Johns said he was either the "bravest or dumbest man in Lake County."

I was picked up at the hotel kitchen and brought to the field under guard. Morgan didn't come and I sat with Puff Johns in the Alliance grandstand, which like the benches on the other side of the field, was freshly cut pine, and we sat on newspaper to keep sap off our coats. I sat with twenty company men and at least two hundred men carrying Springfield rifles. On the other side of the field, behind us, and sitting on the hills, were thousands of men.

The stands were full of guns and whiskey. The Alliance men wore heavy coats with big fur collars. I saw pistols with pearl handles, revolvers, and derringers. In a wagon behind our grandstand six Alliance thugs manned a Gatling gun. The miners wore black hats, which they pulled over their ears as the day got colder, and black greasy coats that didn't look warm. Some carried rifles. Ed Boyce, president of the WFM, had called for every miner to get a rifle and a good supply of ammunition. Looking at those cold, armed men, I wondered if Mr. Frederick Jackson Turner, who so eloquently lamented the passing of the frontier, had ever been to Colorado. But maybe these were the men Turner was talking about — where could they go that a company didn't own? Who could they fight who couldn't summon the law? These pallid men weren't fighting Indians. They faced a private militia and, if Governor Thomas got nervous, troops.

Gamblers sat among the crowd. They came in all variety of coats from fur-trimmed with velvet to raggedy items you wouldn't bet would make it through the winter, but they never stopped dealing: money, whiskey, even guns changed hands. A few dandies strolled through the miners, tipping their hats to the sporting men, and accompanied by women holding enormous feathered hats, over faces red with cold. They were pimps.

I thought the sticky grandstand held about a thousand people. Easily three times that many sat on the hills which were dotted with cowboy hats and men in the long yellow or brown western coats that go from shoulder to boot. Sprinkled among the crowd were a few Indians. The men had their hair in pigtails and wore black hats. A few Indian families huddled under red or yellow blankets which stood out on the gray hills in the gray afternoon. Everywhere I looked I saw shotguns, side arms, bulging pockets. This unremitting landscape of armed men was broken only by horses, mules, and wagons tied to tree stumps, boulders, or stakes hammered into the cold ground. Behind that gray moving sky was Mount Massive, silent and somber.

Though he worked for Rockefeller, Puff Johns wore a diamond in his cravat, western boots, and drank whiskey from a silver flask. Johns was the shortest grown man I've ever met. His pomaded hair and cologne made Frank Robison seem like an English gentleman. Puff showed me a wad of thousand dollar bills. "For the Indian, after the game."

"Where's Morgan?" I said.

"You don't deal with Morgan. You deal with me."

I said nothing. I wanted the fifteen thousand dollars. I wanted to hand it to Saturday and then it would be over: just like it was over between me and baseball, me and Annie, me and Edith. I had gambled on Saturday and lost, but I owed him that money.

He was warming up on the other side of the field. The Indian looked older and had lost weight. The prominent nose seemed bigger, the cheekbones higher, the face thinner, the mouth harder. A scar on the right cheek looked like it had been made by a bullet. Mexico had not been easy. Saturday was tall and angular — his body had grown more like his face. Half a dozen men on that field outweighed him, but Saturday still moved with effortless power and you could see those big, big hands.

He looked very Indian. His face did, as a Cincinnati paper once put it, look "like a tomahawk." The Mexican sun had made him almost black. Several Miner players spat in his direction. I wondered if they'd spit when the game started. The crowd booed. Saturday was a scab and an Indian. I didn't like it and I didn't like sitting with the Alliance. Profanity and spit came our way too. Saturday stretched, ran thirty-yard sprints, and threw a football to a lanky, pock-marked teammate. Saturday was taller than all but two. He wore a white headband, and his sleeves, unlike his teammates, had red and white stripes. Saturday had marked himself. The Leadville paper referred to him as "King Carlos, best footballer in the Arizona Territory," but the crowd called him "Injun," and, "Nigger." This wasn't a whooping bunch of easterners for whom an Indian was sideshow. These men needed something to hate besides their lives. It was hard to blame them. Saturday was another company hired gun.

The Miners wore white jerseys. Some of them had brown canvas vests to protect their shoulders and torsos. The Alliance wore black jerseys — all had brown vests. Both clubs had quilted canvas pants, though the Miners' pants were older. Everyone's shoes had scrimmaged. Several men wore nose guards, which looked like leather snouts, and as the afternoon wore on, gave them the look of odd, soiled birds.

I was angry at the crowd for jeering and angry at Saturday for being on the wrong side. Did he care whose money he took? Did he ever play for anybody but himself? The Indian paced the field. I think he was looking for rough and level spots. Saturday looked angry. There was none of the indifferent concentration that marked his behavior on the diamond.

The Miners got the ball first. The flying wedge was outlawed in '94 but no one in Leadville insisted on Walter Camp's rules. Pony Donovan was quarterback which meant he lined up inside the wedge. Most of these men, certainly the ones who played in college, knew about locking shoulders and could make the twenty-legged beast that is the driving wedge. I don't like football. It's not a game of solitary coordination and reflexes. It's intimidation. It's fighting. It's pain. Where are the numbers in fear? Where are the statistics to ponder all winter? Football is like international relations. Saturday loved it.

On the first scrimmage he lined up at left rush end. The ball was snapped and chants of "Scabs," "Scum," "Redskin," punctuated the saloon and brothel profanity of the west. "Get the rag off his goddamn head!" "Kill him!" which I've heard at many an athletic contest but never in the company of so many capable of doing it. Saturday slipped, and the wedge burst up the middle for fifteen yards. There were no yard markers though there were sidelines. Two big fellows tried to get Saturday's headband — I heard one, a behemoth I saw play for Penn, say, "No feathers, Chief?" — but Saturday dodged them, and got up with a smile. A bad sign for the Quaker.

The Indian didn't fall on the next play. Lining up ten yards to the left of the wedge, he gave an excellent example of the best, no, the only defense against the flying wedge. He took a running start and threw his body at it. The center and guards were as big as he but not as fast and — what is most important — not as ferocious. He hit them like a bowling ball crashing into ninepins, and the men behind him buried Donovan. Saturday came out of the pile with his headband crooked, but still on. As he walked back to the line, the big fellow from Penn took a run at Saturday's blind side. I doubt the Quaker could have gotten the drop on Saturday in the dark, let alone on a football field. Just as it seemed he would get clobbered, the Indian took a quick step and the man flew by him. The referee didn't see it. He was breaking up a fight between the Miner center and the Alliance right rush end.

On the next play the right side of the Miner line braced itself but Saturday hit the wedge more viciously, throwing an elbow into the stomach of the right guard. Donovan was swarmed under and limped after the play. The Quaker tripped Saturday after the play and the Indian got up smiling — another bad sign. The Alliance rooters yelled, "Take care of yourself!" The other side yelled, "Scalp the scab!"

The Miners tried the wedge again. They unbalanced the formation to get more protection on their right. It didn't work. Saturday lined up farther back and hit the formation harder. The Miner tackle left holding his right arm and didn't return. Coaches used to say anyone could break up the flying wedge, if he were willing to sacrifice his body. Frank Hinkey of Yale weighed 155 pounds and was as feared as Heffelfinger who weighed 210. Football is the ability to inflict and withstand pain. The man who does it longest is best. Saturday knocked down three men, and his teammates went through like the Greeks into Troy. Donovan was buried under a bigger pile. The Quaker came up wearing Saturday's headband. He got an enormous cheer. Guns were fired in the air.

Saturday went back to the line without the headband. The crowd jeered and taunted. "Where's the feathers, Chief?" "What you afraid of, you red bastard?" A man on the other side of Puff said, "He's not red, he's yellow." I looked over Puff's ten-gallon hat and said, "Keep your eye on him, fool."

Donovan now elected to go with Penn's "guards back" formation, where two linemen start in the backfield. Both guards looked happy to be farther away from Saturday, and happier still when Donovan handed off to the halfback for a modest gain around left end. Saturday wasn't involved in the tackle. A full minute after the play, the Quaker took a run at Saturday and tried to put a shoulder into the Indian's knees. Saturday didn't quite get out of the way and they both went down. King got up slowly. The big fellow got up smiling. Saturday smashed his face with his forearm. It was so quick, the crowd was silent. Somebody yelled, "Fight!" but there wasn't any fight. The man from Penn's jaw hung crookedly from his face. Blood spurted out of his mouth. Saturday removed the headband, which had blood on it, and put it on his head. Had he taken a scalp, the crowd couldn't have been angrier. They hissed and howled. I was afraid he might be shot. The Quaker was helped off the field.

The crowd may have wanted Saturday's blood, but the men on the field had to get it. For the rest of the half both clubs played instead of fighting. No one took a run at Saturday. I don't mean he didn't take his licks. That Miner club was tough, but they played cleanly. But for Saturday, they were the better team. The crowd began to cheer for the game, not blood. By the second quarter, they stopped yelling at Saturday. I truly don't like football — a back carrying the ball looks like nothing so much as a man attacked by dogs — but as Saturday made long runs, dragging or throwing off opponents, hurled himself at opposing players, caught Pony Donovan from behind, kicked two field goals, and wreaked havoc, they began to cheer him. The game was his, and football, I feared, was his game. This suffering and inflicting in the midst of exhaustion — this beauty at the edge of fear — brought out something in him the diamond never did. Perhaps Saturday wasn't so much an athlete as a gladiator. Perhaps he needed pain. His headband was bloody, his face was bloody, he limped, but he kept playing. He dominated those hard men, and on every play he could have been knocked out of the game with a busted knee, broken leg, or arm pulled from its socket, as happened to men on both sides. He kept running, inflicting, suffering. He loved it.

The second half was different. Later I heard players on both sides were threatened. The injured were replaced by men whose only skill was fighting. It wasn't a game. It was a chance to pile on, kick, bite, slug. The play had no rhythm. It was a brawl. Each side fumbled near its own goal and there were cries of "Fix!" An Alliance man left the field with an arm dangling hideously from the elbow. A Miner had his leg broken so badly the bone stuck through the skin. The referee drank and fired his gun in the air when the fights went on too long. Score was kept on placards displayed on a donkey led up and down the sidelines by an Indian wearing a top hat. The beast was slapped on the rear and driven into the hills after an Alliance touchdown.

Snow fell harder and the mountain wind hit our faces. By my count, Alliance was leading 17-11, but the referee fired his gun and announced the score was tied and but five minutes remained. The field was frozen mud and the players were indistinguishable, except for Saturday who had the blood-soaked rag around his head, and Pony Donovan, who had a jerky, deceptive running style. They played in the midst of the brawl. Both limped. Donovan, I learned, had cracked a bone in his left foot. Saturday had a badly bruised thigh and twisted right knee. Neither could dominate and neither could turn the bloody farce into a game. With Saturday hobbling, the Miners drove for a score. Donovan, running in obvious pain, made a brilliant run cutting shrewdly between two defenders, and would have scored but Saturday somehow got him at the two. They helped each other up.

Before the next play, a bullet whistled over the Miners' huddle. Pony Donovan lowered his head and walked off the field. Gunfire erupted on all sides. People ran on the field and players ran off. The Alliance crowd stood up and began to shove. Two men fell off the grandstand. Bullets went over our heads. Several men tried to lower themselves between the planks. Their hands were stepped on. Puff Johns jumped. I was right behind him.

With the Alliance militia around us, we got to carriages parked by the Gatling gun. I rode with Puff Johns and two men who kept their pistols out. The driver struggled furiously to keep the horses steady in a race of teams, men, and mules heading for town. Leadville was madness. Men ran down the sidewalks firing in the air or at saloon windows. Horses and teams jammed the streets. Gunfire rattled in the distance. People ran into alleys and beat on doors. Snow came down harder.

Puff got out at the Pioneer Club. I scrambled after him. A man coming toward us was run down by a team of galloping horses pulling a driverless wagon. The street was full but we were alone. Puff handed me five thousand dollar bills and said, "Five now, the rest later." I reached in my coat. "Go ahead," he said. Two wagons collided at the end of the street but the little man didn't take his eyes off me. I knew he had the money, but I didn't pull the gun. I just didn't do it.

Thirty seconds later, two men came out of the Pioneer, and Puff walked away with them.

4

King Saturday sat with his back to a gold-trimmed mirror in the bar of Puff Johns' private railroad car. In the mirror I saw a three-inch gash stitched up on the back of his head. A large gold eagle which topped the mirror seemed to hover over Saturday's head. The Indian wore a heavy fur coat. His arms were spread on the bar in either unconscious imitation or parody of the eagle's wings. Saturday's right leg rested on the back of a red swivel chair. He still wore football shoes but the canvas pants had been cut. The leg had a contusion from the middle of the thigh to the knee. The knee was swollen. He downed a shot from a gold jigger and refilled it from a silver decanter that had an eagle spout. A carpetbag sat on the bar

Saturday poured another shot. "The money, little brother."

I put five thousand dollar bills on the bar. "That's all Puff gave me."

Saturday laughed.

"I had the gun. I didn't use it."

He poured again. "You want me to go back? You want me to die?"

"I was afraid. I couldn't . . ." Even now I wonder if he wasn't right. Was my cowardice lethal? Was that my revenge? I don't know.

Saturday laughed a mirthless laugh. "I knew they'd cross me. I sent you because Frank would fight. Frank would be dead. I bet you wouldn't fight. I bet your life."

"This makes us even?"

"Even," he said.

We heard two shots close-by. The train started to move. Snow, mixed with sleet, hit the windows. The car was lit by a Tiffany globe — a glowing representation of the world in green, yellow, red and blue glass, that stood on the bar on a brass base bearing a metallic representation of the Declaration of Independence. Saturday, arms spread like a condor, battered leg extended as if he had just punted, filled the red car. His head almost reached the ceiling and I realized the car had been built on a scale to make Puff Johns look like a normal-sized man. Red chairs had short red legs. The blue sofa was only a few inches above the red Oriental rug and its gold tassels must have measured less than a quarter of an inch. The ceiling was so low one wanted to sit down. It was quilted in tight folds, each held in place by a rose button. Snow and hail pelted black windows and I saw myself framed by red drapes held by golden cords. The decor must have been inspired by a Neapolitan coffin or a whore's underwear. Embedded in a gold leaf cornice was another clock, more brass eagles, four silver cupids, and an alabaster nymph in each corner. This was a place where a little man might sweat in a padded suit while unbuttoning the bodice of a secretary.

"This is the last deal," said Saturday. "I win. We get a club."

"How will you get the money?"

"At Puff's game."

"You're on his train going out of town. Morgan has you."

"Morgan is going to buy his life."

"You're crazy," I said.

Saturday laughed. His scarred, contradictory face was alive. He was playing again, lying, gambling. "I told you I would own a club." The Indian was an eerie sight laughing in Puff Johns' saloon car. The globe gleamed at his side, an electric jewel. Eagles, clocks, cupids and nymphs floated in the red air.

"You can't beat Morgan," I said.

"Morgan is going to kill me."

"What?" I said.

"In a few miles the train will stop. Some men will get on and kill me. But, a mile before this happens, the train will stop and we'll get off."

"Why is he trying to kill you?"

"I took money and didn't kill Lopez. They told me to kill another man. Tonight. Instead they will kill me."

"Ned and Morgan were together?"

"Little brother, sooner or later everyone does business with everyone."

We heard gunfire muffled by wind and falling snow.

"You didn't have to take their money," I said. "We have money."

Saturday put his leg down and no longer looked like a spavined giant. "Ned was the richest white man I ever saw. Then Morgan. I got close. I waited. Now I win. You want that, little brother."

I looked at a red window and listened to the train pull its way through the night.

"You're afraid and you don't trust me, but I tell you we can beat them."

"You can't beat Morgan," I said.

"They tried to buy you, didn't they, Harry? You said no. They bought me, but they have to fight me."

"What about Edith?" I said, throwing her name up like a shield.

Saturday looked at me. The frantic calculation and excitement left his face. "Who can explain women, little brother?"

"Why didn't it work?" I said. "She loved you."

Saturday drank from the gold jigger. I'm sure he'd thought about it, but whatever he thought, he didn't tell me. His shoulders dipped, as if he were vaguely acknowledging the unavoidable and impossibly sad order of things, then he smiled. "You want a club?" he said, looking at the windows that threw back a red reflection. "Bad enough to fight?" Saturday was quiet. Snow pelted the windows. The train moved slowly. "You know why Monte Ward's league didn't survive?" he said softly. "Ward was smart, Harry. He was a lawyer. He didn't have enough money."

Saturday took off the fur coat and laid it on the bar. He opened the carpetbag and removed four sticks of dynamite.

"All my life," he said, removing the canvas vest and jersey. "I've waited for the right deal."

"Money?" I said.

"No, little brother, for a man. A fight."

So that was it, I thought: Saturday did have a game. He had a plan and he had anger — a long-buried fury that broke out in flashes, but like everything else in his life, had been under some kind of violent control. Saturday had waited. The game wasn't baseball and the plan wasn't money. It wasn't football either, or the pleasures of the night, or Edith. King Saturday wanted a boss, a fight, and most of all he wanted to choose the fight — the time, place, stakes. How deliberately this led to Robert Morgan and Leadville, Colorado, I don't know — it could have been anywhere; I suppose Saturday could have made his stand in Cuba or Cleveland or Maine, but he let his life happen until he found his man and his deal and the man was off-balance. I saw myself in a black window, framed by red and gold superimposed on the obscenely quilted ceiling and realized I was incidental — as incidental as the cupids and snow — and I was going with him.

Saturday strapped the dynamite to his chest with two leather belts, and ran a wire down his right arm, securing it at the wrist with a red sleeve-garter. He put on a brilliant red shirt that had an embroidered front, then a yellow jacket, which, like the shirt, must have been Mexican. The jacket was dazzling and covered with a green pattern. Holding onto the bar, Saturday eased off his canvas pants and put on yellow trousers. He wore no belt.

The train picked up speed. Ice had formed on the windows. Saturday looked at me and said, "You people are funny. You can have anything unless you really want it."

Whether he meant me, Edith, or the white race I don't know. A bullet shattered a window between us.

The train stopped and we all got off. Annie looked tired and heavier. She didn't speak to me. Annie could be quite Puritanical.

A wagon and two saddled horses were waiting. Frank pulled me aside and said, "Harry, yesterday at the Pioneer, I saw the man who ruined the Cleveland Players' club. The same fellow who put cash money on the bar at the Stillman Hotel on August

274

first, 1890. I don't like it. Jesus, Harry, you'll freeze." Frank gave me his slouch-hat and a pair of yellow sheepskin gloves.

Saturday got off last. He stood on the steps of the railroad car, hatless, in his fur coat and Mexican suit. Snow swirled around us. The Indian drew a .38 and fired a bullet through the Tiffany globe.

5

Saturday and I rode back to Leadville. He held the reins of my horse in his huge hand. I held on tightly and the snow came down hard. The Indian seemed to know the way. It was a good thing he held my horse. I've never liked riding, and we were in the mountains at night. I don't know how we got to Leadville. Sometimes we left the trail. Sometimes we couldn't see the trail. Twice we stopped and Saturday studied the trees.

We rode with snow and wind cutting our faces. My hands and feet were numb and I thought about winter: Indian-killing winter — winter and disease, the white man's allies. From the time of Cotton Mather to Kit Carson there was no better trick than burning crops and letting the snow come. I clung to my horse's neck and remembered a picture of frozen corpses at Wounded Knee, South Dakota: the last Indian "battle," if that word can be stretched to mean armed men butchering civilians, which is what most of the "battles" since the beginning of time have been. I was cold and frightened, wondering if I were going to die in Saturday's war with bosses, whites, history — whatever it was. I had chosen him again and I was going to pay. His time was my time, and I had to pay for my choice, my anger, my betrayals. One of us, I was sure, was going to die.

All I could see was the neck of my horse and the rump of Saturday's. I thought my horse might slip, or Saturday would lead us into a ravine, or we might be shot. It was all mixed up with snow and fear and a morbid but thrilling sense that it was all going to be reckoned up and paid for in a matter of hours.

We stopped at a spring on a hill outside Leadville. Saturday broke the ice with his bare hand, and the horses drank. He pointed at the town. The snow let up and we saw empty, frozen streets, and snow gusting around dark houses, boarded saloons, and over tents and shacks outside town. Soldiers patrolled in irregular bands.

"Pioneer Club," Saturday said. "Puff's game."

"Are you sure?"

"I have to be sure."

"There's a lot of them," I said, overcome with dread.

Saturday smiled that cryptic yes-and-no smile I once thought meant so much, and now suspect may have only been a mirror. "We could . . ."

"Never forgive a debt, little brother."

"Even if . . ." I couldn't finish the thought.

"Yes."

We stood over the town looking at the few winking lights and empty white streets. I'm sure Saturday had no doubts. Had he hesitated, I would have run. Even our Lord had his moment in the garden — but King Saturday mounted his horse, his right leg stuck out like a club, and we rode into Leadville with its guns, gamblers, and yellowlegs. We rode in silence — I watched his tangled, icy hair, the muscular body struggling to hold two horses, and the dark, wet neck of my own horse.

Our horses' steps were muffled by the snow and our tracks disappeared. We stayed off the main streets. Saturday took a back route down side streets, dismounting at each corner, and looking before we crossed a street. We saw no soldiers. At the end of an alley we tied up behind a frozen pile of broken crates. It was very late — maybe three in the morning. We were behind a row of low buildings covered with snow. Snow had stopped falling and the air had a cold, brilliant clarity. We stood in the alley, rubbing our arms and shaking our legs to get the feeling back. A block away a man with icicles in his beard and a rifle in his lap slept in a doorway.

278

Saturday touched my elbow and whispered, "The football gave the yellowlegs time to get here."

I nodded.

"Scared?"

"As hell," I whispered.

"You should be."

"Aren't you?"

"Little brother," he said, tapping his chest. "No white man wants to die."

I was no exception.

"When I send you out of the room, they'll know I mean business."

Before we walked out of that alley, I asked one question. Of all I could have asked — why he was in Morgan's office that May morning, whether he loved Annie, why he didn't stop throwing games — this is what I said: "Why didn't you play football at Holy Cross?"

Saturday turned around. Moonlight sparkled on his icy black hair. He looked immensely tall. "I didn't want to hurt my knee."

We moved silently through the snow. The air was so clear we could have been seen a mile away but the man hunched in the door didn't move. If he had, I'm sure Saturday would have killed him. We stepped over him.

Saturday must have known the back of the club. I followed in the dark. We crawled. I could see nothing and held his coat belt. We moved slowly, inching through a black room over rough, warped floorboards, around the sharp corners of boxes and hard round ends of barrels. I hit my head on a spigot but managed not to cry out. I don't know how Saturday found the door, but when he stood up, and turned a knob, we were in a hall and light shone around a corner.

The Indian took off his fur coat and gave it to me. He pulled the wire out of his right sleeve, attached a rubber ball to it, and closed his right hand. I started to ask if he needed the gun in his coat but he put his hand over my mouth, and whispered, "Keep your gun out. Cover me."

He moved down the hall without making a sound but the floor creaked as I moved. I thought the world could hear me, but we stopped and heard voices. Saturday got to the corner.

He looked around it and signaled me to follow. We were in front of a gray door. Light came through a grimy transom.

Saturday put his hand on the knob. He tried to turn it but the knob didn't move. He motioned me. "Kick it in," he whispered.

"Me?" The word was inaudible.

He shook his head and pointed at his leg.

I stood in front of the door and, having only witnessed such things on the stage, raised my foot wondering if I were only going to make myself ridiculous, die, or both, then kicked it as hard as I could.

The door flew open and Saturday rushed in. "Don't move!" He held up his right hand. "Dynamite." With his left hand he ripped open his red shirt.

"Dynamite, indeed, Mr. Saturday," said Mr. Robert Morgan. "We concede the point."

"If I let go it goes off," Saturday said, showing his fist to Morgan. "If a sniper shoots me through the head, you die a second later."

"We concede again." Morgan signaled to two confused soldiers by the front door. They laid their rifles on the floor.

"Hands on the table," said Saturday. Five pairs of hands appeared on the table. Saturday and fist towered over the table. "If my grip loosens." He shook his fist and tore away half the red shirt so they could see the dynamite.

"Come in, Mr. Harrison," said Morgan. "As usual you're half in and half out."

I stepped in. Five men sat at a round table in the room with the slot machines and animal heads. The windows were boarded. A lamp hanging over the table provided a circle of light. Two cigars burned in a copper ashtray and the smoke made a halo around the green lamp shade. The light was low so the men couldn't be seen from the street. The billiard table, bar, and gambling machines were shadows. The animal heads gave the darkness a sinister, almost living depth. A telephone, whiskey bottle, five stacks of chips, and a large pile of bills were on the table. Robert Morgan watched me. He wore a blue suit and green tie. His smooth ageless face was so assured one might have thought he enjoyed this, except that he didn't seem to be aware he was drumming the table with the fingers of his left hand. Puff Johns was white. His hands shook badly and he looked so small I thought he might slide under the table. Next to Puff was a pale, bewildered Lyndon Blunt, who looked like a man trying to wake from a dream. Two westerners, presumably high-rolling mine operators — both had lined rugged faces, string ties, and cowboy hats — looked scared. The heavier man, who had both hands on his cards, which were face down, said, "Look here, Indian, we didn't know . . . "

"Shut up," said Saturday. "Harry, count the bills."

I put my gun in the pocket of Frank's sheepskin jacket and counted a stack of bills with trembling hands.

"There's twenty-five thousand seven hundred," said Puff.

"That's right," I said, though I had only counted twenty one-thousand dollar bills, and probably hadn't done that accurately.

"Take it and you're an outlaw," said Morgan.

"Take it," said Saturday.

I put the bills in Frank's jacket.

"Mr. Saturday, you have the regrettable habit of taking money for services you don't render, but I didn't know you were a thief."

"My price went up," said Saturday, holding his fist over the table. "We're talking about your life." The yellow suit appeared to absorb the light and the Mexican embroidery seemed to move. Smoke circled the Indian as it went up to the lamp. "I die, you die."

"When you killed eight men and a woman, including a judge, I took care of you," said Morgan.

"Buyer beware," said Saturday.

"And you, Harrison? Where do you go?" said Morgan. "El Dorado? This man may survive on the run, at least for a while. But you? I'll make an offer. Saturday takes ten thousand and his dynamite, and gets one hour. You may take any gun in this room and point it at my head for that time. At the end of that hour you, like Mr. Blunt, will become my assistant. The terms of your employment are that you never mention what has transpired in this room. I do this only because Ned Phillips was one of the finest men I've ever known. Henry, work for me, or run from me. What will it be?"

"Little brother," said Saturday. "You'll be dead thirty seconds after I leave this room. Take the money. Go. This man and I will deal for his life."

"How far will you get?" said Morgan.

Once or twice in a lifetime, we do something inexplicable. I have no idea why I did this — it was without thinking. "I want Blunt," I said.

Saturday nodded.

"Get up," I said.

Blunt rose, utterly stupefied, and walked by the two soldiers, to the front door, without taking his overcoat.

"There's a price on Saturday's head," said Morgan. "Walk out that door and there's one on yours."

"See you in hell," I said. We left Saturday, shirt open, fist closed, standing with his arm raised like the Statue of Liberty.

We took my horse and rode hard. Blunt kept saying, "Why?" Tears ran down his face. We were by the stadium when we heard the blast.

6

I lied to get Frank and Annie to leave Leadville. I knew if I said Saturday was dead Annie wouldn't go and Frank wouldn't leave her. I told them we were meeting Saturday in Chicago in eight days. We took a buggy to a town called Climax, and in three days of wagon, horse, and train, got to Colorado Springs. The state was full of stories of brutality in Leadville. Three mine owners had died in the "Colorado's Haymarket" as the newspapers put it. Travel in and out of Leadville stopped. Governor Thomas sent troops. We heard of reprisals of every sort: the jails and bullpens were full again. After forty-eight hours the papers said the explosion was either a private grudge or an accident. There was no mention of a Rockefeller man or a ballplayer.

On the train to St. Louis I told them Saturday was dead. Frank suspected it. Annie wouldn't believe it. "Were you there? Did you see his body?" No, I said, I did not see the body.

I do not know exactly what happened. I believe King Saturday had a plan. I believe he is dead.

Frank said little and drank. I was silent — sometimes drinking, sometimes staying near Annie — she didn't want to talk and refused comfort. Annie clung to notions that got more fabulous as we went east.

"Where in Chicago, Harry? Where?"

We had money. We got the best Pullman sleepers, but didn't sleep. We ordered the best meals, but didn't eat. Frank and I sat for hours in high-domed observation cars and smoky saloon cars watching telegraph poles, towns, the night. We rarely spoke.

I didn't understand the Indian, but I believe I was on his side.

"The man who broke the Players, Frank. The man you saw. He died in the Pioneer."

Frank said nothing.

"You knew Saturday as well as anyone. What was wrong, Frank?"

"He didn't love baseball."

I do not know for an absolute certainty King Saturday died in the Pioneer Club. I will not pretend he didn't. I do not know if he died by accident. One of those men may have panicked. I believe Saturday came face to face with something he had to kill.

For years I tried to find a connection between Robert Morgan and the man who killed Saturday's father. I found none.

Annie stayed in Chicago for three days. She wouldn't leave the Illinois Central Railroad Station and would have been arrested for prostitution but we paid porters and policemen. Annie refused to take money. She said Saturday gave her money. After three days Annie took a train west. I never saw her again.

Frank wouldn't take money. He said Saturday gave him money. We decided to go to Maine and buy a stone. I telegraphed Edith. She arrived the day Annie left. They didn't see each other.

Edith didn't wear black. She said that was Annie's prerogative. She said I looked terrible.

Edith was older. The playful athletic sparkle had been replaced by a careful irony. Blunt had been to see her.

"I loved him, Henry. In all ways."

We went east with our grief.

Epilogue

"The sporting public will be pleased to learn that Miss Edith Burns, daughter of Mrs. Emily Burns and the late Leland Burns, wed Mr. Henry Harrison, formerly of this city, and president of the Rochester Eastern League baseball club, yesterday, in that city. Mr. Francis Ember, manager of the Rochester club, was best man. After the season, the couple will honeymoon in Bar Harbor, Maine."

— *Cleveland Plain Dealer,*
May 13, 1900.